CORRIDO: *A narrative ballad or folk song of northern Mexico and the American Southwest. A means of preserving an oral history of important events,* **corridos** *celebrate the deeds of great heroes, lament the cruelties inflicted on the innocent, and honor the memory of the dead.*

Corrido

Corrido

Mandy Keifetz

fleabites press · New York 1998

Library of Congress Catalog Card Number: 97-95371

ISBN 0-9662835-0-3

fleabites press

Box 20229 Tompkins Square Station NYC 10009

Acknowledgments

This list is huge, so bear with me. For their tireless efforts on my behalf and willingness to gamble on such a long shot, I'd like to thank my agent, Malaga Baldi, and my publisher, Maddalena Polletta. Ditto for the silent partner of Fleabites Press (ever a gambler) whose silence makes his Herculean contributions to the cause no less noteworthy. Let's just call him Murray the Cop—he'll know what I mean.

For expert info on every conceivable subject I'd also like to thank: Sheelagh Bevan, Tauno Bilstedt, Yvette Blanco, D.L. Bowman, Bob Burns, Tomas Christensen, Brooke Corey, Tom Cushman, Joyce Engelson, Yesenia Figueroa, Liz Fitzgerald, Suzanne Goldenberg, Lisa Hale, Tom Hale, Beth Jacobson, Chris Johnson, Brom Keifetz, Norman Keifetz, Darius Knight, Michael Lewis, Ali Liebegott, Phil Liu, John Murray, Dean Pappalardo, Henry Rader, Bess Ratray, Sam Spake, Jeff Tompkins, Mark Tompkins, Steve Tompkins, Kath Van De Water, Amy Verdon, John Welch, Susan Willmarth, Sarah Wright and the mysterious "Mickey," he of 13th Street, access to whose last name I have long since, regrettably, lost.

I've taken any number of liberties with reality in this work, though, so let it now be said that any such error, intentional or unintentional, is entirely my own.

For their grace, care, and, most of all, time, I also need to thank Bob Hershon of The Print Center; the book designers, Modino Graphic; and artist, Eric Drooker.

Finally, and there's no way to do this right, short of giving him the keys to my kingdom, which, of course, he already has, I want to thank David Tompkins. This book, my heart, and half my dog are for him.

In addition to the lives we lead,
we also live lives we don't lead.

H.L. Goodall, Jr.

O Western wind, when wilt thou blow
That the small rain down can rain?
Christ, that my love were in my arms,
And I in my bed again!

Anon., circa 1500

Those are people who died, died.
Those are people who died, died.
They were all my friends.
And they died.

Jim Carroll

1

Only Five Daughters

*Doll, my plan is this: Get what I need and get the hell out of town.
It's not a great plan, I know. It's even, I guess, an old-fashioned plan.
But my head feels a thousand years old and it's the only plan I can
think of. This is a two-fold plan, Doll. It also involves you. Get what
I need. Get the hell out of town. And then get my ass over to your
bedroom. That can even be the new address for my ass: Flan's Ass,
c/o the Doll's bedroom, NYC. It's got a ring to it, you have to admit.
New York City. Molly's bedroom. Be still my sour old heart. You said
in your last letter that you missed me upside down and backwards,
wanted me there. You also said I was not to take your letter as bait
for consoling words. So, Doll, I hope these words don't console you.
Or something. Please pick up my trunk—big black leather sucker—
at Kennedy Airport around 3:30pm, Thursday, the 20th, and I'll
meet you at Fee's that night. Love, Flan.*

I wrote that exactly two weeks before my probation was up. I
rolled it out of the typewriter, folded it into an envelope
addressed to Molly and slipped the whole thing into the back
pocket of my jeans. It was broiling in Mapache. The driest Fall
New Mexico'd ever seen and even so I had to wipe the sweat off
my chest with a clean towel before putting my shirt back on.

I opened the door to my shack. The endless rows of ugly cotton shimmered wetly in the huge sun and the Organ Mountains
made a bruised green shadow across the farm, a rising shelf of
darkness against the glare. The Organ Mountains are really just

the foothills of the Rockies. They do look like pipe organs, though. Great purple cylinders as if the whole farming community in this God-forsaken southern tip of New Mexico was one huge Catholic church. Fucking poets these Mexicans are.

Nary Totonac, old and bent, deep red lines etched into his face, was struggling with his pecan trees, of course, and I started across the field to give him notice. Nary'd been good to me. He'd given me the job and the brown adobe shack to live in when I got out of prison, claiming that my grandmother, the madam, had done as much and then some for him.

I hated to let Nary down. He'd kept me on even after the pecan weevil and the drought had come up from Juarez, destroying half his winter crop. I felt terrible about leaving him in the lurch, especially after the fine meals I'd shared with his family, but the truth was, there wasn't much I could do to help him save his farm. It was out of our hands.

If I stuck around, it'd just be me salivating after his beautiful sixteen-hand gray appaloosa, and shooting longing glances at his youngest daughter, Sonia. She was fucking gorgeous. Nary himself called her his red hot tamale. She had those eyes you read about in crummy pulp books, Spanish Eyes, flashing black eyes, and bleached white hair down to her ass.

I'd been trying to get her into the sack for close to three years now and every time she'd bat those glittering eyes at me and giggle prettily, "*mañana, mañana.*" Of course *mañana* never came which was the thing I hated most about the Southwest. It's always *mañana* with Mexicans and they almost never come across.

Thinking about it, I felt the bile rise in my throat. My black boots were cracked with three years of hard farm labor. They were just about ruined. All the cracks were a dusty tan brown from the bone-dry dirt. I felt the sun on the back of my neck and I knew I looked almost as red as a Mexican myself.

Yeah, I had to get out of Mapache, away from this burnt-up culture. I figured a few years in clammy, brutal New York were just what I needed. The whole time I worked at Nary's, and even more when I was in the slam, I'd hallucinated about going back East. In fact, my whole damn life has been one long struggle to get to a place like New York and stay there; but somehow or other I always find myself back in the Southwest, sweating and choking, my mouth full of gritty dry dirt.

New York made me think of Molly and I took the letter out of my pocket and reread it as I made my way toward old Nary, who was throwing dead pecans for his german shepherd, Vulf. I knew Vulf was going to eat about a thousand pecan weevils and then get sick and shit green all over the farm; and Nary's wife would beat him with a beaded belt. But I'd had that fight with them hundreds of times and my face hurt from the glare, so I kept my eyes on the letter.

It was pretty good. Picturing Molly reading it, her long black hair falling into her eyes, I got hard. I had a much better plan than the one I'd described to her, of course. One that involved a load of peyote and season tickets to the Mets; but I was afraid Molly wouldn't help me unless she thought I was finally gonna settle down and become some kind of fat, pipe-smoking philosopher.

See, Molly's a strange girl. If you saw her walking down some street in New York, struggling under a ton of books and papers, patiently addressing invisible demons, hair in her face, tight black jeans, blue sweater over perfect breasts, you'd never think she could know someone like me. And God knows no one I come across would ever dream there was a person like Molly. An Easterner? A Hungarian? A professor plagued by an entourage of ghosts? It's like we pull a fast one on God every time we kiss.

But I met her in a bar. And, well, bars are like that. Everybody's got to drink. And two very different people can end up with the exact same thirst for the slick burn of tequila. Molly's eyes are gray-blue, huge, the color of an old black-and-white TV purring all night in the corner of darkened trailer. She's tall, taller than me, about 5'10" or 11", taller in the black boots she wears.

Black hair. Blue eyes. Black jeans. Blue sweater. Black boots. Blue smoke curling around her fingers. Black and blue and black again. A guy could look at her and get the idea that bruising's gonna enter into this soon, and in a big way. But it isn't like that. At the college where Molly teaches, they call her Doctor Silence.

When I stepped up close to Nary he was bent over Vulf, showing him a handful of rotten pecans. Black weevils squirmed in his palm.

"You see this, Vulfito? Is terrible. Just terrible."

He stood up, shaking his head and closing his hand around the infested pecans, crushing them. I hoped he would say "terrible" again. I liked the way he said it. He rolled the R's out into a low long growl. He sounded just like Vulf, in fact. He dropped the nut fragments into the dust and wiped his hands on the sides of jeans. I saw a couple of half-dead weevils clinging to the seams. He clapped a great red hand on my shoulder and I set my face hard so I wouldn't grimace. I felt sorry for Nary about the weevils but I didn't want the bugs on my shirt. I was going into town.

"Nary," I said.

"Flanagan. You see these wee-bowls? It is terrible."

Vulf barked and I grinned. Of course Nary didn't know that was the name of a kid's toy and I didn't want to tell him. It would be embarrassing. Nary was sensitive about his accent, a crazy mixture of Mexican, German, and Vera Cruz Indian. I knew the suits at Molly's office would probably eat him up; but he didn't like to talk about it, and that was okay with me.

I picked up a pecan and threw it for Vulf. It was a good throw. He leapt up and caught it right at the peak of the arc, his tan legs at least three feet off the ground, then trotted back to us, dropping the nut between Nary's legs.

"You going into town, Flanagan?"

"Yeah, Nary, I..."

"Af, you leave us soon, Flanagan. So, don' look surprised. I know you. Your probation almost up. Now you move on. This is good. Now you been with Nary. Now you stay out of trouble. For your beautiful grandmother, God rest her soul, I never do less. Tonight you eat with us, hokay? We drink the tequila we brought up from Juarez. Very good. Sauza Blanco. Special. Special night. Vulf he 'ave some too. Dogs love the tequila."

He squatted down on his dead farm land and scratched his ratty dog behind the ears. Vulf thumped his tail, his mouth hanging half open in a big stupid grin. Nary looked up at me, squinting in the sun.

"You take Arturo into town, Flanagan?"

"I was thinkin' about it."

"Af." He spit and stretched. "I don't know which you love

4

more, Señor Flanagan, my horse, or my daughter."

I wasn't sure what to say. He'd never talked like this before and I didn't really want to get into it. I was anxious to get to town. It was true I loved them both, but probably not as much as Nary would've liked to think.

"They're much the same, you know?"

I laughed.

"Sonia and Arturo?"

"You laugh, Flanagan, but it is true. Arturo, he is very pretty, is he no, with his spots?"

"He is, Nary. The best Appi in the county."

"Yet I ride him into town, sitting up there sixteen one, maybe two high, and what do the ranchers say as I pass? Go on, you tell Nary. I heard before."

"They say he's an idiot horse, brains in his spots."

"But you know Arturo is very smart, gentle, one in a thousand, a million."

"Sure, but what's the point?"

"Sonia, she is a very pretty girl, so people think she is not so bright, hah? Her brains in her," he carved the figure of a woman in the hot dusty air.

"Okay, Nary, I get the point."

He sighed, picking weevils off of Vulf's coat, then shook his head, swivelling to take in the entire sight of his ravaged farm.

"Af. I'm not sure you do, Flanagan. But anyway it don't matter. Not you I worry about, truly. This land, my family. I worry what will 'appen. I wish I could sell this land, take Mrs. Totonac to Atlantic City. Always she wanted to live classy like that, back East. You think I care who I sell to? Another farmer? The Church? The Army? Af. They talk in town about these greedy developers but I don't care. I would sell to anyone. No one want this terrible land. Not in five acre lots like it must be. And little Sonia, she need her mother. Sixteen and still with no real prospects? Af."

At the sound of Nary saying "terrible," Vulf started barking. Nary shook his head, unscrambling his tired old brains, and smiled.

"Never mind this, Flanagan. You go to town, never mind the crazy talk of a crazy old man."

I stood from my crouch, waiting for the old farmer to spill it, watching him trace patterns in Vulf's mangy ruff. He was quiet a few minutes and when he finally spoke his voice was hushed and level.

"You do something for me, Flanagan, now you are leaving?"

"Yeah, Nary, anything. Shoot." Extending his thumb and fore-finger, he pulled a silent trigger at me.

"You must stop to tease my Sonia, hah? She like you but no can 'ave. *Hay un chingo piche de putas hembras en este puta mundo, pero solo hay cinco hijas,* many girls, you understand, but only five daughters. I rest easier on this terrible farm knowing that my Sonia, she 'ave nothing to fear from you."

His face was all smile but I knew he was dead serious. Anyway, it was no problem. Sonia was a pretty little girl but I was thinking about Molly again. I'd need that tequila. Even though Sauza Blanco is just about the worst shit ever squeezed out of a cactus. It tastes like liquid candy corn.

"Sure, Nary, no problem."

"Good," he said, and smiled at me, full of teeth and mirth this time. "Stop by hacienda on the way to town, Flanagan. Ask Mrs. Totonac if she need anything."

Nary always called his wife Mrs. Totonac. I didn't bother to stop by the hacienda, though. I knew his asking was just a for-mality, a way of including me in the family, and I figured I'd already done my part with the oath of chastity to their young daughter. After all, what could Mrs. Totonac possibly want from a tiny town like Mapache? Chintzy turquoise earrings, a boiler-maker from El Cabra, the bar, or maybe I could pick her up a nice cold six of absolution from the church. That's all they have in Mapache.

I suppose I could have borrowed the truck, or even Arturo, Nary's genius horse, and gone into Las Cruces where they have a Skagg's Alpha-Beta, the giant Mormon supermarket chain, but I was itchy to get to town. I was working on a big deal, something that could easily keep me out of the Southwest, and away from the questionable charms of the Totonac girl, forever. I didn't want to take any chances.

6

2

Doctor Silence

He spoke slowly, in a cutting nasal rasp. It was a wheedling kind of voice and in it, behind it, ten thousand smarmy echoes.

"But what about *your* name," he said.

"My name? What about it? Do you mean is my name a Rigid Designator? Is it subject to the Problem of Universals? Is it causal or denotive? Or do you just mean why is my name what it is?"

Jasper Nitz maintained his even smirk, not answering, and in the shuffling quiet that followed, I felt the class realign itself. The power lines were a little screwy, but I was used to that by now.

Every year, in every class, some kid asks me why I publish under the name Dr. Silence. Usually it's a tiny boy, dressed all in black, Converse sneakers, greatcoat, face a cross between Pierrot and a weasel. A Beat geek. And each one has a grinning point man, a sidekick, crouched inevitably in the shadow. I recognized Jasper's flunky. He was my new teaching assistant for an undergrad lecture in Language Acquisition, a gangly boy with a faint Amish accent and a new-wave tonsure. I couldn't stand him.

But as I say, I know the drill by now. Jasper Nitz was unusual only in the girl he'd picked out to perform for. I cast a glance her way and froze. The rest of the major points in the day's discussion, which had been pristinely demarcated in my head, melted into murk. She had a blunt power to her, Louise Brooks hair and China Doll cheekbones. But that wasn't it.

Perched neatly on the ripped black shoulder of her Nico T-shirt was a pint-sized version of the demon I call John. He kicked his feet into her collarbone, leering at me. Normally, I wouldn't care. Normally, my demons are such an easy, familiar part of the architecture of my day, I don't even blink. But I've found through years of, I don't know, attrition, that somehow they tend to occupy the same unnatural place in my brain as public speaking, and as a result, I'm fucking useless as a teacher when they're around.

The classroom was hot and smelled of wet flannel. On the stage of Nico Shirt's slender shoulder, a tiny drama unfolded. A blond, square-jawed demon emerges from a rectangle pat of butter light, lugging a rocking chair out of sight, down her lightly sloped back. In front of him, oblivious, minute, my father shrugs elaborately. Bulge in his tiny pocket and I know he's brought his opium ball along (he always called it his opium softball), rendering him useless, and I wanna say "hey, stop him; he's stealing the chair," but now my father's squinting at me, concerned, insensible, opening his toy mouth, saying,

"*Nyugi, nyugi, Édesem.*"

"Is that an answer?" Jasper Nitz, seizing control. "What's it supposed to mean?"

"It means," I whisper, "hush, hush, my sweet. In Magyar."

"What's the point?"

"No point, Nitz. Just something my father used to say."

He rolled his eyes, raising his arms in a lost-cause flap, a gesture I've grown accustomed to over the years, a gesture meant to imply: the chick's bughouse, but what do I care? Of course, if he knew my reputation, the gesture would've been superfluous; just as if he'd actually read my work, he'd already know why I published under the name Dr. Silence. But why would he? Who'd pick up a dusty treatise on psycho-linguistics? Or read an article in an obscure New England journal?

Looking up, I saw Nico Shirt's shoulder blessedly free of demented parasites. I cleared my throat, then fell silent. I didn't want to be there. Teaching smartass graduate students is not exactly the ideal job for someone who regularly hallucinates hours of machine-gun dialogue with an entire bestiary of demons, even if that person has a facility for learning new languages akin to that of Captain Sir Richard fucking Francis Burton. As usual, I resented being made to feel like more of a fraud than I already was.

But I was determined to earn my keep. The syllabus concerned the Language of Madness, a subject some might say I was ideally suited to take on. Also a subject on which intimacy renders me mute. It all depends on how you look at it. But if I couldn't teach them what was on the syllabus, I was nonetheless prepared to teach them something; to stake out a claim, to charge in. To take no prisoners.

I was gonna play draughtsman extraordinaire and, early, draw them a field map for the mine fields, find them an inexhaustible source of rocket fuel for the imagination, and thus for the study of Linguistics as a whole. Better that, better anything, than diminishing speech by counting the rocks in the speaker's head. Anyway, that was the plan.

I wasn't sure how to go about it, exactly, but it had something to do with the truth. The truth and carbon dating. The truth in pith helmets. The truth and the silence of the dig at night. The brutal shape of the pick, artifacts in shadow: the cast of language, the die of language.

Alright, so I'm full of shit. But I was gonna have to read their papers for the next four months and I was determined about at least this much: if I was gonna read their stuff, I wanted to watch them listen first.

Besides, Jasper Nitz was a smug little bastard but the kid'd asked me a legitimate question. I guess it is pretty stupid to publish academic work under a wacko pulp fiction name like Dr. Silence. To tell the truth, even given the fact that it's common knowledge among the higher philological circles that I'm mad as a fucking hatter, I can't believe I've gotten away with it this long. So I told Jasper Nitz the truth, told him,

"It was Flan's idea."

He gave me this look. This really impressive look. This mean, squinty look which said "I know exactly what you are." He said, "Is that your boyfriend?"

"Not exactly. Want me to answer your question?"

He shrugged. "Not exactly," he said, in a precise imitation of

my voice. No mean feat, that, the nervous crash-down on sylla-
bles, the barest glaze of Romany; and so, delighted with him, I
decided to tell them the story. It's a long story, and it's pretty
goofy but, fuck, it's true. At least it's true.

First time I met Goliath Flanagan was in this scummy bar on
Ludlow Street. I was wild, desperate to come up with a proposal
for my doctoral thesis, and I'd been on a three-day drunk with
this guy, Spin Burke, who claimed he was a shinto-bassist. I never
heard him play, in fact I don't think he even owned a bass, so I
have no idea what the fuck that means, but cut me some slack. I
was a young widow, drunk, probably half mad from grief.

Spin had the requisite skull ring gleaming on his knuckle and
this long ugly face that just slayed me at the time. Anyway, I was
sitting cross-legged on a table and Spin was knuckling the shellac
with his Keith ring when this dream in a black leather cop jacket
shows up. Goliath C. Flanagan.

Flan looked about the same in those days. Bar light suits him.
He was a pinch more hungry then maybe, a tweak less worn, but
he hasn't aged much in the decade-plus I've known him. He looks
like a wrecked angel. He's all wide square angles, rib cage out to
here, insane mop of auburn hair, baggy eyes of the murkiest
green. And always a cigarette angling his jaw. Just about half a
beer short of perfect, in short. Anyhow, he casts the briefest of
appraising looks over Spin's slumped body, turns to me, and says,

"Jesus, Doll, that face. Let's cruise."

"I'm with him," I said, nodding at Spin.

Spin raised his head, looked at me, at Flan, sighed, and settled
his head on the table. He had a kind of resigned zeal about bar
fights. Flan caught his look and grinned at me.

"What if I hit him?"

"Then I'll be with a hit guy."

"What if I beat him to a bloody pulp, Doll?" he said, and now
I sighed.

"Then, I guess, I'll be with a bloody pulp and I'll be mad at you."

"What if I kill him?"

I looked at him.

"Then I'll be with a corpse and you'll have me for an enemy."

Flan looked at me a long time. He was back lit by a Rolling Rock sign. His nose was a knife in the shadow. He rubbed his hand across his jaw and burned it on the cigarette dangling from the corner of his mouth. He jumped back, dropping the cigarette. Just about half a beer short of perfect.

He said, "Jesus, Doll, you love him that much?"

"He's alright," I said. "I'm with him's all."

"Well," he said, coughing, "that's an answer."

I laughed at him. He was acting so fucking hard-boiled. But whatever my erstwhile faculties, and they were probably at their lowest right about then, I knew a sap when I saw one. Flan's hard all over. But he's a swooning romantic fool. His eyes get wet at baseball games and he addresses dogs on the street.

After a minute, he laughed too and his face softened some. He bought us a round, then another. Then I bought several. Shitty bar tequila. It suited us. Spin had a few words with the bartender, followed her up to the office, and came back with a bottle. Passing it around, the long pulls burned at my gut. Spin probably knew he was licked by then but we all played it out cheerfully.

For about an hour, I drank, consorting silently, as was my wont, with an endless parade of hatted phantoms. I think at one point I must've borrowed a crushed brown fedora from a greasy mongoose named Cump, a favorite specter of mine back then, a dapper anarchical fellow possessed of the sheer joyful exuberance of "Surfin' Bird." I'm certain I felt it poised rakishly on my head when I turned, tuning in on the boys.

They were arguing baseball. Spin was a die-hard Yankee fan. It went with his long gray face, his cool eyes. Flan, with quieter vehemence, was a Mets man. It flushed his skin, a slow burn. I didn't know about the Mets then. Everybody talked about the Yanks. They were the magic men, could do no wrong. Everyone talked about the democratic fairness of the designated hitter, the Yanks, the *wunderkinder*.

Unless you follow baseball, just about every player you've ever heard of is a Yankee. Babe Ruth, Mickey Mantle, Joe DiMaggio. Lou Gehrig, the tragic Iron Man. Bill Dickey off the '27

Murderer's Row. Yogi Berra's blather. (C'mon, you've probably said "it ain't over 'til it's over" dozens of times, admit it; and what do you know about baseball?)

Like I said, I didn't know about the Mets then. Sweet. Balletic. Tough. And mortal. Incredibly mortal. The tang of strive and failure, of labor in obscurity, underdog magic, long muscles stretching under sweaty skin. It's one of the main things Flan gave me. But that was later on. At the time, I watched my two drunk suitors, listening, drinking.

Maybe you think I'm a little too hip, gnomic, an asshole; and Flan's a little too smooth, working that big tough-guy seduction game: a pair of assholes. But such, as Flan might say, were the numbers we were running. We were young. We were in a bar. Seated. Drunk. We were seated in a bar drunk. We were all kinds of fucked up.

After all, this story has a point of sorts. I was trying to tell about how it came to be that this long talker, this tall drunken girl, not two months a widow and in reckless need of a shape to her dementia, how it was that this girl came to call herself Dr. Silence.

If the story's kind of slick so far, I guess it's because madness can be slick that way. And so can tequila. In the right company. The point is listen. Listen to how you listen. Listen to me.

Toward the end, almost at last call, almost at four o'clock in the morning, Flan was having two conversations at once. He was talking to Spin about what a cool girlfriend he had. Me. And he was talking to me about, well, me. He said,

"What are you so drunk for?"

I told him. I told him that Evan was dead, coughing out the words "my husband"; told him that, tripping, he'd walked under a bus. (That one time, I kept the dope-sick part to myself. I wasn't ashamed, but it seemed so over-determined, somehow, like he'd died in a motorcycle accident or got eaten up by syphilis.)

I told Flan that, including creoles, I spoke 39 languages. He blinked at me like a lizard. I told him I had next to no interest in any aspect of my chosen profession. He nickered and shook his head sadly. I told him I had to have the proposal in in two days or lose my funding and all I really wanted was for someone to pay me to sit around acquiring new languages. And, as I told him this, he whipped his head around, saying to Spin,

"And do you know what the coolest thing about her is, what I love, what I've been looking for all my life," beating him up with the words. Spin shrugged.

"She just sits there, absorbed, absolutely silent. Or watching you speak. She measures every word. No cop could make her talk. Her silence is her bond," whipping his hard face back to me, "your silence is your bond."

I remember the moment perfectly, Evan. It was the first time you ever appeared to me. Goofy, your severed head floating and grinning. Now we're pals, sure. Now I can take it: Evan the honor guard, Evan the apparition. Maybe I even like it better than when you were alive.

But that was the first time. I was startled, cool, startled. How many times had I addressed you in the weeks after you died? A thousand times? A million? And you chose that instant, a drunk instant, wild, flirtatious, a brink, to make your schlocky entrance.

You hovered inches over an ashtray, one long shock of your bloody balk hair curling into the smoldering butts. Someone came by collecting empties, grabbed the ashtray out from under you, and your head shot straight up like a jackrabbit. You teetered, off balance, against a Slits poster, then gracefully double-somersaulted your way across the table 'til you were hanging right between Spin and Flan.

Isn't nostalgia sickening? Viscous and patently absurd, the way it slaps that sepia clarity on everything? "Now there's a notion, Chica," your dumb head said. "Silence. Damn. It's got a ring to it, no doubt about that. Damn, Chica. Get a load of the cowboy."

I turned my attention from your severed head to the raving guy your head had indicated. Out of the corner of my eye, I saw Spin raise *his* head from the table, look askance at Flan, raise his eyebrows, shrug again.

"Okay," I said, cool, knuckles white, my voice a little high. "Silence it is. Dr. Silence. Makes sense. Can't choose a facet of language, make it no language at all."

"That's how it happened. Suit you?" I said, inserting myself into the tired quiet, into their boredom, their desire, the quiet catch of breath. Jasper Nitz shifted in his seat and grinned. He'd won, apparently. He'd won his battle of Bohemian Honor. I'd expressed emotion about something. I was wearing myself on my sleeve. But of course I'd won because he'd listened very carefully to my story, measuring it for, whatever, for phoniness, I guess. Anyway, I won. That much was clear.

I gathered my papers, looking over the sluggish faces. Nico Shirt, smiling, cleared her throat. Her voice perfumed the room.

"So, did you write your thesis on silence?"

"Well, actually no," I laughed. "The next day I got a bunch of stolen chicory blossoms from Flan and a call from Uncle Sam. I did a small job for the Feds and kind of slipped into an assistant professorship on the strength of that."

We were ten minutes over and at the far end of the table, watches were checked repeatedly, amid nervous coughs and twitches. I was happy. I'd rather talk about just about anything than *Naming and Necessity*.

"But I'll tell you about that another time. And you can check the thesis I did end up writing out of the library. I won't be here Thursday. I have to pick something up for a friend. We can get back to how loons talk after that. Finish the Althusser memoir and I'll give you each five bucks if no one has any questions about it. Stay out of trouble."

Right. Get back to how loons talk. As if we ever left.

14

3

Fat Man

I was drenched in sweat by the time I reached town. I bought a Chihuahua beer and stopped to catch my breath in the center of Old Mapache Plaza. The restaurant I was going to, El Cabra, was right across the street on Calle del Oeste and I could watch to see when my friend, Hezekiah Johnson, stumbled in. I knew he'd be hungover, if not still drunk from the night before, and I didn't want to see him until he'd had some coffee and a beer. Hezekiah, a doctor, was at least half crazy and I was a little afraid of him.

There was a pocket of shade cast by the San Arcadio Church on the north side of the plaza and I leaned into it, reading one of the wooden Official Scenic Historic Markers that dotted the entire plaza.

This one said "The Spanish explorer Oñate reported passing an Indian village on this site in 1598. In the 19th century Mapache became popular as an oasis on the long stagecoach journey between San Antonio and Los Angeles. A flag-raising ceremony on the Mapache Plaza on November 15, 1854 confirmed the Gadsden Purchase which established the 118° Mexico Boundary. (See Other Side)"

Old Mapache Plaza is a state monument, because of the Gadsden Purchase and because it's where Billy the Kid was scheduled to be hanged. I remembered when they put the markers up, hoping to attract some tourist trade to the miserable little burg. It hadn't worked, but anyone caring to break up the concrete

15

under the markers would find a preserved condom I'd pushed into the wet cement when I was a kid, drunk and out of hand.

I regretted doing such a stupid thing, especially after I got caught, but I couldn't help feeling that the rock-encrusted rubber would be a much more telling symbol for the town. It was certainly more Mapache's stripe than a bunch of plaques telling a trumped-up, whitewashed history.

The real truth was that the Gadsden Purchase took place a full day's ride away in Union and, of course, Billy the Kid escaped before the scheduled hanging. He had his own plan, a bloody death to seek, but Mapache was his hide-out for a spell, and his initial capture there was important to the feeling of the entire outlying area. Even though that was the last Mapache had to do with him, Billy the Kid is a town hero. There's a couple of stores named after him, two or three highway bars, the nearest motel, and even a pew in San Arcadio Church.

The town council—two morons, two criminals and a sycophant mayor who's a little of each—grins sheepishly and calls it tourism, but there's more to it, I think, something futilely romantic. Billy the Kid drums in their heads. It's part of being a border town. It's an edge of sorts, a crack between pride and shame.

The Gadsden Purchase is the same sort of thing. There's a neat explanation, carved in ornate wood standing on the plaza. A proud historical moment. But underneath, the Purchase cleaves the town. I learned all about it from Lobo, my cell mate. Lobo was a short Mexican guy, a con artist, smart as a fucking whip. He spent all his spare time in jail working over this scam he called *el Tratado de Mapache*, which is what Mexicans call the Gadsden Purchase.

The scam is a good one, a classic. We called it Robin Hood last time I was in New York, though if you've heard of it at all, you probably know it by its Cop Name which is old as the hills, the Handkerchief Switch. On the streets, of course, these things evolve pretty quickly, and once I learned the truth about the Gadsden Purchase, I decided el Tratado de Mapache was an even better name.

The Gadsden Purchase was a seven million dollar deal. We got the Mapache Valley out of it, which extended as far as what is now Arizona. Mexico got the seven mil, which a general named Santa Anna blew on high living, the people never seeing a single peso. General Santa Anna. He's the same Santa Anna that we remember the Alamo about. Part of the original deal was that we would protect the Mexicans from the Indians, but that fell through early in the proceedings.

It was a deal between fat cats in Washington and *El Manda Más* in Mexico City. General Santa Anna lived like a goddamn king, apparently, and even though he was later exiled, he lived out his life in the British Bahamas. Poor fucking guy. The Secretary of State, a guy named Marcy, dined out on the glory of the Gadsden Purchase for years. It's a small tale of border corruption, nothing compared to what goes on nowadays, but the simple flag-raising ceremony, commemorated by the plaque on the Plaza, sticks in everyone's craw. Lobo said that even Mexican-Americans still consider it a flag-*lowering* ceremony and call it, "*La enaboracion de la Bandera.*"

Robin Hood, or *el Tratado de Mapache*, as Lobo calls it, is an old scam which requires constant reworking, but it's one of the best. All it requires is a victim with a guilty conscience and some fast talk. Guilt is the key. On the streets of New York, a city for the very very rich and very very poor, you appeal to the gutless liberal gooeyness buried in the rich. You appeal to their guilt. With enough shills and operating capital, you can work it indirectly for a big score, by convincing the mark he's helping you beat the system. Or, for easy small change, you can take it to the streets.

I knew this Jamaican chick, Moneytree Davis, who worked the direct, or street, Robin Hood everyday in midtown. I met Davis on a marijuana run—we were both carriers—and she was the queen of the short con. Friendly, without a touch of malice, her eyes soft, voice sweeter than rum, face chiselled night, she'd sidle up to you. Fear and innocence crowding her voice, she'd ask for directions to the YMCA. After a few minutes of talk, she'd ask you to hang on to her life savings for her while she went to find the Y.

Then a friendly flush of panic and suspicion would sweep across her face and you'd find yourself putting your own money in a paper bag with hers, just so she could be sure. You'd hold the bag for her. And wait. An hour after you met Moneytree, she'd be in a bar counting your money, buying a steak for her brown poodle Trixie, and you'd be standing on a street corner holding a paper bag full of old newspaper.

It's a simple scam, really. When a person can really work it well, we say he has the gift of GABS: Guilt, Appeal, Bait, Switch. But someone probably should've told Lobo he was too nasty and too political to pull it off. He had a terrible temper. And I doubted the power of the guilt white people feel toward Mexicans. The line between North and South, between pride and shame, is too clearly marked by the border. Still, the name, *el Tratado de Mapache*, was very funny. Lobo'd kept us entertained for hours at a stretch in prison, and I wished him all the luck in the world.

I saw Hezekiah go into El Cabra and followed him about ten minutes later. He was sitting in the back, behind the big parrot cage and the tank of piranhas. He had a mug of coffee in one hand, a beer in the other. He was alternating gulps, his fleshy eyes closed in ecstasy.

A tourist family in brand new ten-gallons was crowded around the piranhas, the mother holding a baby in one arm, a jar of Cabra's green salsa in the other. The parrots cawed jealously at them. But apart from the tourists, the place was fairly empty for a hot afternoon; and I worried that Hezekiah had put the word out that he wanted the main dining room to himself, which probably meant unwelcome work for me.

I sat down across from Hezekiah, wiping the sweat out of my eyes. It was cool in the restaurant. Overhead fans spun slowly, turning the hot, dry air into spurts of breeze, slicing the table into moving ribbons of shadow. A waitress came up and Hezekiah raised his head.

"Coffee," he said, "*corto*," cut with milk, "for my friend. And a beer, yes, Goliath?" I nodded. "And *chile con queso* for us both, corn tortillas."

The waitress smiled and walked away. She had a huge ass. I watched her move into the kitchen, feeling Hezekiah's eyes on me.

"Goliath," he said. "My friend."

18

"Hezekiah. How are you?"

"Goliath is a strong name, a man's name, that is how I know you are a good man. Otherwise, I am sometimes not so sure. Me, I am not so well. I have a problem with our Rosalita. She must go to the hospital and she is very frightened, the poor flower."

"Didn't you call Molly like I said?"

"Yes. I called your friend, this Molly. She is very helpful. A good woman she is, I can tell, though her name is very ugly. Molly, this a witch name, a name for a *bruja*, you understand?"

Hezekiah will never shut up about the sound of names, evil names, honest names, biblical names. Once he gets a good start, he can go on for hours. Even though he himself, an obese Mexican Indian, had obviously adopted the ridiculous handle, Hezekiah Johnson, when he came North to go to medical school. If you point this out to him, he'll just ignore it, so I kept my trap shut, hoping he would finish the story and not go off on a tirade about how no good could ever come out of a person named Molly.

"I tell her my little wife, Norma Jean, she yell at my illegitimate daughter. (I don't like this word, 'bastard,' Goliath. It belongs to the gutter.) I tell her Rosalita come running to my office, crying to me, saying only this thing 'bapa-tada-mana, pada-naba-tama, nata-daba-mapa,' like this, over and over again. Now, Goliath, you know our Rosalita, always she is a little different. It is a mark, maybe, from being born out of wedlock; but this talk we feel is too much. Your friend Molly she tell me these letters, which are they? B, D, M, N, P, T..."

He counted them off slowly on his fat fingers.

"That these are the letter made at the front of the mouth. She asked about my flower, little Rosalita, if she has an infection in the back of her mouth, or an abrasion on the roof of her mouth. I tell this woman, your Molly, that I will check. And then she tell me these sounds are the first sounds little babies make, that perhaps my Rosalita is regressing to infancy. This, I feel, is too personal, no insult to you, Goliath, but everybody is not always as polite and respectful as perhaps they should be. So, I thank this woman Molly, many times, I bless her children, and I hang up. I hope I have not offended her, Goliath, but I had nothing more to say."

He looked up at me earnestly. I think the two-bit capo was legitimately worried that he'd offended this woman, as he called her, this friend of a friend. The sudden fear of it pounded in his ugly little eyes.

"Don't worry about it, Hezekiah. You couldn't have offended Molly. She doesn't care about that kind of thing. She's got bigger fish to fry. But what happened? Did Rosalita have an infection?"

"You don't mind my saying so, Goliath? But this idea of your friend's is wrong. I feel I must speak. Good manners are important for all of God's children."

I sighed, taking a tight sip of coffee.

"I don't mind your saying so, Hezekiah. What happened to Rosalita? Why does she have to go the hospital?"

A tear crept down Hezekiah's fat cheek, slowing at his chin, collecting momentum. It hung for moment, then dropped onto his stubby hand. He licked it off and sampled a spoonful of the creamy *chile con queso* before answering.

"I get off the phone with your Molly and call my little flower into my den. She is not crying but her face is very serious, not pretty for a little girl. And she says this thing: nada-tama-dapa, very careful, yes? Like she is trying to tell me something. Open your mouth, I say, and I peer in with a surgical light, very good light, fiberoptic, mounted on a metal tongue depressor. Still, I cannot see. So I give her a shot, she looks at me so trusting, Goliath, it breaks my heart. When she is sleeping I get out my new retractor. Special. A precision tool from a surgical supply store, all the way from Santa Fe. The Dott-Dingman mouth gag it is called. I have been looking forward very much to using it."

"Jesus Christ, Hezekiah," I said.

Hezekiah is crazy and sometimes he's hard to take. I hoped taking the Lord's name in vain would distract him so he wouldn't tell me about the Dott-Dingman mouth gag. I didn't want to hear about it.

It seemed to me that far from being cured, Rosalita had suffered further sadism at the hands of Hezekiah and his imbecile wife, whom I guess you could call her parents except that they don't really acknowledge her. The poor brat wasn't even baptized.

Anyway, I didn't want to have to tell Molly that her advice had been used to hurt a kid. She talks a lot about language, but I know Molly. She believes in the sanctity of the flesh. No one could be that good in the rack unless they thought they were committing some kind of sacrilege.

The waitress came by with a fresh pot of coffee. Despite the fans, I felt hot again and I waved her away. I didn't want any coffee.

"It is a very good retractor, Goliath. It pushes the tongue and jaw down, very wide, wider than she can open herself, and there is a good ratchet on the tongue blade. This opens her mouth wider still. It has special hooks to hold the lips away from the upper teeth, so my Rosalita does not get pinched. And two cushioned side bars rest here and here, like so, stretching out her cheeks."

Demonstrating, he ran his forefingers down his face from pouchy eye to triple chin on each side, and I grimaced.

"Great, Hezekiah. So, was she okay?"

"You are impatient with me, my friend? You do not understand that a good doctor still needs good tools. Modern tools. A good doctor must learn to blend the ancient wisdom of his people with the new advances of science. The wonderful tools. The invisible rays. The special lights. This is essential to good medical care, yes?"

"I guess so, Hezekiah. Was she okay?"

He nodded solemnly and scraped up about a fourth of the chile with his coffee spoon. He swallowed, new tears coming to his eyes, this time from the spicy food I think, and polished off his beer before he spoke again.

"Yes. She did not have these sores your friend spoke of. I was very relieved, Goliath, as you can imagine. But it has been three weeks. I come home from Juarez and still she is saying this thing over and over again. It is not natural for a child of thirteen. My *pobre* Rosalita. So I have decided. She must go to the hospital. My wife tells her this and she cries and cries. The tears, Goliath, I think they have broke my heart."

"I'm sorry, Hezekiah."

It was obvious that Molly was right. Hezekiah's "little flower" was escaping the only way she knew how from this vile ass-end of

21

nowhere. She was becoming a baby again. Hoping, no doubt, that if she was completely defenseless, pity would save her. Silently, I prayed it would work, but I didn't hold out much hope. The strategy was kid stuff, and her demented father was just too powerful.

Still, I'd had all I could stomach of Hezekiah and his fucked-up family. I knew I'd have to come up with some story about the kid for Molly when I saw her in New York and I wanted some time to digest what he'd said so I could turn it into a more palatable lie. I drank some beer and watched, irritated, as Hezekiah took out his wallet, laying half a grand on the table between us.

"Goliath, Norma Jean and I were thinking, perhaps, you are going away, you should buy a suit."

I didn't touch the money, uncertain as to where this was gonna lead.

"What's this about, Hezekiah?"

"It is about nothing, Goliath. Always you are suspicious. You think we are not generous, sweet Norma Jean and I, that for a friend we would not do something special?"

I just waited. Hezekiah never mentioned his wife, a beauty-pageant imbecile, unless he wanted me to do something for one of her brood of half-wit children. I usually didn't mind, especially for the oldest son Chris, but I was sick and tired of the dance. I looked at him.

"Okay, Goliath. It is because you are a hard man that I turn to you in times of need, so I must be patient and overlook your hard ways. It is about Chris. He needs some help out at the airport, some little playing-card thing he wants to do. I thought maybe you could dress up, take a part in his small dream."

"You wanna buy me a suit so I can shill for Chris in a Monte game? At the damn airport?"

"Monte, yes, that is the word he used. You know I do not always follow these American terms the young people use. And Chris, he admire you so very much, Goliath."

I knew he knew damn well what three-card Monte was, and his son was the last person on Earth who you'd think of running a Monte game. It would never occur to Chris to do something like that. Besides, an airport, filled with private business and crawling with security, was the stupidest place I ever heard of to try and pull one off. A showy scam like that wouldn't last five minutes at an airport. I figured he wanted Chris out of the way, way out of town, for some reason of his own.

"Forget it, Hezekiah. I don't want a suit and Chris is too inexperienced. I'll take him with me out to the airport on Thursday, if you want, though, show him why it's a bad proposition."

He put the money back in his wallet.

"Yes, Goliath. You are a good man and very kind to my family. I knew you would think of a good way. It is all in the name. Goliath C. Flanagan. A name like that is like a healing salve, waters blessed by the very Virgin."

I'd had it, and ground my teeth to choke back what I had to say. I would've just walked out except that Hezekiah was holding for me and, unfortunately, played a pivotal part in *my* small dream.

"It's no big deal, Hezekiah. How was your trip?"

"Ah, my friend. Always impatient. I do right by you, of course, what do you think? I have brought you back a special present. Not peyote as you had hoped. Something much better, unknown. Secret, Goliath, special. A special fungus of my people, part of the ancient wisdom. *El hongo antiguo, 'Yendo con La Sonrisas.'* A translation from the ancient tongue, you understand. It is an important mushroom. I know you will use it well."

I stared at him.

"It's called 'Going Away with the Grinner?'" I said.

"There is a problem, Goliath?"

"For Christ's sake, Hezekiah. I can't market a drug called 'Death.'"

Hezekiah crossed himself, then smiled impatiently.

"Goliath, my hard American friend, so literal you are. How little you understand about names. You will sell my little drug to the hippies, yes?"

The hippies. Well, there was no point in taking exception to *his* terminology, especially while he was in the middle of taking exception to mine, so I just nodded, and he nodded with me, raving.

"You will sell the fungus to hippies. And you will call it something that appeals to your customers. These people do not need to know of Death. 'Smile,' perhaps. Or 'Makes you Smile.'"

I barked a laugh.

"Or 'Smiley,'" I said.

"Or 'Smiley,' Goliath, if you think that works best."

Hezekiah patted my hand, then reached under the table. He handed me an oversized red flannel shirt, folded several times, and a bible. The shirt weighed at least three pounds. A veritable ton of hallucinogen. I smiled at him, feeling grateful and uncertain, hoping that this at last would make my life-long association with him pay off.

"I will, Hezekiah, and thanks."

"Pray for me, Goliath C. Flanagan. And for my little flower. Do not thank. And if you would do something for me, marry this woman, this Molly. Give her some children, an honest name. Children are a great blessing and also a curse. You will do this thing?"

"Yeah, Hezekiah, I just might."

Right. If she'd have me.

4

Feck

Or: How Are the Mighty Fallen

By Thursday afternoon, the day of Flan's arrival, time was collapsing and expanding like a fucking accordion. I sat in my tiny office, behind two locked doors. One door was gray, the better to blend in with the gray hall of the Linguistics Department which it opened on. The other door, smaller, and only an arm's length from the first, was pebble and glass, criss-crossed with wire, flaky black stencil paint reading "Men's Room." The door does not lead to a men's room, but to a utility closet which I've slowly filled with books, papers, tapes, maps and dog treats. When I'm really in trouble, I sit in there.

Thursday I was too nervous to hide, though. I sat at the desk, also gray, throwing milkbones at my dog, who was crammed into the consultation chair across the littered table top. Kaspar's a real dog, let's just clear that up at the outset: fur, teeth, dulcet meaty breath. He never really got a handle on catch, though. He prefers to be pelted with whatever you're throwing for him. I guess he's kind of a freak, my dog, but then, what do you expect? And when you get right down to it, I've really made no effort to discourage his little eccentricities.

I let one fly, my mind on Flan and the fifteen papers on Mario Pei, overripe for grading, piled up in the corner. Kaspar cocked his head, craned his enormous Alaskan body half out of the chair, following the bone's trajectory and then, very purposefully, knocked his head into it, snapping at the air. The treat caromed off his head, falling to the floor. After he let four or five collect, he jumped off the chair and hunted them down, gulping them whole. My intercom buzzed and Kaspar whipped his head up, banging into the bottom of the desk.

"Yeah?"

The department secretary, a slinky leather-jacketed girl named Sharon Ackerman, coughed into the phone. "There's a Special Agent Feck on the phone for you, Dr. Veeka." She affected a stage whisper. "I think he's from the FBI?"

"Yeah, Sharon. That's okay, thanks. Put him through."

Henry Feck, the slash-hound scourge of Academia, my oldest (living) friend. I picked up the phone.

"Hey, Feck. How's tricks? And why are you tormenting my secretary?"

"She's got a cute voice. Far Rockaway Red Hot?"

"Buzz. Gum-cracking Motorcycle Mama."

"From?"

"From Elmhurst, Dr. Feck. You are Dr. *Henry* Feck, are you not, author of the definitive *Word Geography of Outer Borough New York*?"

He was quiet and I worried that I'd offended him. He was always like that, a terrible sparring partner, backing out without warning, just as things were getting tasty. And somehow I always fell for it. I knew he took no special pride in the book of dialect maps, even though it's widely quoted as the ultimate work on the subject. He told me once that he drew the isoglosses, the lines which separated the various New York lingoes, on a gas station map, using a crayon he'd borrowed from a little girl seated next to him in a coffee shop.

On the other hand, the project had been foisted on him in his first weeks at New Mexico State University. He'd taken it on grimly, amidst the roaring scandal of his dismissal from Columbia, which scandal centered on his predilection for young students. And given that I myself had been one of his earliest conquests, though not, thankfully, one who squealed, I suppose calling attention to that dismissal was arguably offensive. But we were old friends, our association predating even my marriage to Evan, and

26

I figured "fuck him if he can't take a joke" was the only attitude that would, at this date, wash, so I waited.

I was comfortable with the choked silence, of course, clearing my head of the buzzing voices, the veers and curves which taunted from the corners of the room. At last, warming my toes under the sleeping malamute, I heard Feck light a cigarette. He coughed elaborately.

"I need to talk to you about something, Molly."

"So spill it, Svengali. You know you don't need an invitation."

"No. In person. You won't do it if I ask over the phone."

"Do what? And what do you mean in person? Are you in town? They let you cross state lines now?"

"Yeah."

I looked at my watch. It was almost time to pick up Flan's bag. Knowing Flan, I figured I was probably aiding and abetting a felony luggage scam or something, but what Henry Feck didn't know, even if he was inclined to masquerade as a Federal Agent, wouldn't hurt him.

"Does it need to be now?"

"I guess."

"Yeah, okay, Feck. You can drive me to the airport. But don't show up at my door in that ludicrous truck, it's embarrassing."

"You love my truck."

"Okay, I do. But that doesn't mean I want the Dean to see me jump into a metallic grasshopper-green monster and roar up Sixth Avenue. I've got a reputation, or had you forgotten?"

"You've got the reputation you deserve, Kid, as a brilliant psycho. My truck isn't going to affect that one way or the other. But I flew in anyway. I rented a Buick."

"So, no truck? Really?"

I was genuinely disappointed. I'd lost my virginity in the splintered wood back of the old Ford, a '74 Custom Deluxe. I'd crouched hidden in the cab for more than thirty hours the morning after Evan's funeral, weeping and beating back phantasms. I knew every creak of its chassis. After Flan, the truck was maybe my favorite person.

"No truck. But if things work out, you can see the ol' girl next week. My department needs your expertise."

"Christ."

"Would that he were available."

"Downstairs in twenty?"

"Check."

True to form, Feck was waiting downstairs for me, probably all along, sitting in a cherry red Buick Skylark. I ducked to check my lipstick in the darkened window, gesturing to Kaspar and the locked back door. Feck reached behind to let the dog in. He was wearing a suit. He opened the passenger door for me, kissed me chastely on the cheek, and raised his eyebrows in question.

"Kennedy," I said.

Henry Feck was tall and impossibly thin, concave, cadaverous, almost. His hair, when he had it, had been a patchy ginger color. Only a few shaved wisps remained. He had watery brown eyes, a red rep tie, and was missing the ring finger from his left hand. He's every bit a soft-science professor, but now and then he likes to play Fed, flaunting his hacked hand, dressing up in a bland suit, twitting young girls like Sharon Ackerman, and talking like old FBI. None of that polite, polarized anonymity that's so popular in the movies. He turns the air blue.

"A mutt but no luggage. Where're you off to with no luggage, a proper chick like you, a full professor with a *reputation*?"

"The airport."

"The airport, right."

He revved the engine in response and took off across Houston. The Skylark gave a good smooth ride, insular, just the kind of car you'd expect a Fed to have. Nothing like the lovely old truck. Feck dodged in and out of traffic, purring along toward the highway. I sighed.

"I'm picking something up for a friend. Nice suit."

"Flanagan, right? Christ, is he here too?"

He fished a cigarette out of his jacket with his right hand and tried to light it, bending the match over the strike area with his thumb and flicking up. His gnarled left hand was on the wheel. After a couple of tries, he succeeded, shaking the flame out and tossing the match book on the seat between us.

"I can't get away from that guy. Drive all the way out to San Miguel to grab a beer in a farmer's bar, cop a little privacy, and there he is. Run out of toilet paper and drive to Skagg's, there he is, on a goddamn horse. He's like Banquo's fucking ghost."

"Oh yeah, and what's he supposed to be reminding you of?"

He paused.

"If I answered that, Dr. Veeka, I'd embarrass us both. The point is, he's always hanging around."

"Look, Feck, if you expect sympathy from me because a figure from your past's always popping up, you're askin' the wrong—"

"When are you gonna give up on that two-bit con and marry me?"

"You're a linguist, Henry Feck, or you used to be. Are you familiar with the expression 'when hell freezes over?'"

He shook his head with a half smile, a rueful smile, then gritted his teeth, jutting his bottom jaw out hard. Normally he had a kind of weak chin. The gesture gave him some character.

He said, "You oughta drop this Dr. Silence thing and bill yourself as Gun Moll-y Veeka, Queen of the Underground."

"Cute, Feck," I said. He laughed hollowly.

"I'm serious, Molly. We'd make a great team."

"Henry, I couldn't marry you. Where would you wear the ring, on a chain around your neck? You'd always be chasing young tail, and, as I recall, you're a goddamn disaster at finger fucking. You don't even have a hand."

"Alright, drop it. I give up. Light yourself a smoke, Dr. Stiletto."

"Besides," I added quietly, "I thought you liked Flan. You said at the time it was the best thing that ever happened to me."

The city, silent from within the rented car, articulated a cuckoo-clock minuet, etched maroon out the darkened windows. I turned in the seat, boxing with Kaspar who had his chin on the headrest behind me. I was content to wait out Feck's quiet sulk for the whole ride if that's what it took. I knew he didn't really want to marry me. He went for kids.

"Damn, Molly, what was I supposed to say? You were maybe

the greatest student I ever had. You flipped after Evan died, disappearing for weeks at a time, blowing off prelims, hanging out with that idiot, the faux-guitar player, what was his name?"

"Spin Burke. And one says 'air-guitar' nowadays, Mr. Safire. And it was a bass. Or, I guess, a not-bass. And I'd been 'flipped,' as you so stately put it, forever."

"Crazy, yes. A four-star fuck-up, never. If you hadn't met the cowboy, you'd never have agreed to take on that thing with the Feds. He sort of straightened your wig; am I right or am I right? And if you hadn't done that, where would you be now?"

"Jesus, Henry, in a shitload of trouble, I guess. Is that what you want to hear? How much I owe you? How you got your one big break, a chance to play copper for real, and you had to give it to someone else? We've been friends forever. We slept together for a while, more than fifteen years ago. You're not driving me all the way out to the airport to rehash all this."

"No, I'm not."

"So? Your department needs my so-called expertise. What the hell for? You taught me everything I know. And you work in an English department. I don't *have* any expertise in English. What is it? NMSU rookie with a great future ahead of him only he's got a stutter and no one knows what he's saying? The Las Cruces cops have a catatonic witness? Or some retired Colonel with the Stars and Stripes tattooed on his balls who got worked over in a back room and now all he does is pick his toenails and sing '*Deutschland Uber Alles*?' Jo-Jo the Dog-faced Boy? I mean, what could you possibly have out there that you couldn't handle yourself?"

I rolled down the window, Kaspar immediately vying with me for the air space. Outside the car, Roosevelt Avenue stretched in the soot. At 126th Street, Shea Stadium loomed up round among the zooming cars, the factories and parks, twinned by the old World's Fair site. I was quiet waiting for Feck to talk, watching the El pull out of the Willets Point station, the women in finger waves descending the steps. Queens is huge, a whole secret world to me, with its vast stretches of cemeteries, blocks and blocks, entire neighborhoods of the dead, and subway tracks plowing through among the rows of stone.

30

Tell you the truth, I wanted to get out there with Kaspar, dash across the black lines of highway, jump off, under the El track. I wanted to stand, dog in hand, on the Willets Point platform, staring down into the open emerald of Shea, but the stadium flashed by and I turned, a little sadly, to Feck.

"Molly, I wanna go to the MLA."

"Come on, Feck. The Modern Language Association? You know what they're like. It's a Shriner's convention for steamed-up word trolls only you don't get to wear a fez."

He laughed.

"They said we might get the fezzes this year."

"Yeah, so?"

"So, it's next week. In New York. And you know I'm on permanent probation."

"Well, granted I'm not exactly the world's expert on academic etiquette, but wouldn't that be *good* for NMSU?"

"So you'd think, but they don't look kindly on my cancelling classes for a week to attend a conference in the wrong field and they won't find me a substitute."

"And you want me to cover your classes?"

"Yeah. Would you?"

"Why me?"

"You've got tenure. And you're a whiz kid. They'd come all over the place to have you. And you're on the reading list, so most everybody'll show up for class."

"I'm on the reading list in your English class?"

"You bet, cutie. Though it's not exactly an English class."

"What book?"

"*Metaphasis and the Drunkard.*"

"My thesis —are you kidding?"

"'Fraid not, Sis."

"Just what is it you're teaching those farmers?"

He hunched further over the wheel and smiled sheepishly out of the far side of his mouth. Kaspar whinnied and I turned. My father was curled next to him on the back seat of the Skylark. Spats and suspenders, filthy brown pilled-wool trousers, my mother's gold coin necklace around his grizzled head like a halo.

He was sucking on a stogie, his face wrinkled, straining for English, pupils clean and full.

"You know, always I think on your demons, Little One," he said. "Good they are, nice. Like when you are little. Not your soul they want, but your furniture. As you go, how you say," his face engulfed in wrinkles, "*hajo-hoz*, see you no trade them for more greedy ones."

"Toward what ship, Pappa?" I asked.

"Ship there," he said, pointing at nothing in particular, and blinked out, the vanilla cigar smell lingering, a stinky reminder of a thousand and one tenement nights: my childhood.

Coming in particular from a man who never did an honest day's work in the new world, I resented all that rarified immigrant wisdom. Besides, damn his bohunk soul, what business did my father have talking all sage and great guns about my demons as if he weren't one of them, one of the peskiest? But I suppose he had a point.

"Alright, Feck. Spill it."

"What airline?"

"Braniff. I think."

"Hmph," he said, "Braniff. Figures."

He turned down the ramp and I sighed.

"Jesus, Feck. Never mind that shit about Flan. What are you teaching?"

"One section of 'Vocabulary and Grammar Review.' And then 'Metastisizing Praxis, Phenomenological Vertigo and Other Diseases of Meaning.'"

"Huh. 'Vocabulary and Grammar Review?'"

Feck sighed.

"Molly."

"Well, what do you want me to say, Feck? 'Metastisizing Praxis?' What the hell is that? An English class? A Philosophy class?"

"It's, you might say, *in-ter-cur-ric-u-lar*," he said, savoring the phrase.

I laughed.

"That one's your personal baby, right?"

"Give the girl a cigar."

A cigar. In a car that was already a chorus-line of cigars. I lit a cigarette to add my own smoke, tangible, to the mix.

"What about my classes?" I said. "And the seminar, my ten little brilliant Indians just dying to know what's next in 'The Language of Madness?'"

"Does this mean you'll do it?"

"No."

"What's to what? Give'm a long assignment, a week off, and pick out the one that shines to put in charge 'til you get back. That cute secretary of yours'll cover for you."

He rammed the Buick into a parking space, and I started, bumping against the glove compartment. It was idiotic sitting in the car arguing, knowing on some level I was already hooked, suckered by the chance to prowl around in Flan's world. I wasn't even interested in talking about it anymore. What I really wanted to know was what Feck was presenting to the MLA. But then, we were on a roll, and I'm an idiot that way. Old habits die hard. Or not at all.

"None of them shine," I said.

Evan landed with a thud on the hood. He pressed his bayou face hard against the glass; his soft bicycle-spoke eyes peered into the car. He was wearing a ludicrous ironed blonde Nico wig. Legs hanging off the hood, pounding his fists into the windshield, he started to sing in a spooky, sepulchral voice. Not his style at all. No really. Even though he's dead.

I recognized the old Nico song. Funny how one's head is filled with these cornball anthems to regret. It was Evan's way of reminding me there was someone in the seminar I respected, Nell, the Nico-shirt girl. My dead husband, in squeaky falsetto, distorted by the quarantine interior of the new car, I could handle. My dead husband in a blonde wig, going for icy Germanic hauteur, I could handle. But Evan and bad music? It broke my heart. If things like taste began to confuse Evan, it didn't speak well for the clarity of thinking in the afterlife. My stomach dropped away and I winced.

"Feck, do me a favor? Move the car right up against that column."

He complied, jamming Evan into the steel post. Evan twisted and rolled, tearing off the pinned leg and saluting me with it as he foundered into nothing.

"Maybe there's one girl."

"So, you'll do it?"

"Yeah. If you'll grade fifteen papers on Mario Pei."

"Deal. What changed your mind? My unbelievable charm or your enduring sympathy about how far I've fallen from grace?"

"Evan thinks I should. Besides, it'll be Halloween. And I'm always up for a frolic with the dead."

"As long as you'll do it," he sighed.

I yanked at the door handle.

"Wait for me, okay? I'll be right back."

"Okay."

"And watch Kaspar?"

5

In Line for the Egg Clan

The flight was okay. I had on clean jeans, a new blue work shirt, a gray vest and a bolo tie with a silver coyote clip that I bought at the airport gift shop. I'd polished my boots and had a new ox-blood cowboy hat. A luggage scam is pretty easy to pull off at Kennedy, especially with an airline like Braniff, which is going down the tubes so fast, they probably really do lose most of their passengers' bags. But I like to stick with stylized characters when I'm working. People are more at ease that way. And of course this was a little trickier than most luggage scams. I had a ton of mushrooms in the trunk and I didn't want Molly to get in trouble.

Braniff doesn't even serve meals. Midway through the flight they pass out a mint and a stick to bite down on. The rest of the time you're on your own. Of course you can buy a drink. I had a coke. I thought if I had any booze, I'd want to smoke even more and I was already fantasizing about eating the unlit cigarette in my mouth.

I thought I was used to dry air because of all my time in the desert but the air in a plane isn't just dry, it's wrong. The seats were scratchy, the color of dried blood, and outside the window there was nothing but white.

The woman sitting next to me was drinking a coke too. She was about fifty, wearing a blue dress with close to a hundred pockets sewn onto it. She weighed around 300 pounds. Out of the corner of my eye I saw her reach into one of the pockets on her left tit and pull out two packets of Sweet'n'Low. She added them to her coke, took a sip, nodded, and turned to me. I lifted my hat and smiled.

"Ma'am."

"I'm the Pocket Lady," she said.

"Chris," I said, giving Hezekiah's son's name, the name I'd used to book the flight. I'd bribed him with a sack of Nary's rotted pecans for the privilege and we'd both walked away from the deal feeling like a goddamn king, though I think Chris wanted the pecans more for the weevils than the spoiled nutmeat. The kid was hard to figure.

"Do you know what a pocket lady does for a living?" she asked.

"No, Ma'am, Ah'm afraid Ah don't."

"Well, just what do you think I have in these pockets, young man?"

Resisting the urge to say "condiments," I smiled and shrugged.

"Surprises! Presents! Treats! Tiny plastic sunshine for the weary soul! Toys that bloom a smile on a young girl's face! Games that wipe the frown off a young lad! Something for everybody!"

I cleared my throat.

"Waal, Ma'am, Ah don't know much about pocket ladies, but thet seems like a right nice job."

I started to turn away from her and she grabbed my arm.

"Oh, it is, Chris, it is. It's a wonderful job! Look here, you give me a dollar and you can reach into any pocket you want and pull out your toy. I guarantee satisfaction."

She let go of my arm and peered into my face, smiling eagerly. Weighing my options, I reached into my vest and pulled a buck out of the lizard-skin wallet Nary'd given me as a going-away present. I handed her the dollar and she slipped it into a large pocket hanging over her enormous right thigh. There was a green pocket sewn onto the hem of the dress and I reached in. Her dress was moist to the touch. I pulled out a white plastic worm. It was molded into an S-shape and had a big red grin painted on its face. I turned it over in my palm, then slipped it into my vest.

"Thank you, Ma'am. Thet's a right nice worm. I'm gonna give it to my godson jest as soon as I get into New York City."

"Oh, you have people in New York?"

"Yes'm."

She nodded and looked at me expectantly. I was sorry I'd taken the worm but there was no getting out of it now.

"How 'bout you, Ma'am? You goin' visitin'?"

"Oh, no, Chris. I'm on an important mission. You see, I've been researching my family history and I've discovered something incredible."

She paused trenchantly and I shifted the soggy cigarette to the other side of my mouth before answering.

"What's that?"

"I'm in line for the egg clan. Isn't that something?"

Bingo. People like the Pocket Lady always sit next to me. Freaks on the Greyhound offer to trade cocks. Young girls at the next table enlist my help in shoving the sugar bowl up their noses. Languorous men on park benches follow me for miles, hounding me to buy one red checker. It's a fucking parade of the deranged. Molly says it's because I jangle the air around me. She also maintains that everyone is interesting if you know how to interview them.

I decided to cut it short. Molly'd be disappointed in me but she usually is when it comes to stuff like this. I can't afford to be like Molly. Her life is always messy, cluttered with unfinished business, because when you listen to people like Molly does, when you draw them out with infinite patience, you have to be around to help them sew it all back up. In some way, you take a piece of them with you back into your life. In my life, Molly herself is just about all the extra information I can take.

The Pocket Lady was staring at me, frowning slightly. I wasn't sure how long I'd been thinking.

"Waal now, isn't thet something," I said. "You know, it don't surprise me one bit thet providence'd smile down on a pretty ladybug like yourself."

She giggled, satisfied.

"Why, thank you, Chris. It isn't often a woman of my years

gets to meet such an understanding gentleman."

"Naw, the pleasure was all mine, little lady. And thanks again for thet worm. I jest know my godson will love it. Now if you'll excuse me, this ol' broken-down cowboy's gonna try to catch up on his sleep."

She patted my arm. I turned in my seat and lowered the hat over my eyes.

"You have a good rest, dear," she said.

I didn't really have a good rest. Molly kept gnawing at my brain, nudging out my plans for unloading the mushrooms. And I wanted a cigarette so badly I kept thinking about crawling out on the wing. A couple of times I thought about throwing out the wet cigarette in my mouth and putting in a fresh one but I didn't want the Pocket Lady to know I was awake.

Finally, I changed the cigarette and got one of Molly's letters out of my carry-on bag. I could feel the Pocket Lady staring at me.

Dear Flan—

Nothing much to report, Green Eyes, just I was walking Kaspar up along Delancey and the place was so goddamned layered with memories of you, I thought I might vomit from longing. Why was I walking Kaspar all the way up along Delancey? Well, we're temporarily banished from the park because last time we were there, Kaspar stole a dog. He ran up to this shivering little chihuahua, sniffed it a couple of times, picked it up in his mouth, and took off running through the fish market with it.

We finally caught up with him next to a truck full of shad. He was shaking it in his mouth, toying with it, looking puzzled. I guess it wasn't too satisfying an experience for him. The chihuahua's owner said his dog was traumatized but he didn't look any different to me. Those dogs are all fear. Fear and bug eyes. I trashed Kasp but I don't think he got the message. He seems to think there's nothing wrong with stealing a dog. That's your influence, no doubt.

What else? Well, it's an oven in New York. I went up to Cooperstown to see Johnny Bench get inducted into the Hall of Fame. It was an oven upstate too, but the sight of Johnny Bench's bald head brought on my period so that was some relief. Red Schoendienst was there too but he didn't seem to have any effect on my body.

Speaking of which, my body I mean, I keep having this insane dream. I'm chasing Kaspar and the dink up through the fish stalls. The chihuahua's owner's chasing me, screaming, waving a machete. I can see up ahead that it's too late. The chihuahua's already dead, Kaspar's big teeth meeting neatly over its crushed frame, its head and hind quarters flopping lifelessly on either side of his huge jaws. The owner is hysterical, bearing down on me. Kaspar's spitting little pieces of chihuahua as he runs. I'm winded, and the owner is closing in but it doesn't matter because suddenly I find myself

running toward you,
MV.

Molly can never seem to understand that Kaspar is a big dumb malamute. All he cares about is fun. He probably thought the chihuahua was a squirrel. He's a beautiful dog, 90 pounds of muscle and ruff, bright white with a gray and black mask forming a perfect widow's peak between his eyes. But he's got the personality of Dennis the Menace and Molly's his Mr. Wilson. She's the ideal foil. He'll pull a stunt like taking the chihuahua and Molly'll chase after him, all long legs and awkward grace, screaming in this ridiculous deep "authority voice," "Kas-par Hau-ser."

It was a pretty old letter but I couldn't help wondering all over again who Molly'd been sleeping with that it was a relief she got her period. It made me mad. I started grinding my back teeth and unfortunately for the Pocket Lady, it was at that moment that she chose to speak to me. I looked up to see that she was reading over my shoulder.

"I feel I should say something to you, Chris," she said.

"Ma'am?"

I wanted to kill her for looking at Molly's letter. Keeping my face calm, I imagined burning her fat forearm with a cigarette; the round puckered scar. She reached over and grabbed the cigarette out of my mouth, crumbling it into pieces between her huge sausage fingers. I set my teeth hard.

"Ma'am," I said again.

" A handsome young man like you...Should! Not! Smoke! It's

39

very bad! Especially since you have a young lady! Don't you think she worries about you?"

That did it. I grabbed her chin and put my face up to hers. She gasped.

"Look here, lady," I said. "You don't know me. You wouldn't care if I got run over by a bus, what do you care if I smoke? I'm not even smoking. You think that dime-store worm makes a connection between us?"

I let go of her face, shoving her against the seat; she rose and lumbered down the aisle, muttering to herself. Putting my hat back over my face, I slid down the seat. It was hard to think about Molly. I knew she'd be mad about the scene with the Pocket Lady even though she'd sympathize about the cigarette. She's an unregenerate smoker, my Molly. She even smokes in the shower. Still, she'd say I did have a connection to the fat bitch because I'd listened to her. It made me uneasy. I knew I'd have to calm down to pull off the scam. Finally, imagining Molly's black hair hanging over me, brushing my face, banishing the Pocket Lady from my mind, I fell asleep.

So, as I say, the flight was okay. While I was waiting in the Braniff Customer Service area, looking worried about my luggage, scratching my cowboy head, I saw Molly dragging my trunk out the door. She looked beautiful, her hair up in a Mets cap, the loose tendrils digging under her cheekbones. The Customer Service rep followed my gaze and I arranged my face sheepishly.

"Legs like that do a man's soul good," I drawled.

"I'm sure," she said, drawing her body up in the tight Braniff uniform. "Now, there's nothing to worry about, Mr. Johnson. You just go on and enjoy your stay in the Big Apple. We've got your address and we'll send your trunk over just as soon as it arrives. Probably tonight!"

"I'm much obliged, Ma'am, but what if it don't turn up? I got some right expensive presents for my godson in there."

"Now, I'm sure that won't happen, Mr. Johnson. Think positive! If somehow you baggage has gone awry, Braniff will reimburse you for the losses. Why, you can pick up the forms right at this office. At Braniff we treat every passenger like a V.I.P."

"Well, thank you, Ma'am. I think I just might do some sightseeing this afternoon, but you call just as soon that trunk turns up, y'hear?"

"We certainly will, Mr. Johnson. And Mr. Johnson?"

"Ma'am?"

"Thank you for flying Braniff."

6

Mets Fuck

The build-up was huge. Spectacularly romantic. No mood seemed too expansive to match our reunion, that heroic clash of cultures. The thumps of my heart were almost craven in their prosody. My pounding throat alone told a story so eloquent I could hardly stand it.

But I was a fraud by profession, my eye on the disguise. So I worried about all that hype for just me and Flan, two dumb bandits, profane dolts, skulking the sleazy border towns, the outskirts of order, passing empty-eyed through those great throngs of fate's swaddled cuties.

And as the moment of truth approached, I didn't feel like a princess or a damsel or a lover, or even, exactly, a girl. I felt like a minor league pitcher, hammered into a corner, behind on the count. I walked Kaspar slowly through the late October rain thinking: Can I get us out of the inning? I stared down my own heart, the monster in the batter box. The stands full of scouts, all watching me, watching me. Can I get us out of the inning?

I waited for him in a booth at Fee's, this bar on Avenue B. When Flan and I hung out there, more than ten years ago, it'd been a sort of junkie bar. Local riff-raff slumped over cokes, Velvets on the jukebox. Fee, the owner, was always half wired, though, and he liked it when we came in, drank beer, kicked up a fuss.

In some ways now Fee's has lost its edge. It's become sort of a stage stop on the slumming trail. Beautiful kids haunt the place, their eyes bright, flaunting tattoos. Fee doesn't care. He whomped up a kind of Ukrainian motif and pretends his is one of the old-time neighborhood bars. Real prole. He even sells spiked tea in a glass. During the day, tiny, wizened Polish guys come in to play pool and they drink the stuff like it was going out of style which, I guess, it is.

I like the place, its red ripped booths, dark, cut tables. I have history there. Fee's unchanged behind his thick glasses and stringy brown hair. His life etched hard in his dead white face, he always gives me a free drink.

Kaspar sat across from me, happily eating a giant peanut bowl full of ice. Kaspar's gullible. He thinks ice is food. He was crunching three cubes at once, slavering, his nose in the air, when Flan walked up to the table. He looked great. He leaned down hard, hunched up his shoulders and thumped the dog. Kaspar batted him with a front paw and, boxing with him, Flan cleared his throat.

"Jesus, Doll, that face," he said, lifting the big dog out of the seat, cradling him in his red arms, "let's cruise."

Then, laughing, he slid in next to me, around me, the dog in our laps, fur in our mouths. We kissed, yes, hard, our teeth clanging. A long kiss, an incredibly long kiss, a kiss like no previous kiss even was a kiss, Kaspar whipping us with limbs and tail as he squirmed in the booth.

Excited, Kaspar scrambled up on the table and started howling, really more a strangled "woo." I bit Flan's lip, and we separated, trying to coax Kasp off the table. Fee ambled over to us, scowling. Seeing Flan, his eyes lit up the scowl. He scooped Kaspar off the table and tossed him to the floor, then reached out a hand, clapping Flan on the shoulder.

"Goliath, man, good to see you again," turning to me, "Molly, you wanna get these two beasts the fuck out of my bar?"

"Sure thing, Fee. Sorry. Just a little publicity stunt."

"Hmph."

Flan broke in, smiling, reaching into his pocket. He held out his hand and Fee scooped up the glassine envelope sitting on it.

"Everyone should enjoy a family reunion," Flan said.

"You, know, you're right about that, Goliath," Fee said, palming the envelope. He leaned over, kissed me on the cheek, and nodded, studying my face.

"Good to see you all together again. But take it outside, huh? You're scaring the clientele. Most of these people ain't seen passion like that since the war."

Flan lifted his great auburn eyebrows at me and stood up. We didn't know what Fee meant by that, which war, or whether that was some line he usually reserved for the old men who made up his day clientele, and we didn't, at that moment, care. I dragged Kaspar out from under the table.

"Wanna go home, boy?" Flan said to him.

Kaspar cocked his head and Flan grabbed me from behind, holding my shoulders hard.

"That was some kiss."

"Yeah, it was," I said, laughing. "Did you come?"

Flan snorted.

"I don't know, beautiful girl. Why don't you check with Red Foley?"

Red Foley's a sportswriter, one of the official scorers for the Mets, and I guess that's sort of an in-joke between us. Hard to believe we still *had* any in-jokes after all our time apart. But you know what they say: Old Mets don't die—their balls just get heavier. Or something.

We walked down Avenue B, past the green gizzards of Tompkins Square Park, past the zombies, the college pretties, men in undershirts, kids shrieking in fire-hydrant spray, through the persistent tango-sweet wail that poured out of cars. Kaspar ran up ahead, sniffing garbage, panting in the thick air. There's nothing he likes better than pizza that's been run over a couple of times. Axle grease is his favorite topping.

We crossed Houston onto Clinton Street. The streets got tighter, quieter, more desperate. Quart bottles of cheap beer and bins of socks crowded the sidewalk, pushed up against the densely packed short buildings. Pregnant women leaned out of shadows offering us dope, Brown Scum, Eagle Man, All American. At the cross streets, cafeterias glowed a sick fried yellow on each corner.

It was a long walk down to my apartment, a half-converted warehouse on Fulton. Flan was quiet, taking it all in. We stopped once on Catherine Street, absorbing the chanted bravado of a gang of teenage boys, outrageous hats festooned with fuzzy car dice, wispy moustaches, Tommy Hilfiger jackets in color combinations you'd normally associate with a Finnish loge team. It seemed to buoy Flan. He laughed, shadowed funny in the street light. As we got closer to my house, tourists dotted the streets, looking for the South Street Seaport, the smell of fish bulging out their eyes.

What's sex with Flan like? Well, searching for a metaphor, it's not geometry, exactly, or big, melting slabs of dialogue. It's not sliced parts or the honeyed down-home homeyness of Elvis Presley. I guess if it's like anything, it's like, well, a certain kind of live unpolished music. That is to say, out of noise, out of darkness, out of pure chaos, hysteria, long hair caught in a bass drum, a broken chair leg bulging out the lead singer's cheeks, fingertips sliced on strings, blood running down the rounded body of a flat guitar, slippery picks sailing across the room, out of all of this rose one clear sweet note, catching us, carrying us, exploding in our ears.

What gets me about it is, well, yeah, of course, the blessed fucking quiet. It's just me and him. No Evan, no Pappa, no basilisks in greatcoats, animate blenders, mocking window panes. For all that peace, for noise so amiably despotic it chases away everything else, for the barest of moments as a beatified little sucker, a girl can put up with almost anything. Remember that.

Round Three. Flan's beard stubble burning my cunt. Softly, the question from between my legs,
"Did you miss me, Molly?"
A bite, a gasp, hand scratching a fish-hook scar into my thigh, my voice a squeak.
"Yeah, Flan. Not as much as I miss the Kid, Mex, Roger, Straw, Mookie, Nails...but I missed you."
A tremendous growl and he's looming above me, hands on my shoulders, throwing my head against the bed,
"did."

Hands hard around my wrists, his breath in my face,
"you."

Knuckles against my jaw, my teeth on fire,
"miss."

Again my head slammed hard against the bed, my shoulders under his calloused paws,
"me."

Biting my lip, a little distance, "Yeah, Green Eyes, a lot."

He flopped over on his back next to me, reaching across my face to grab the cigarettes off the window sill. He put the cold ashtray on my stomach. Cigarette poised over my body, flicking over the tray, a tiny weight in my gut as the ash falls.

"You're a cigarette hog. Gimme some."

He nodded, hoisting himself up, resting the 'rette in the ashtray between my ribs. Bearing down, he opened my mouth and blew smoke into my lungs. He gave me the cigarette and, propped up on his elbows, began tracing patterns on my face. Then, taking it from my mouth, he held it ember-down, making a sound like a diving plane, and crushed it out hard in the ashtray, forcing the air out of my lungs. He laughed, stroking my collarbone.

"You're a real piece of work," he said. "Think you know everything about the Mets?"

"Uh-huh."

We started fucking, the ashtray between us, digging a red circle onto his chest. Flan moving effortlessly above me, hip bones piercing bruises. Small moans and an evil crinkle around his sharp nose.

"You didn't know shit from Shinola about baseball when we met."

"That," hips up to meet him, a spray of ash in my face, "was then, and this," his body chasing mine, pinned to the bed, "is now."

"Think you could pass a Mets test?"

"And if I can't?" His teeth on my arm, his hair a mess, cadence carrying the challenge.

"If you can't, I'll stop."

"Oh yeah?"

"Yeah."

"Okay, shoot."

"What," a fast grind, a slow withdrawal, raw flesh, "happened in the sixth game of the '86 World Series?"

Voice choked in hard exhale of breath, "the whole game?"

A soft kiss, a short stab, teasing, "can't you do it?"

Eyebrows raised, muscles tight in my left leg, "Oh I can do it alright," arms around his neck, riding, "the question is if you can hold off coming that long."

A hard smash, knees against my thighs, eyes on fire; a short silence, bouncing, a huge groan.

"Maybe you're right," he said, blowing air hard. "Just the tenth inning."

"You're serious?"

He slapped me.

"Dead serious."

Breasts hard in his hands, "Okay, they kept Hojo in to play short. The, um, center fielder homered."

Cock pelting hard, upping the ante, "Uh-huh. What was his name?"

"Hen-henderson."

"Good."

A quieter drive, an inducing rhythm.

"Owen and, oh, Schiraldi struck out."

"Uh-huh?"

Flan acrobatic, a great circular wallop, pulsing snake sinew, Kaspar scratching at the door. Very fast, the words tripping,

"Boggs doubled and Barret singled, scoring Boggs, then he stole second on the throw to the plate. B-buckner got hit by a, god, pitch, and then, oh shit, how do you *do* that?"

"Shh," Flan said, stroking the hair off my forehead, blowing on my face, saving me, crushing my mouth down before Rice lined out.

"Shh." A final parry, a flutter of kisses, contorted faces, a pair of screams, Kaspar howling in the living room, then Flan erupted into laughter, hurling the ashtray across the room.

"What's so funny?"

Laughing hard, his red face full of mirth,

"You're such a geek."

"Fuck you," I said, laughing too.

"I gotta hand it to you, Doll, I never expected you to be able to do it."

"Yeah, well, a girl learns to keep busy when her man's working off his probation in a fucking desert."

"That was then, and this, Doll, is now," he said and grabbed me to him, pressing away the years apart, smiling for us both.

I watched Flan's angled face move in sleep until the morning sun streaked it. I think I breathed once or twice.

7

The Ice Cream Man

Molly was awake when I got out of the shower, sitting on the table, her legs on a chair, staring out the kitchen window at the business on the river. She was wearing my blue shirt, unbuttoned, and huge ratty cut-offs. Her hair was all over the place. In less than five days she was going to be in Mapache. But I wasn't thinking about that.

"Don't you ever sleep?" I said.

She pondered this question with utmost seriousness, drawing her long legs up to her chin. I should've known better. Throwaway dialogue is wasted on Molly.

"In the first place, Flan, you haven't slept in a bed with me for five years, so what do you know about my habits?"

There was no point in answering. I knew she was only just getting started. Besides, watching Molly rave melts my heart a little.

"In the second place, I didn't sleep last night because you're so fucking beautiful, I can't take my eyes off you and in the third place, to answer your question, no, I try not to because when I sleep, I dream and when I dream, things go all fuzzy and irrational. Don't you think I get enough of that shit just going through my paces?"

"I guess, Doll, but what choice do you have?"

Molly was wound down some, but as she considered my question, she hoisted herself off the table and started banging around in the kitchen, setting up the percolator, throwing open cabinets, tossing ice trays out of the freezer, which set Kaspar to howling, thinking he might get some ice.

"Well, you know how they say a person is the author of his dreams?"

I nodded. The visual comedy of all this was so breathtaking, Molly throwing herself around the tiny kitchen with her big exaggerated motions, huge dog tangled at her feet, so like a Buster Keaton movie, that I could already foresee the outcome. As she spoke, each disparate motion told the whole story, the punch line coiled in her muscles, but I let her play it out. Her clipped voice rushed the blood in my ears.

"Well, I'm not the author of my dreams. I'm the tailor or the fabric technician or something. I just go along merrily with whatever my brain serves up, taking in the floor show. And then, sooner or later, something happens that doesn't make sense. And bang, I'm not the hero at all, I'm not the central character, I'm just a crew member. I'm part of the dream staff. And I'm off and running, frantically crawling up the walls of the dream, snaggletoothed, stitching, trying to hold it together, trying to invent some plausible reason why you're standing on your head in my pediatrician's waiting room when you're supposed to be in prison and I didn't even know you then; or what I'm doing in a high-school Greek class not having done the homework in god knows how long when I know I've got my PhD diploma hanging on my wall and anyway I didn't learn Greek 'til grad school and the teacher suddenly unzips his pants and whips it out for no reason at all. Or else it's something like I'm trapped on a dope boat to nowhere which is a totally absurd idea to begin with and everyone I've ever known is huddled in shit-caked blankets staring at the blasted landscape and instead of offering some explanation about how we came to this miserable state, they're all arguing about whether it's cool to score at Clignancourt which I know is a Paris Metro stop and we're on a boat which doesn't seem to be stopping anywhere."

Molly, freakily graceful, scrambled onto the sink ledge to reach a high shelf, knocked a salt shaker into the sink, and jumped down into the hysterical clutter on her kitchen floor.

"I spend the whole night desperately trying to keep things in line and I wake up exhausted and grouchy. So, no, I try not to sleep. Okay?"

"You're out of coffee, right?"

She turned and smiled, holding an extension cord.

"Right."

"Well, I gotta go out, how 'bout I make like a boy and bring you some?"

"Wait, where're you going? I'll take Kaspar."

"I gotta see a guy about a horse."

"Flan." Her voice was rough, wary. When you're treading on dangerous territory with Molly, she scrapes her lower teeth against her upper lip. She makes a face like a bulldog.

"It's kind of an unsavory horse, Doll."

She threw her arms up and came out from behind the kitchen counter. Heaving herself up on the table, next to me, she said,

"This is where I came in."

I felt my temper flare and Kaspar, who'd been placidly trying to chew three huge steak bones at once, raised his head and growled a warning at me, his ears erect. Molly was absently burning at the loose threads on her shorts with a cigarette, her brain going a mile a minute.

I took a deep breath. She was right. We'd been through all this before. The last time we'd split up over it. That was right before I'd gone down on the sour deal in Cruces and when we got back together, Molly tracking me down through her old connection to the Feds and flying all the way to New Mexico to visit me, we'd agreed not to talk about it. But it's hard. I don't believe in mixing business with pleasure. No con does. And I can't shake the feeling that Molly sees my life as some kind of anachronistic adventure.

But I watched her ram her bare feet into bashed leather sneakers, and something gave in me.

"Listen, I'm sorry, Doll. You really wanna come?"

"Yeah, it'd be fun."

"Well, it's okay with me. Maybe you'll bring me luck and god knows you have one hell of an early warning system. Any sniff of trouble and you'd have Kasp to say nothing of Evan and your father and Noah's fucking ark down on you in a second, dragging you out of the fray."

She smiled and I kissed her, her huge eyes opening into wells.

"It's just it rips me apart inside to think of you in the slam, Doll. Hang on, I gotta get something outta the trunk."

Bending, I unwrapped the flannel shirt and portioned out a couple of mushrooms. I felt Molly's eyes on me and my hands clenched into fists. Alone in my adobe shack, thinking I'd pay a million dollars just to have her with me for a second, I forget what a pain in the ass Molly is. She wants everything to be just so. She sat down hard on the floor under the kitchen window, kicking her foot against the ground, her bulldog face in place.

"Were those mushrooms in the trunk yesterday?"

"Yeah," I said, "what do you care? You think the DEA's gonna stop a couple of egghead professors driving around in a Buick?"

"That's not the point, Flan. I was carting that thing around all day. You should've told me."

She was right, again, damn her gloomy eyes. I should've been straight with her about it. Hell, it was the least I could do. Anyone else working a scam with me, I'd've laid it all out and cut them in besides. Dragging that trunk through airport security was probably a quarter of the risk in the whole operation. It's just hard to tell how to play it with Molly. She's not exactly straight and she's not exactly crooked either. I wasn't sure what to say to her. Slipping the mushrooms in my pocket, I lay down on the floor, my head in her lap.

Molly curled a hand and ran the ring I gave her along my jaw-line. The polished wolf tooth was cold on my face. I closed my eyes and waited. See, most girls in a situation like that would be sweating rivers into black lace, shrieking anything they could think of, trying to figure an angle. You feel like an asshole and they try to get an edge; but Molly was quiet. I knew she was try-ing to assimilate the information, trying to think of a way to make it okay between us and I figured if I left her alone, she eventually would. Molly never forgets anything but I've never known her to use old beefs against anyone either. When it's over, it's over.

A man who's been in jail, like a boy who comes too soon, eventually learns how to stretch each moment into a game of concentrated focus. Of course, when it comes to Molly, it's a little harder because against all my best interests, I actually care what she thinks of me. On the other hand, from knowing Molly, whose damn brain never stops whirring, I've picked up a lot of little tricks for keeping my mind occupied. So I was startled, absorbed in what kind of soup Nary would be if he were a soup, when she brushed her hands together suddenly, wiping the slate clean.

"What the hell, Flan. You can make it up to me next week. Come with me to Feck's class. I'll use you as an exercise."

"You want me to go back to New Mexico?"

"Yeah. Will you? It's just for a week."

I sighed. There was no graceful way out of it and I did want to be with her. In fact, I didn't want her out of my sight and certainly not in the fucking Southwest where the people are so stupid they'd probably lynch her as soon as buy her a beer.

"Will you take a probably?"

"If you kiss me," she said.

"Doll, it's what I live for."

That's how I found myself, with a pocketful of hallucinogen, a malamute on one arm and a beautiful girl on the other, walking across Fourteenth Street. I was happy as a clam. I love cities. The streets play music. We were treated to a Beirut serenade as kids on both sides of us set off pre-Halloween firecrackers. The noise didn't seem to bother Kaspar. He raised his snout, joining in with an occasional "woo."

We crossed north between B and C, over to the island in the middle of the street. I stopped at a stalled ice cream truck and rapped sharply on the barred window. I wasn't sure if Tom would be in. He usually hangs out in the park mornings when the kids are in school and his other clients are still sleeping off the previous night's excesses, but after a few seconds of knocking, his head and arms poked out of the opening.

Half of Tom's face is paralyzed and he looks kind of scary, bald, with his face frozen into a half-rictus, his mouth a plastered grin. He was dressed as I last saw him, in a frayed Nehru jacket open over his bare scarecrow chest. A heavy chrome peace medallion seemed to weigh down his skinny neck. In the old days you could really get his goat by calling it the footprint of the American chicken. For a second, the five years since I'd seen him last seemed to accordion, leaving me still in spitting distance of 35, with a clean record and no questions about the way I was leading my life. I glanced at Molly. She hung back, unsure, then spoke just before he did.

"You were Evan's dealer. You sell ice cream?" she said.

Tom's good eye widened as he recognized me and the other half of his face crept up and joined the smile. He didn't seem to hear Molly and I decided to let it go. Whatever was eating her, I knew she could just as easily tell me about it after I closed the deal.

"Flan, Jesus! It's great to see you. This your woman?"

"Yeah, Tom. You been charging her?"

"Looks like an ordinary New Yorker to me. Why shouldn't she pay for ice cream?"

"No reason, I guess. How you been?"

"Okay, Flan. I can't complain too much. Didn't think I'd see you again, man."

"How come?"

"The city's alive, Flan. It evolves away from you. It eats itself."

I shrugged.

"How's business, Tom?"

"Kids all want dope, coke, special K. You hear of special K out in the fucking desert, man? Goddamned neural toxin. They take it and dance, I think."

"That's what Molly called it, 'the fucking desert.'" I shook my head. "Pair of provincial big city Yankees we got here, Kasp."

Tom wrinkled one eyebrow at me.

"Anyhow, man, kids come up to the truck, heads full of horseshit. I tell'm so, too. They're too young to remember. All want C or D, X, Special K. Do I look like a fucking nursery school teacher to you? Still, supply and demand, what can you do? Ice cream's sellin' as good as ever."

"You sell drugs out of the ice cream truck?" Molly asked. Her voice was flat and dry, like the desert I detest, and I turned to her, alarmed, as Tom answered breezily.

"I prefer to say it I sell ice cream out of my drug truck, little lady, but beauty's in the eye of the beholder, they tell me."

"You okay, Doll?"

She shook her head, that same clearing gesture Nary used, her long hair making her look even more like a waterlogged dog than Nary does.

"Yeah, I guess. Most New Yorkers have paranoid fantasies about ice cream trucks but they run more along the lines of there's a band in there playing the loop over and over again or a clown smoking a cigar's driving or how do they get the swirls in soft ice cream?" She gyrated her hips obscenely. "You don't expect to see the guy who—"

I cut her off. She was making Tom nervous. Kaspar strained on the leash, desperate to chase a black squirrel that was scrambling up one of those stunted trees that grow in the middle of the street.

"That dog's got some kinda timing, Doll. Why don't you take him up the road a ways and give him a fair shot at that squirrel?"

She shook her head and rolled her eyes, her mind a million miles away, and softly, absently, voice alive if not verdant, she said "Yeah, okay, nice to meet you, Tom."

"The pleasure was mine."

We watched Kaspar drag her east down Fourteenth Street, his long tail bouncing, curled over a powerful back. Molly's hair mantled her shoulders, lit blue in sunlight too pretty for an East Side slum. Kaspar pawed the tree, howling, and I turned back to Tom.

"I got something for you, Tom."

"I figured, man, but what's with the crazy lady and the pooch? Nah, never mind. None of my business, you always workin' one angle or another. Just pray she don't go down, man, be the good Lord's own pity what the Tombs'd do to a beautiful lady like that."

"She won't."

"You say so man, I believe you. So lay it on me."

I handed him the mushrooms, and he sniffed them, then ducked out of sight into the interior of the ice cream truck. He popped back up a second later.

"Mexican?"

I nodded.

"You try this shit yet, Flan?"

"Nope."

"Well, you try it, I'll try it. We'll talk tomorrow." He waved to Molly and Kaspar and started to retreat. Popping up again, he said, "Flan, listen, I need someone to run my carriers."

"The Montego Bay run?"

"Yeah, listen it's a real cush run. I know you can't carry anymore."

"Says who?"

He looked at me blankly.

"Well, hey, this is better, right? No risk, you pay all the plane fares but you get a clean third, right off the top, and I guarantee I'll buy it from you, $1600 a quarter pound and we're gettin' six pounds a pop."

"Your runners are getting three pounds of pressed pot apiece into their shoes?"

"Not shoes, Flan. Jesus. How long you been out west, a hundred years? Shoes are over. The dogs are on to it. We do coffee bags now. Vacuum-sealed, and dark rum for the hash oil. It's a hippie milk run, man. Easy as pie. You shell out for the fares. I'll back you for the grass and set up the bribes. It's that same family, remember, the cousin works airport security, the mama puts y'all up in Negril, the sons do the farming out by the cliffs? You dug 'em, remember? Took real pride in their product, their farming technique, not like these Napa Valley assholes with their cellars and blue lights. Of course, you'd have to clean up a bit, cut your hair, go straight, the whole tourist thing—"

Tom broke off. I was staring down Fourteenth Street at Molly, who sat on the weedy broken center walk, her long legs over Kaspar's prone body.

I scratched my head, rubbed my jaw. I really wanted to take him up on it. Back when I carried for Tom, I really envied Jism Jeff, the guy who ran us. Colossally calm and even-tempered, Jeff would move sleepily through the whole process, stuffing his big red face with jerk-pork sandwiches and sweet Dragon Stout, soaking up the rays of the Jamaican sun.

Of course, he had no reason to be anxious. He was, essentially, on a bi-monthly vacation, taking no risk as Tom had pointed out; but still, we all felt he had the situation in hand, making the buy and paying off the guards, and none of us ever feared going down. Breezing through the dogs on both ends of the plane trip, he'd wait calmly, just out of sight. If there was trouble, he'd be there with the bond. And even though Tom has had plenty of hard luck, as his face will attest, no one ever went down on a Jism Jeff run.

I knew I could do it, be Jism Jeff and then some, get what was, for me at least, a straight job, some security. But I felt Tom's eyes on me as I watched Molly and the dog.

"Oh," he said. "It's like that, huh?"

"Yeah." I nodded up the street at Molly. "I'd kill for the run, Tom, I really would, but I gotta play this thing out."

"Love's a monkey, Goliath. I been tellin' you that for, what, ten years now?"

"Yeah."

"Well, listen, man, think it over, okay? I really want you to do it. I won't start asking around for a couple of weeks. So, you let me know."

He retreated into the truck and called out,

"Hey, Flan, about the other, how much you got?"

"More than you could sell if school let out for the summer every day of the week."

"It's coming," he called, "school can't go on forever."

8

I Can't Believe I Ate the Whole Thing

Well, anyone could foresee the hitch, I guess. Foresee it as I see it. It wasn't the clash of cultures that was gonna trip us up. It was the domesticity thing. The quiet awe of it all is deaf in dialogue. Nowhere in "I'm having a beer. Can I get you one?" do we find that tremendous mystifying whomp, the dull beauty of shared lives. It's hard to speak of. It's hard to speak *to*. It's hard to speak.

I left Flan and Kaspar in a bar on Sixth while I ran up to the office to arrange for my week's absence. Sharon, now that she'd met, and apparently spent the night with, Feck, seemed to think the whole thing was hysterical, and agreed to cover for me, cheerfully xeroxing what papers I'd need at NMSU, and calling grad students to sit in for my office hours. The power that man has over young women, even though I was one of them once, never ceases to amaze me.

On the way out, I ran into Nico Shirt, lugging a giant blue bag, big enough for a corpse, big enough, I was sure, for all of her possessions. She stopped, out of breath in the stifling hall, and cleared her throat.

"Um, Dr. Veeka?"

"Nell. What's up? Please don't tell me you have a question about Althusser. I'll shrivel up and die right on the spot."

"No. Um. I can't come to class next week. Do you think you could, I mean," the barest of tragic glances at the corpse bag told me all I needed to know about what she meant.

"Well, since you spared me the pontificating, I'll letcha in on a little secret. No, wait, scratch that. I'll make a deal with you."

"What?"

"Do you like dogs?"

In response, she unzipped the bag, rooted around in it a second, and came up with a photo album which she handed to me, her pretty young face a mixture of triumph and gravity. I leafed through it. Pictures of dogs. Mostly a tan and white English bull and a grizzled chocolate lab.

"Jerry, that's the bull, died last year—died like a rock star, choked on his own puke. I've got Mary tied up downstairs."

"Is she friendly?"

"Yeah. She wouldn't know evil if it came up to her and bit her on the knee."

"Well, then, how 'bout this? I'm going out of town for all of next week. You and Mary could stay at my place, take care of my dog. Would that do anything to affect your inability to show up at class?"

Relief, disappointment, gratitude, suspicion. A volley of emotions played connect the dots on her freckled face.

"Yeah, it would, thank you. I mean, but if—"

"If I'm going out of town, what do you need to go to class for?"

"Yeah."

"I guess you don't, but I don't wanna cancel class 'cause then we'll all get in trouble. So just show up and talk about the reading, or whatever."

"Okay, Dr. Veeka," she sighed, impatient with me, and I laughed.

I gave her the address and we arranged for her to meet Kaspar that night. Of course, everything working out so neatly was predicated on getting Flan to agree to go out west with me, but I figured I had all night to work on him. Just the sight of that fresh, daisy-faced damsel would probably go a long way toward convincing him it was the right move.

She smiled and hoisted the bag onto her shoulder, starting off down the hall. Feeling happy, like maybe there was something worthwhile about being a teacher, remembering all Feck had done for me, that partly exalting hard swallow of accomplishment, I choked down the usual overpowering humility I feel about being in a position of authority over my students and called out to her.

"Nell?"

She turned.

"If you'll forgive a little unwelcome advice from someone who's been there, don't try to be a grad student living out of a bag. It's not cool. It's not insouciant. It's just a colossal drag. And it's too fucking hard. Graduate school is an exercise in accommodating stupidity. If you're gonna pull it off, you need a place to decompress, bounce off the walls. Get it together or take a term off. I'll help you make sure you don't lose your funding."

She froze and then nodded, saying nothing more as she walked off down the hall, the bag goosing her, hitting her legs as she moved. Her reaction pleased me. She'd think about it but she didn't want to talk about it. A girl after my own heart.

When I went to meet Flan he was standing by the jukebox, staring at the changing lights, lime, rose, blue, and listening to Johnny Cash. I thumped Kaspar and slipped in behind him, tugging the belt loops of his black jeans.

"Hey, guy, you ready to talk about the ice cream man?"

He turned, eyes a little wild, and started to follow me to a table, then stopped, grabbed my shoulders, and spun me around. He got tangled around Kaspar and went down hard. I helped him up. The bartender snickered and Kaspar howled.

"Swift. What were you gonna say?"

"Molly, you know I'm tripping, right," he said and laughed.

"Literally," I said.

He rolled his eyes.

"No, Doll. I—"

"I know what you mean, Flan. But I don't think that matters unless you really mean you're tripping and you think you're an orange and oranges can't talk. Or you're tripping and sounds have colors and the timbre of my shimmer is so loud you can't hear a goddamn thing I'm saying."

He shrugged and brushed the hair off my face.

"Nah, Doll. I just wanted you to know."

"I knew. But consider me warned."

"Okay, then, let's do it."

I sat at a table in the corner while Flan went to get me a beer. I was uneasy with the situation, trying not to know it, or even think it to myself. My little unholy visitations seem to come hardest and heaviest when I'm ill at ease and I was in no mood for a bunch of unwelcome advice from my unappointed, undead praetorians and their goddamn Warner Brothers familiars.

But I couldn't shake the feeling, a kind of sick ardor. I'm not the kind of girl who thinks everything can be settled with one big wet-eyed huggy "talk," and as far as I was concerned we were embarking on this stupid conversation more because I owed Flan an explanation as to why I'd acted like such a freak after insisting he take me along than because I wanted his reassurance.

But as long as this thing was in the way between us, I figured I had to tell him the truth, and the truth, as is so often the case, was fucking complicated.

He came back to the table with a pitcher and two glasses, and, shoving Kaspar over, slid in next to me.

"I gotta tell you, Doll. I'm not sure what this is about but if it'll make you feel any better, I won't deal with Tom anymore."

"Me neither. And no, that wouldn't help."

He rubbed the heels of his palms hard into his eye sockets, wrenching his wrists around, then sighed and took the cigarette out of my mouth, sucking on it, his cheeks floating inward, looking simultaneously sneaky and bedeviled. And beautiful. What's a girl to do?

"Listen, Doll," he said, "you know I'm not too at home with these rarified subtleties of yours. But you realize Evan was fucking stupid, don't you? It's not Tom's fault a guy with a serious dope habit ate five tabs of acid and walked under a bus."

"Why isn't it?"

"What do you mean why? Because your husband, God rest his soul—"

"I wish."

I could see it in the curl of his shoulders: he resisted the urge to look around the room, peering instead, intently, into my face.

"He's not here, is he?"

I laughed.

"No."

"Good." His posture relaxed. "Because Evan knew he was sick, knew what the acid was when he took it. He didn't have to be alone. He didn't have to leave the house. I mean, c'mon. Give the guy a little credit. What would you have wanted for him? No fire? No passion? That he just said no?"

"No, Flan. But I'm not too sure about just saying yes either."

"Okay, Doll. Granted. It's serious business. Dangerous. The guy had balls. He gambled and he lost. You feel mixed up about it. You don't wanna make a sweeping statement one way or the other. I understand that."

"But?"

"But I don't know. How're you gonna break it up? Say yes to legal drugs but not illegal? Organic but not chemical? Ups but not downs? Safe but not exciting? Masculine but not feminine? Eaten but not injected? Mind-expanding but not escapist? Affecting you but not the people you care about? This dealer but not that one? How are you going to decide?"

"I'm not going to. And certainly I'm not going to decide for anyone else, least of all you. But I think everyone has to. For themselves. Make some kind of accommodation. Any kind—"

I lit the filtered end of a cigarette and dragged hard on it. Flan ripped it out of my mouth, set about lighting me a new one, tapped it into my mouth, lingering, his rough fingers on my lips.

"Respect drugs," I coughed. "Bifurcate them."

"There's a slogan. I can see it all over town, spreading like tumbleweed. Respect drugs: bifurcate them. What the hell is that supposed to mean?"

"I don't know."

"Well, okay, Doll. Lemme ask you this. How do *you* 'bifurcate' them?"

"I don't know, Flan. I take hallucinogens because, I mean, what's the point of not?"

"Fair enough."

"I drink for the hell of it. I don't take speed because I like it too much and then I can't do anything else and anyway I think it makes my breasts shrink. I don't take any prescription drugs because all the ones I've tried, like because I'm insane?"

He nodded, egging me on, me, the queen of awkward silence, talking up a blue streak, maudlin, goofy, unable to shut up.

"They fuck up my language facility and if the whole point of them is to level my mood and make me into a good little economic soldier then why bother if they take away my livelihood? I don't take any of that rave shit because I'm too old and because I hate that bliss-out, affectless feeling like poison. And I have reasons like that for everything else. You want me to go on?"

"What about dope?"

"I don't know."

"How 'bout you don't take dope because you think it killed your husband, probably, and your father?"

"Yes. No. That's not a good enough reason. And it's certainly not a good enough reason for you to act on out of consideration for me."

"Okay, so what's the problem?"

"The problem? What's the problem with heroin?"

"Right, Blue Eyes. Give."

"The problem with heroin is."

"Yeah, Doll, what?"

I stretched back, then brought my arm down around the dog's back like he was my movie-theater date and I was trying to cop a feel. Kaspar licked my face. I had no idea what I was going to say, but I couldn't let that stop me. I opened my mouth, and the words tumbled out unbidden.

"You're gonna think this is crazy, Flan But to me, dope is like you're the lonely fat kid in the 'I can't believe I ate the whole thing' T-shirt, wandering around an amusement park, thick-glassed, waddling like a coolie undertaker, right?"

"I guess."

"Right, so you're galumphing around, eating everything in sight, and you buy a ticket on the grossest, fastest, spinningest, most upside-down ride there. The ride they advertise on TV. The big one. The Matterhorn, The Krakatoa *West* of Java, the Oscillator, the Extinction Express. And you get up there and the best-case scenario is you're gonna buckle in, get to the top, and vomit a great stinking deluge, enfilades of puke, on the people waiting in line to get tickets. That's the *best* thing that can happen, right? Total fucking humiliation?"

"If you say so, Doll."

"I do. And the worst thing that can happen is you just die. Your tiny, fat-slabbed heart just gives out. And the in-between thing that can happen is you're trapped in there forever, just spinning around, chubby fists beating on plexiglass, your chunky face contorted by something, something major, the biggest thing that's ever happened to you, but from the ground, no one can see what it is: ecstasy, rage, horror, recognition, numbness. It could be anything. And there you are, still spinning while everyone else goes home.

"And the really sad part is: all anyone wants to know is why. Why did you buy the ticket? But it doesn't matter why you bought the ticket. Because you thought it might be fun or because it was cool or because the most popular girl in school hurt your feelings out by the log flume or because you saw something so beautiful in the trained elephant's eyes or you were running away or you wanted to hurl yourself off the top. What matters in the end is, what? Nothing. Just that you're on a wild ride. Alone. And that's why I don't take dope."

Flan stared at me.

"Because you don't want to be a fat kid in an 'I can't believe I ate the whole thing' T-shirt?"

"Right. Because it's too private."

"Private." He nodded at me slowly, making up his mind. "Okay. How 'bout if I keep working with Tom but I don't ever deal dope? Would that work for you, Piggy?"

"Yes."

We staggered out of the bar into a quality of light that is absolutely endemic to staggering out of bars in the middle of the day. We blinked in the clammy, stinging brightness and Kaspar started to pull on the leash, almost as if he knew he was about to embark on a week-long fling with an older woman and couldn't wait to get home.

Kasp and Mary got along famously, as it turned out, racing in tandem through the cluttered apartment, barking at the passing garbage scows; and not even Flan could bring himself to split them up by nixing our trip.

9

Anyway, Virtue

It wasn't Molly's fault. Part of me, the part my mother raised right, knew that. But I was mad at her anyway. All that talk made us shy with each other, like a couple of kids in a schoolyard, an incredible waste of time. And then my big move East had lasted a grand total of five fucking days. She'd been cool about it; cool, practical, magnanimous, saying of course I could stay at her place, that she'd be back in less than a week, making a big show of not asking me to come, giving me space, not rubbing me the wrong way.

But I wasn't about to freeload at Molly's house and I wasn't about to let her traipse around my turf with Feck, that pointy-headed satyr, even for the few days he'd be around. Molly, for all her supposed genius, was absolutely convinced the guy had no real interest in her. For a girl who can talk to anyone, she's fucking illiterate when it comes to stuff like that. I knew he was in love with her. I could smell it.

I hate the Southwest. I despise every cactus, every coyote, every mesa, every stringy jackrabbit, every single stunted pecan tree. And most of all I hate running into Molly's own Ichabod fucking Crane everywhere I go. I go to the track, he's there. Nary and I stop for a shot of tequila on the pecan delivery, he's there. Always with a different twenty year-old chippie on his bony arm.

But even given that I detest the Southwest, it's the place I know the best and picturing Molly and Feck driving southeast along highway 10, the huge sky canopying them, the top down, music blaring, that pink air they put up at dusk, speeding with no fear of reprisal, I got sick.

What Molly doesn't understand is that she can't help but rub me the wrong way. She can be cool. She can be silent. She can be fucking gorgeous. She can be every con's ideal. But she can't make it so we fit together exactly right. It chafes when she's with me, from jamming our lives together, and it chafes when we're apart. My cock chafes from fucking her, my heart chafes from looking at her, my fists chafe from hitting the stucco walls of her living room, thinking of her, my girlfriend, the package deal: a chick, a dead gypsy hophead in a snap-brim hat, a squashed junkie, and ten thousand animals in period costume. She makes me raw.

So I wouldn't fly with her. I couldn't. I didn't want to watch her angelic face, composed, listening with rapt attention to some bore sitting next to her, nattering away in Chink, some bird doctor with a twitch, some one-legged Mormon, some bright-eyed punk smuggling a rat in her leather jacket. Or worse, bringing that same palpable attention to someone who wasn't even there. It pissed me off. Besides, I planned to break at least five state laws on this trip and I'd be damned if I was gonna ditch my luck by flying in on the NMSU budget.

I made plans to take her to dinner that night. Feck'd put her up at the Quinta Inn out on 28, too damn good for the Billy the Kid Arms which was closer to the school and had a friendly mom 'n' pop management. That was another thing. I had to laugh when I heard where Feck suggested Molly and I rendezvous when I'd nixed picking her up on the NMSU campus. The Doña Ana County Municipal Office Building. I knew the place well because my mother was conceived there.

Back in the '20s and '30s, the Doña Ana County Municipal Office building was the biggest cathouse around for miles. It was an ornate two-story house, full of plush red velvet and dark polished wood; all around the central area, in two stacked rings, were little rooms where the johns went once they'd chosen their lady, though I guess the filthy leftover fruit-pickers and hopped-up young soldiers from Fort Bliss or Los Gordos didn't particularly care which whore they got.

Anyway, each room had a sign with the girl's name over the

door and when the place was turned into the Citizen's Bank in the late '40s, some wise guy with a misplaced sense of irony, probably an Easterner, had left the decor exactly as it was, name tags and all. By the time the County bought the building, it had got to be sort of a tradition, so they left it too.

My grandmother's room, still called the Esperanza room, was a whole five-salon suite. The head judge had his offices there, and that's where Feck thought I should meet Molly. I guess he thought it was quaint. Or maybe he thought he could get points with the judge, dragging a hot-shot intellectual like Molly around and making introductions. Or maybe he wanted to get me bagged.

In any case, I had no intention of hooking up with Molly there. The place made me laugh; some poor sucker doling out justice from the very room where my grandmother had given cowboys head for 25 years. But I stand firm on my position. Quaint is quaint, but there's nothing worth seeing in Mapache.

For that matter nothing good's ever come out of NMSU besides the world-renowned NMSU Experimental Pepper. Developed in the seventies, the flat green pepper is mildly pungent and easily digestible, an accomplishment which is interesting only if you like chile, which I hate. The Aggies, the big NMSU team, couldn't even cover the spread against UTEP, their biggest rival, another bunch of losers. I arranged to meet Molly at the motel.

I took the crack-of-dawn flight into Dallas/Fort Worth and changed for El Paso. By the time I rented a Chevy Corsica on Chris Johnson's American Express Card it was still only noon so I decided to take my time, cruise around a little, and go to the track. I bought a racing form and some chow off the bartender in an El Paso dive.

Working my way through a plate of *arroz adobo*, I studied the horses. I'm a rotten gambler. I spend hours painstakingly applying formulas, changing lengths into time, getting a feel for past performances, but when I get up to the window, I always go by my gut.

Summer Sage, the 2 horse, was the indisputable favorite in the 12th. The morning line had him at 9 to 2, and at 6 and a half furlongs, placed so close to the rail, the four-year-old was a sure thing, but I couldn't bring myself to circle him on the form. I puz-

71

zled over it all the way to the track. I didn't think he would win and I figured if by some nasty fluke he did win, the odds were so lousy, it would be like finding a buck on the street. The pool at Sunland Park is puny and if some Texas big-spender coughs up even a sawbuck, the odds go all to hell.

But I felt good. My anger had faded to a little knot in my gut and I still had almost two grand in my pocket from Tom, payment for the first pound, five hundred of which I owed to Hezekiah; but Tom had promised to unload it all plus another five pounds if I could get them, and turning a fifteen to one profit on every hit, I figured I was sitting pretty.

It's true Tom operates at a low overhead. I guess he must get paid a regular salary by the ice cream company, but he must have also been getting close to forty bucks a pop to make this worth his while. A decent hit'll cost you twenty easily in New York, and that's assuming you know where to *get* a decent hit. I wasn't gonna question it though. Some things, you look at them too closely, it sours your luck.

Besides, Tom is a freak. He might have decided to break even on the deal just 'cause he liked the high. It *was* good, maybe the best I ever had. I'd saved some out, smuggling them back to New Mexico, to celebrate when Molly finished bailing out that jerk and we could finally go home.

I paid for valet parking, tipping the kid five bucks, and bought a program and a sweatshirt for Molly. I was even looking forward to taking her to Cabra's, though I knew she'd probably ask the waitress why the place was called El Cabra, the goat, and I'd get an earful about Pat Garrett, Billy the Kid, the Old West.

I was in time for the sixth race, a simulcast from the Fairgrounds at Louisiana, but I let it slide. I know it's sentimental, but I like to at least know that I could look at the horses if I wanted to. I always thought it was degrading to drive all the way out to Sunland just to stand in a crowd of Texans, squinting at a little color TV.

That's something I'd have to get over if I was gonna adjust to life in New York, where they have an OTB every mile and you could go ten years without ever seeing a horse, but maybe just getting away from those moronic Texans would do it. The only Texans at Aqueduct sit quietly in the reserved clubhouse, smoking cigars and counting oil wells on their pudgy fingers. You don't have to rub elbows with them if you don't want to.

At Sunland Park, which is technically in New Mexico, but only technically, you get a different class of Texan and they make me sick. They wear powder blue suits, loud flowered ties, and big red boots, and they mill around with their bored young wives on their arms, acting like they know everything there is to know about the horses. Of course, if they knew anything at all about racing, they would figure out how to get their damn state to legalize gambling so they could have their own track, and get the revenues; but it's widely known that most Texans are so dumb, they can't think their way out of a hangover, so I don't know why I'm surprised.

At Sunland, the door is level with a huge marble platform, a stage almost. The bar is on that level, and the betting windows and bathrooms. There are steep stairs, very ornate, which lead down to a glass wall overlooking the track. All along the stairs, flush with a full third of the track itself, are tiers of tables, crowded with Texans. I walked all the way down to the bottom and took a table right up against the glass. There's a duck pond right in the middle of the track and I liked to get close, close enough to see the horses' eyes, close enough to watch the ducks and wonder what they made of their strange life, those great sleek monsters thundering past them every twenty minutes.

I ordered a shot of tequila and had a fight with the waiter, who insisted that a gentleman of my apparent stature should be drinking Cuervo Gold, that the house tequila was for wetbacks. I guess that kind of line works on Texans but I wasn't drinking the bar stuff out of stinginess. Cuervo Gold is too sweet and smooth, it's tequila for broads, you may as well be drinking a milk shake. I wanted an irritant, something to fire up my luck, cut through the phlegm, set me slightly off balance. The whole thing annoyed me. I brooded about it and by the time I got my drink and downed it, post time for the seventh had come and gone.

The horse I'd wanted, Golden Slew, a five-year-old from Thatcher, Arizona, won handily. There was no point in agonizing about it. Either my luck was queered or it wasn't. I tested the waters, placing a random bet in the eighth, a two dollar exacta box on two mares, Street Chick and Strait On Line. Neither of them came in.

I had about an hour 'til the race I really cared about, the twelfth, so I paid up and wandered around. I went to the bathroom and washed my face thoroughly, drying it under the blower, a trick my mother taught me for when you're losing at poker: sit out a hand, excuse yourself, wash your face thoroughly, concentrating all your attention on the task at hand. You get back to the table and your mind is clear. The slate is wiped clean and you can begin courting your luck again, slowly, calmly, with humility.

Seduction, she claimed, was mostly a matter of flattery, of giving your complete attention, and it didn't matter if you were trying to nail fate or the girl next door; if you were preoccupied, you weren't gonna get any. My mother, who spent the early part of her life as a fat lady, and her later years as a professional gambler, had died of a heart attack at a poker table behind a chicken coop in Vado, a fistful of nothing, nine high, I think they said, and I usually took what little advice she gave me pretty seriously.

I took a different set of stairs back down to my table and ran into Hezekiah, who was sitting with a young blonde, working his way through a mountain of onion rings. He nodded me into a chair, his mouth full, his chin shiny with grease. He didn't seem at all embarrassed about being with the girl and he didn't introduce her, but he didn't have to. It was Sonia Totonac, looking good but a little sleazy for my tastes, in tight pink leather pants and a see-through white top, some kind of halter.

I took the five C's out of my wallet and laid them on the table. Hezekiah, without looking up, still chewing, grunted and put them in his pocket. Waiting for him to swallow, I caught Sonia's eyes and she giggled at me. I didn't care one way or the other about the girl's defilement. Nary's old-fashioned and thinks he can protect his beautiful daughter but the truth is most girls choose their own debauchery and like everything else, it's mostly a matter of luck, being in the right place at the right time, when they decide to go down.

Finally, Hezekiah choked down the last of his food, and looked up at me.

"Goliath, my friend. I'm glad that you should be here and see this. It is a great day for medical science. All over the world, I am sure, the ill and depraved are sitting up in their beds. This beautiful girl, this Sonia, has decided to go into nursing."

Sonia giggled and stood up, shaking out her curtain of wavy platinum hair. A long lock brushed Hezekiah's plate and, dipping the end into the oily ketchup scum, he sucked it clean.

"*Voy a apostar,*" she said.

The nurse was going to bet. It was post time for the eleventh race and I gave her ten bucks. I wanted to bet with her. Sonia is dumb as a stone but I figured she was embarking on what was gonna be the biggest decision of her life, fucking the physically repulsive Hezekiah, and because of that, she had to wield some power with fate. I was still feeling out of sorts, not quite in bed with Providence, and before I tapped Hezekiah for more mushrooms, I wanted to offer up something of myself to the racing gods. Whatever divine interest it is that watches over beautiful dumb girls is pretty generous, I've found.

Sonia flounced up the stairs, her ass swaying wildly. I looked down. I'd already played my hand, and I wasn't interested anymore.

"Goliath, you are back sooner than I had expected, but I see now that I should have known better. This place, this Land of Enchantment, is in your blood, of course. You have brought your woman, I think, this time, your Molly."

He shuddered slightly and I stared a warning at him. He patted my hand.

"You do not take offense, I hope, Goliath. I know that soon you will give your Molly an honest name and it will roll off the tongue. Ma-lee." He clucked and shook his head. "These harsh sounds, it has the ring of the *bruja.*"

Actually, I did take offense. Who was he, after all, to talk about an honest name? And if I thought New Mexico was really in my blood, I'd get a fucking transfusion. But Hezekiah, as I've said, is crazier than a shithouse rat, and I didn't want to spoil the deal over something so stupid. If push came to shove, I knew Molly could defend her own name and I know she doesn't exactly consider my name honest. If she were there, she'd probably be more interested in why the sounds seemed witchy to him. So I laughed.

"What makes you think I brought Molly along?"

"Ah, my friend, you are baffled by my shaman's sight, are you? Yes, this I understand. The ancient wisdom of my people has puzzled many a good man. But, in this case, Goliath, I think it is not so very mysterious. It is the Totonac girl, no? It is a rare man who can resist the charms of Nary's lovely daughters. They are like angels. I have known them all. I myself have watched them grow from little babies, pure as the sunbeams of Jesus. Hobi. Becca. Tita. Yesenia. Each more lovely than the next, Goliath. *Yo las enseñe a vivir. Yo las hice mujer.* And now it is Sonia I am helping along the last difficult step to the full flower of womanhood. I watch her climb the steps, Goliath, and I think my heart will burst in two, and yet you show no interest. Goliath, my friend, you do not even look twice. This is how I know, here is a man who is in love with another."

"If you say so, Hezekiah."

"It is something I know, my friend. You are a good man, and every man must love a woman."

Number 4, Sí A Bit, an ancient horse from El Paso, came in way ahead of the favorites and I felt flooded with a sense of well-being. I was sure Sonia had bet on Sí A Bit, the only horse in the race with any Spanish in his name. I studied the card for the twelfth. I still couldn't shake the feeling that Summer Sage was a red herring. I liked three other horses, Icelist, Dakotas Bold, and Two-Edged Sword. But I liked them all the same. None of them really sat up and sang for me.

I decided to play it cool. I still had almost twenty minutes to bet. The day had been so strange, so many ups and downs, I figured I'd leave it to fate. If I could get Hezekiah to commit to the extra five pounds of mushrooms, I'd bet the three horses in a trifecta, every combination covered by an extra buck. That way I wouldn't have to pick one over the others.

And if I won, I decided I'd drive Sonia back to her father's farm. I'd had no idea that Hezekiah had fucked all of Nary's daughters and it made me a little sick. There was no way a stupid girl like Sonia could ever live up to her father's expectations of purity, not in a tiny town like Mapache. Sooner or later she was gonna let some jerk unwrap that Mexican package, what else could she do with herself? She certainly couldn't go into a skilled profession like nursing. But she deserved more of chance than she'd have with a lunatic like Hezekiah, who'd already screwed her four older sisters.

"So, my friend," Hezekiah interrupted my brooding, "you have paid me quickly, much quicker than you promised. You have found a buyer worthy of the ancient wisdom? A good man?"

"Yeah. He loved it, said it was the most powerful experience of his life, in fact."

"This does not surprise me, Goliath. The ancient people of Chihuahua are a very powerful race. He is an Anglo, this man?"

"Yeah. A guy by the name of Tom. Tom Cushman."

"Tom Cooshmon, Tómas, yes?" He nodded to himself, mouthing the name. "Yes, I trust this man. Tom. That is a trustworthy name. The *Yendo con La Sonrisas* will prosper in the hands of man such as that."

"I'm glad you think so, Hezekiah—"

He cut me off. Sonia came back to the table, holding her money in a fan. She fluttered it in front of her eyes, giggling, then counted off sixty bucks into my palm. I kissed her hand. Hezekiah nodded approvingly and handed her one of the C-notes I'd just given him.

"*El caballo trés*, this Summer Sage, my little nurse, on the nose."

He touched her nose. She took the money and ran back up the steps. That fixed it for me. With Hezekiah shelling out a hundred, a truly inane bet, even if Summer Sage did come in, a guy'd be lucky if he got a dime back on his two-buck bet.

"Your friend, this Cooshmon, he would like some more, is this it? He wishes perhaps to be a shaman."

"Well, that's the thing, Hezekiah, around Loisaida, that's the neighborhood where Tom lives, he already is a sort of shaman. Kids trail after him, begging for enlightenment."

I paused, hoping he'd buy it. It was a long stretch, Tom as a spiritual leader, but Hezekiah couldn't know that and my fingers were getting itchy. I wanted to place my bet.

"He said he'd like another five pounds, at least."

Hezekiah smiled.

"Well, Goliath, I will see what I can do. I trust you, as you know. And you will vouch for this Tom, that he is good man, as his name suggests?"

I nodded. I didn't see what difference it made to Hezekiah what kind of man Tom was. He'd never have to meet the guy. But Hezekiah's sensitive about his drug smuggling, having convinced himself he's on some kind of mission from God. And it couldn't hurt to play along. Certainly Tom, whatever the Doll might think of him, was a damn sight more honorable than Hezekiah himself.

"Then it is settled. We will do this thing, Goliath. You may have to travel with me into Chihuahua, my friend. I am a doctor, a man of the world, and in some things I am more understanding than the harvesters of the mushroom. Perhaps they will want to see you for themselves, Goliath. You may even have to go by yourself. I will send Packy as your guide. You know I am having problems with these developers, wanting to make our beautiful town into I don't know what? I will have to let you know. You are staying at Nary's?"

"Nah, I'm not sure where I'll be staying, but I'll call you."

I placed my bet just under the wire and hung around upstairs waiting for the results. I dreaded the possibility of traveling anywhere with Packy Salvo, a man I truly detested. Even though it was because I beat him up that I'd run away to New York the first time, when I was a kid, so in a way he was indirectly responsible for my salvation.

I made up my mind as the results came in that I'd blow the whole thing off rather than go on a road trip with Packy. The thought of sitting next to him in a car tied my stomach into knots.

It was a photo-finish, Summer Sage and one of my horses, Dakotas Bold, nose and nose for third place. While I waited for the decision, I tried to figure out how to get Sonia into my car. It had been a good day all in all and I wasn't about to blow it by breaking a promise to fate.

As it turned out, there was nothing to worry about. When I got back to the table, three clams richer, Hezekiah was totally distracted, fuming about his loss. I offered Sonia a ride back to Mapache and Hezekiah waved us away, muttering under his breath about the hundred bucks. It was a foolish bet he made, and I didn't feel sorry for him.

I stopped at the Loretto Mall on the way back to Nary's. I couldn't very well bring Sonia back to her father's farm the way she was done up. I gave her some money to buy a dress or something decent to wear. But Sonia surprised me. She had a very proper flowered dress rolled up in her purse and she laughed as she climbed into the back seat to change into it.

She gave me back the money and another fifty besides. It turned out she hadn't placed Hezekiah's bet at all and wanted me to have half the money. I'd done half the work by distracting him, she said. I took the money because she would've been insulted if I hadn't, but when I pulled off Nary's property, the smell of pig spice from Mrs. Totonac's kitchen still tickling my nostrils, I balled it up and threw it out the window.

Sonia had pulled off an excellent scam, she'd rolled Hezekiah beautifully, and she'd even fooled me. I wanted to remember the lesson. As I drove over to the Quinta Inn to pick up Molly, I concluded that it was a perfect example of poetic justice. Sonia had seized her own redemption and in so doing she had assured herself of revenge. The story, I knew, would delight Molly, and I was looking forward to running it past her.

10

Enter the Dane

On the flight, things got a little hairy. When details get to be too much for me, I call on Evan, and he usually makes matters worse. Why I keep doing it, I'm not sure. It's like hitting myself on the head with a brick. Of course, he shows up all the time anyway, whether I call him or not, but I'm not sure that's an excuse.

I felt closed in on the plane, which, of course, I was, lonely and scared of the silence in my head. I crammed Feck's syllabuses into the seat pocket in front of me, disgusted, and grumbled under my breath.

This seems insurmountable, I said, mouthing the words. I don't just mean me and Flan. I decided long ago that the improbability of that was so grotesque, I'd just let myself sink into it. By now, the surface of its mire is so far over my head, you can't even see the bubbles of my breath. It'd take a depth charge of some unimaginable proportion to free me. It doesn't matter, though. I love him, and more often than not, that seems to be enough.

I paused, scanning the cabin, and after a minute, the plane reeked of Evan's derisive laugh. I felt immediately at ease, lucky, drinking in his heady scorn. It's not so bad to be beleaguered by imps, really. There's always, well, there's always someone to talk to.

The stupidity of such a system wasn't lost on me, of course. I hurried my point along, knowing it was only moments before the whole construct collapsed, and the idiocy caught up with me, stove me through. The fact that I was addressing Evan, thereby demanding his attendance, rather than enjoying the brief moment of shriven peace, was a problem, was *the* problem, and I knew it. But in common with everyone else, my misery is much more clever than I am. Thus trapped, I figured if he was hanging around anyway, I might as well take advantage of it.

The problems here run deeper than the love story. A love story, despite what we might like to believe about our active participation, tends to iron itself out. A love story invents itself and follows its own crazy course, zig-zagging across time and vast stretches of land, unmoved by convenience or neatness. We're just along for the ride.

But Evan, do you remember the time you met my father? Probably you don't. Why would you? You've got a head like swiss cheese; and it's only for the living that these shadow plays have any meaning. Everyone thinks ghosts are mired in the past, stuck in the cobwebby corner, batting great mummy hands at the sticky strands, frantically reliving that one awful moment. We like to think of death that way. But of course, only warm bodies, flushed with blood and stinking of life, can really exist in the past. You're the camera's fucking flash, Evan, popping only into the present.

I'll tell you the story, though. I had a crush on another guy and I was smoking his brand of cigarettes. Boxed, factory-rolled cigarettes, some stupid brand, the first pre-mades I'd ever tried. I'd been rolling my own since I was ten, my parents' since I was six, twirling the rich tobacco in chubby little kid fingers. You bought the brand too, that same week, a way of sucking me, you said, and I was quite taken with that. It was, after all, precisely what I'd been doing with the other guy, but I never would've come right out and said so.

We ran into my father on Second Avenue. He was eating a barrel pickle, half-sour. He was as short as you were tall, thin, and preternaturally healthy despite his gray pallor. He was high, but just a little, my favorite of his moods. Of course, I don't have to tell you, his moods were strictly predetermined by his drug consumption, and I grew to like that about both of you. It made you predictable.

Pappa squinted at you, Evan, looking up and down your long frame. He grinned at your ratty red and black T-shirt which read "better drunk than dead," and he made a gesture that I can only imagine Eastern Europeans have been making since time began. He moved his body a little too close to ours.

"So, *Édesem*," he said, "last week, for the short rat-face *gajo* you start in to smoke these wasteful *gajo* cigarette, this week, tall blond *gajo*, he smoke them for you. Perfect," he laughed. "From one *gajo* to another, these cigarette, and nothing to do with you! This I like! For what you need this silly yellow box with its lid, how you call it?"

I laughed.

"Flip-top, Pappa."

You were a lovely Louisiana liberal then, Evan, New South all the way, not yet a junkie yourself, and maybe a little shocked. I could see the little wheels turning in your swampy eyes, those spikes of uncertain color. My job is not to find this ruffian charming, your own quaint programming went, but to love-him-as-thoroughly-and-bawdily-as-possible. Nevertheless, you found him charming which, of course, was what he wanted.

"'*Gajo*?'" I think you said, "is that Hungarian or Romany?" Pappa laughed, saying nothing. He clapped you on the back and ambled off down the street.

What's the point? The point, my poor dead dear, is that dreadful embracing movement, from one gajo to another, one voice to the next. There I am, right? Listening *hard*. My pupils wide in the fetid half-light that lurks between words, waiting for the click that precedes the pattern. That's the way I've learned everything I know about language, from sign language to the labyrinthine dance of Czech, from autism to empathy. Total immersion, a baptism in syntax, is the key. But what about the rest of the time?

Look within yourself? Are you kidding? By myself, inside myself, not that you guys give me much opportunity to experience that particular prank of human existence, but when I'm there, I see nothing, the big black zilch, a slick gooey vacuum, and guts. Look within myself, Evan? That's the wisdom of the dead? Look within yourself and find the bluebird of happiness fluttering against your esophagus, pecking lovingly at your uvula? Shitting white joy on the maze of your capillaries?

"It's not the wisdom of the dead, Chica," Evan said, settling in next to me, bending his long skinny legs into themselves four times each, on invisible hinges. "It's the wisdom of the sane. Man, I hate planes."

"Yeah. That's what Flan says too. 'So, you feel like shit,' he says. 'Retreat, Doll. Don't try to think your way out of it. Go lie down.'"

"I told you, girl, you should listen to the cowboy."

"Yeah, Evan, you told me. And Flan is cool that way. But his system doesn't work for me. I don't know how to not do anything. Oh, I can lie still for a few minutes thinking how miraculous it is that I can feel so miserable, thinking, yep, that's pain alright, that's pain, desperation, anxiety, more than you'd think could fit in a girl my size, but sooner or later a new feeling creeps in to exacerbate the agony."

"You get bored."

He grinned at me, looking immensely pleased with himself. I nodded.

"I get bored. And then I seek consolation outside myself. I mean, way outside myself, as outside myself as a girl can get. I mean, inside other people. I seek the salve of distraction. So I set every neuron to singing, matching the timbre of someone else's agony, the dips and fits of other speech. That and only that drowns out the empty echoes, the goose-flesh terrors—"

"Yeah, yeah, I know, Chica. It's die and become, enchanted reaffirmation, and it's got your name written all over it and all that jazz. But don't you see that's your particular genius?"

"No, you fucking reticulated swamp rat, I don't see. I can talk to anyone but I can't hear myself. Is that a blessing or a curse?"

"Is that what this is all about? All that rocky-grinned smiling through tears, muttering to your dead husband on an airplane, calling me across time and space, and what you want to know is, are you in with God or aintcha? Is it a blessing or a curse? It's like everything else that's interesting about people, you dumb cooze, it's both. And neither."

Disgusted, Evan did a slow dissolve, just to annoy me, I guess. He knows I hate that campy spook stuff. I sighed and reached for the first syllabus, ironing it slowly, back and forth, with the side of my fist. It was probably just as well. Fatuous affirmation was never his long suit.

Smoothing the paper, I felt better. There was nothing there I could really hang my hat on. Just a quick shot of something, something profane and slovenly, something to dog my cats, to get the juices flowing. I figured he was a peach to put up with it, a peach and a pal. But fuck, if we're going, let's go. Let's get there already. Away from me.

The sun, apparently, loves the Southwest. Whole ragged patches of mountain were etched in gold as I drove along the highway, following Feck's nervous instructions. The bouncing truck glittered in the light.

An incredible wind swept across the highway, throwing bizarre desert plants against our windshield, muttering bitterly in its howl about the land and the light. Land's supposed to be promiscuous, a feral trollop, shifting and opening itself to any element strong enough to stroke its fetching passivity. But something in the 'scape belied this. The precisely lit arroyos, those corrugated sloughs of brown and green, the glistening blood on a squashed coyote, the massive stretches of horizon that seemed to quiver, all this suggested that the land and the sun had a real thing going, an actinic tryst, a couple's arrogance, something no mere wind, no ravages of man could penetrate.

We drove through a town called Vado, dairy farms, cows, as far as the eye could see. The smell of shit nearly knocked me off the road. My eyes watering, I rolled up the window, and Feck cackled with glee.

"Hey," he said, nudging me, "you cut one Molly? Didja toot?"

"Aren't you supposed to be a teacher or something, an example to all the little boys and girls, just the facts, ma'am, and all that kind of thing?"

"Yeah, except I drove through Vado, and Anthony, which is even worse, with the damn committee and the guy we were picking up from the airport, this real high-class Danish guy, I'm not sure what he's all about, says 'who farted?' and you'd've thought they all fart through a deodorized hole in their wrist watch, the way they freaked out, fanning the air and coughing these dainty little coughs like they were out of a shit-ass restoration comedy."

"What committee?"

"The Committee. As in capitol Tee, capitol fucking Cee, as in Terminal Crap."

"Or Tiny Cock. What committee?"

"A bunch of so-called 'sensitivity trained' moralizing idiots, actually one of them's okay, the guy who said 'who farted.' You'll meet'em this afternoon. They're keeping a lid on me, or so they say."

"Or Ty Cobb. You didn't tell me I'd have to pass a fucking test, Feck."

"No. But you're okay, Kid. Flan excepted, you don't fornicate with small animals."

"How would you know? Anyway I see them, small animals I mean, in full, four-color regalia, smoking, and talking trash about the savior."

"Did you read the syllabuses?"

"No, Feck, I used them to roll joints. Great stuff, too. Only I think maybe it was laced with something 'cause I got really fucked up, like paranoid, you know?"

"Finished?"

"Yes."

"Damn, Molly. You really didn't read them?"

"Not yet, Feck. So what?"

"Well, when we get to the committee, just talk like you're talking to a pastor."

"I never met a pastor. Don't you know the expression 'only a dead gypsy needs a preacher?'"

"You know, you are even more of a pain in the ass than you used to be. Hasn't age mellowed you at all?"

I didn't answer, busying myself with the highway, the roaring blur and parched sweet air. I pulled off the road at a stand of trees, mostly dead from the bottom, crowned at the top with a bushy violent green.

"What's the story there?"

"That, you parochial Dead End Kid, is the parasite mistletoe, famed in song and story for its powers to attract the elusive kiss."

"And it kills these trees?"

"It lives off any tree it pleases, and no one can stop it."

"That sucks."

He slapped his thigh with his mangled hand, laughing, an obscene gesture really, if you know his preposterous dimensions. With no perceptible change of expression, he said, "What the fuck's wrong with you, Veeka?"

"I don't know, Feck, the sky's too big. Teaching something called 'Metastisizing Praxis, Phenomenological Vertigo and Other Diseases of Meaning' makes me nervous. Teaching 'Vocabulary and Grammar Review' makes me nervous. Fuck, teaching *anything* makes me nervous. Morals committees make me more nervous than teaching. I'm pissed off because you didn't tell me I'd be subjected to a HUAC job talk. Evan won't leave me alone or else I won't leave him alone—we haven't quite figured it out yet. And I don't know what's happening with Flan."

"Well, Jesus, Kid Gloves, put the radio on and crank it up to ninety Em Pee Aitch. Fucking pinko academic, whaddaya wanna do, join a self-help group? Wait, I got a tape. You're priceless, you know that? Your brain goes into a stall for four fuckin' minutes and you think it's the death of the goddamn life of the mind. Just cruise, don't think so much."

Driving that fast, and listening to some ancient Frank Sinatra compilation, we pulled into the ridiculous campus about forty minutes later. Fatuous affirmation, as it happened, *was* Feck's strong suit, and I discovered it made me feel even worse. What kind of comfort can you really expect to derive from a man who thinks "Witchcraft" is driving music?

The grounds, cheerful and unbelievably modern, were saved from absurdity only by the throngs of trees slowly being sucked to death by mistletoe. I knew it was trouble the minute I walked into the briefing room, Feck's hand biting into my shoulder, whispering garlic breath into my ear,

"Trucker's Clap."

He turned to the four inquisitors, propped stolidly in leather chairs.

"This is Doctor Veeka. Doctor Veeka, The Committee, from

left to right, Doctor Orrinson, Lucas Christensen, he's the guy I was telling you about, Dean Wolcraft, and Professor Raju."

I tossed my mental quarters for something to say, perusing their faces, the low-wattage scrutiny.

"Your names are an acronym for 'Crow.'"

A sea of empty visages. Christensen, the Dane, smiled wanly, and flinched, pinching the bridge of his nose, his apple cheeks pale and contracted, set off by a black silk Italian suit. Floating over their heads, the dramatic reappearance of Cump, his hat askew, drawing a long furry paw across his throat, the "cut it" gesture.

Behind me I sensed Feck squirming. Christensen felt his breast pocket for a pack of cigarettes, just touching them, then bringing his arm down robotically. I took a chance.

"*Du ligner ikke en der tilhører en moral komité*," I said. You don't look like you belong on a morals committee.

His blue eyes laughed and it seemed to cost him something. He winced before answering.

"*Det er precis derfor at du skulle vaere glad at jeg er her. Hvad ligner jeg så?*" Precisely why you should be glad I'm here. How *do* I look?

The Danish carved out a space for us and I went on, less tentative, on certain ground. I knew nothing about the geography but his accent was easy to mimic. How did he look? Big, awkward, happy, something like a great dane puppy, in fact; simultaneously robust and washed-out, the crooked black lettering of a rock T-shirt barely visible through his starched white dress shirt. How did he look? I went on, in his tongue, courting him.

"Sort of...hungover."

"That I am, and enchanted. You sound just like my mother. Surely you are not from the Faroe Islands?"

"Not even close. You mean these squishy vowels? I picked them up from you."

"From me? When?"

"Just now."

"Wonderful! I'd heard of course, but I could not believe it."

"I'm glad you think so. Just what is the real low-down here, Bub?"

I had trouble with that last one. It tasted absurd in my mouth and I ended up with something that sounded for all the world like Dylan's Mr. Jones. *Ven, hvad sker der her i virkeligheden?* Ridiculous. You'd be sapped before you got it out. But I'd dropped my voice into a Bogart lisp and I think he got the idea.

"Orrinson is dimly aware that you're insane and hopes it won't affect his budget. Wolcraft thinks Professor Feck is a hippie and I'm not sure she's wrong. Raju is an idiot and for myself, as you say, I am hungover."

"Tough crowd."

"Perhaps. I for one would be most grateful to have Henry out of the way for several days. We are competing for the favor of a young farmer's daughter by the unlikely name of Virgen Santísima Blanco. But I suggest we put an end to this little *tête à tête*. Wolcraft's face is distorted in a particular way I've come to recognize and detest in literate Americans."

"Good Lord. Meaning what?"

He sighed mightily. "Meaning she is about to say 'There's something rotten in the state of Denmark.' A little joke."

"I think there's something rotten in the state of Denmark," Wolcraft said. She was about my age, her face at once pinched and fat, little wire-rim glasses, heavy on the facial hair.

Christensen and I laughed. Feck, cringing, took a seat at the table.

"Are you ready to proceed, Dr. Veeka?"

"I guess. Well, no. Not really. Proceed with what?"

"It's just a formality, Molly," Feck said.

"Now Henry, that is not really true," Raju said. For a guy with a sexy Sikh name, he was singularly bleached out, so tall and white he made my eyes hurt.

"For a solid, practicing Christian with an impeccable reputation, yes, perhaps, this is a formality," he went on. "But your substitute is something of a mystery to us. And her reputation is, well, let us call it *eclectic*."

He said the word the way my father used to say "cop." He did not, however, spit on the perfectly appointed orange carpeting.

"Are you a Christian, Dr. Veeka?" he said.

"I don't know what that means."

"Don't you?"

"Back off a little, Raju," Orrinson said, a goosed P.R. panic flushing his florid face. "You are giving Dr. Veeka a terrible impression." Then, to me, "We're not on what you might call a 'witch hunt,' here, Dr. Veeka. You really must excuse Mr. Raju."

"Must I?"

"Now see here, Jim," Raju said. "I told you this was a mistake and now we're seeing it come to fruition. You reap what you sow."

"This is unbelievable," I said.

"I quite agree," Christensen said. "We had this same conversation when Dr. Feck wanted to use Dr. Veeka's book in his class. Granted we know nothing about this woman's belief system. But we know she's a full, tenured professor, at a prestigious university, and at a very young age. Really, Raju, you have no reason to suspect that this woman has travelled half way across the country to corrupt your student body."

"Not corrupt, maybe, Lucas," Orrinson said. "But we don't want a loose cannon around here. Not with all the scandal, the terrible crime spree. It might affect our budget."

"And you raise an interesting point, Lucas," Wolcraft said. "Just why would a full, tenured professor at such a renowned university arrive to teach a couple of English courses and a, well, whatever that course of Dr. Feck's is?"

What was I gonna say? I come to conquer; take me to your leader? I came because I'm on the reading list and people do make guest appearances now and again? I came as a favor to Feck? I came to see if dwarfism runs in my boyfriend's family? I said what I thought a good English teacher might.

"I've come for the winter sport."

Wolcraft sneered. Christensen laughed. Feck, that bastard, hung his head. Raju broke a pencil. Orrison's pop eyes widened. Cump pointed behind me at the door.

I fished around in my purse for Drum and papers. I rolled a cigarette, slowly, preternaturally, working the thick plug between my thumbs. I lit it and stood. Orrinson opened his mouth and I held my free hand up. He shut up.

"Listen. Just call me when you get this together. For reasons that would probably shock you, I could give two shits that Henry Feck once slept with his students. I have no intention of discussing my belief system with you, not that I stand on ceremony or anything, but discussing it tends to get me tossed in the bin. As for your so-called crime spree, as far as I can tell, this town has a history of untoward behavior that goes back at least three generations. I was raised by criminals myself, and I happen to like that in a town. I'm taking the truck."

This last I addressed to Feck and fled, ignoring his "Molly, wait," Cump high on my shoulders, cackling. Through a maze of identical corridors, he rode me piggy-back, digging his furry feet into my armpits.

Outside, catching my breath, I actually tripped over a tumbleweed. There was a cat-call as I struggled to my feet and I rolled my eyes back. Evan was bobbing from a treetop like a spider, couched all around in lusty green mistletoe.

"Fucking leech," I said.

"Which of us?" he called, and then I was running slew-footed like a little kid, blinking back tears, coughing deep howls into the lean homespun air.

11

Smiley

What I didn't think of, but should have, is that everything happens in El Cabra. Anything that happens on the American side of the border, within thirty miles of Mapache, happens at El Cabra. People cut deals by the piranha tank. Guys propose to the caws of the parrots, over bubbling cauldrons of *chile con queso*. Not that guys propose too often in Mapache. It's a shotgun kinda town and a girl like Sonia Totonac who hits fifteen or sixteen without getting pregnant is regarded strangely.

But once things iron out, and the father completes his often perfunctory waving of the double barrel and the mother dries her eyes, it's a sure bet the whole family's gonna head out to Cabra's to seal the deal. It's such a tradition around here, I've often suspected that Father Burn, over at San Arcadio Church, gets a kickback for every weepy clan he sends next door.

The point is, Mapache being such a small desert town, it's just about an even bet between a kick and a kiss that you're gonna run into at least one person you'd rather not see every time you bang through the wooden double doors of El Cabra.

I wasn't thinking straight, though. Molly does that to me. I get this sap's idea that time with her is enchanted, is other somehow; that the events of the world can't touch us when we're together. You can't even say that I gambled and lost, though that was to be the veritable fucking theme of the evening, because I didn't stop to consider what might happen when I brought Molly, an Easterner and a citizen, tripping, into El Cabra.

93

I walked into Molly's motel room, carrying a potted cactus and a liter of tequila. Molly was sitting cross-legged on the bed, wearing a black bra and a long white skirt that swaddled her hips beautifully, covering her feet; sharp indentations of muscle cleaved her perfect soft stomach. She was smoking one cigarette as another burned in the glass Quinta ashtray, gesturing wildly, her eyes fixed on the bureau. Oh yeah, and she was crying.

I set the cactus down on the cable box, cracked the bottle, and swooped down on the bed.

"Wanna swig?"

She reached out for the bottle without looking up and took a long pull. Handing it back, she swept the ashtray onto the floor and fell back on the bed. I took her chin in my hands.

"Spill it."

Molly doesn't talk too easily about what's bothering her, or rather, she doesn't seem to know how to think out loud. She'll only say what's bugging her in fully formed, perfectly rational paragraphs. But stroking her soft face, I eventually got the story out of her. Before she was half way through, I saw red. In fact, I saw red right from the very beginning. Whatever her pretenses, Molly can really tell a story. I mean, there's no silence in her head. She brought the sordid tale alive, filling the room with ol' Blue Eyes, with the stink of Vado, the roar of the highway.

I was already prepared to think the worst of Feck and his whole crew. They are, after all, just glorified assholes, on the wrong side of the law, as far as I was concerned. And I couldn't stand the idea of my girl driving fast with some other guy, especially Feck. Especially the way Molly drives, maybe the sexiest thing about her. Molly learned how to drive on a stick shift and the gear changing is so deeply ingrained in her, she makes the shifting motions with her hand even when she's driving an automatic, her right hand gliding fluidly over the leather of the seat next to her, doing nothing.

About the rest of it I wasn't sure what to say. I felt bad for Molly, and if she was the kind of girl you could protect, I'd've tracked down the fucking committee and beaten them to a bloody pulp. But that's not the way things worked in Molly's world. I couldn't say what was on my mind, which was: What the fuck did you expect from a bunch of lard-ass teachers?

In some ways the gulf between us is too great. Certainly Molly could've said the same thing when I landed in the slam: What did you expect, breaking the law? But she hadn't, and I'd been grateful, though by not saying it, she'd effectively sealed a deal of silence between us. We passed the bottle solemnly back and forth.

"So you went on a tear, Doll. So what? It sounds like they deserved it and now you bought yourself some time. You can think about whether you wanna stick it out. Besides, that guy is so in love with you, he'd come crawlin' back for more if you stuck a tarantula up his ass."

"That's not what I wanted to hear, Flan."

"Yeah, Doll? Well, I'm not in the business of saying what you want to hear."

A perfect silky pout, her eyes crinkled, "I thought you were."

"Okay, I am. You wanna stick it out 'cause you think there's some kind of connection between what you do and what Feck does and you need to test it out. And maybe you wanna check out this place for yourself after I've been telling you about it for so long, though God only knows what kind of ghosts you're gonna turn up here. And you wanna do it because Evan, a guy who's really starting to piss me off, by the way, thinks you should, right? And for some unknown reason that damn fake fed's a friend of yours and you wanna make things straight with him. How'm I doing?"

She rolled her eyes but a smile was forming under her pale, tear-streaked skin. I felt a little silly telling Molly how she felt, something I assumed she already knew, but girls, even Molly, are like that. They wanna know you know; and the more intricate a girl's mind is, the more she wants to know you follow her convoluted reasoning. It's colossally innocent if you stop to think about it. I'm not playing on Molly's team because I find her thinking valid, although most of the time I do—I stick by her because she's my girl. In fact, I'd say most people would probably use it to their advantage, and against you, if they knew how you felt.

"Listen, Doll, what time is it, eight? I betcha ten bucks that guy'll be knocking on your door inside of twelve hours, dragging you back to the goddamn mines."

"You suck. Will you take me out to dinner?"

"If you put on a fucking shirt."

Tucking a blue and white striped sailor shirt into her skirt, Molly kicked the hotel dresser.

"Damn," she said, "I can't catch a break today."

"What's the problem now, Doll?"

"Evan won't leave me alone."

She shook her head violently, trying to clear it, the ends of her long black hair stinging me as they whipped back and forth across my face.

"What should I do?"

I handed her a mushroom.

"Make him dance."

"You think I should?"

"Why not? You can't get'm out of your head, at least you can paint him pretty day-glo colors."

She hesitated so I took a hit myself, chewing it grimly and chasing it with a big mouthful of tequila.

"Look at it this way, Doll. You're on a job, lookin' for, what do you call it, a higher symmetry. Maybe the Smiley can help you out with that. Besides, this is a drug Evan's never tried. Don't you think—"

"Right. Like I'm gonna take a drug called 'Going Away with the Grinning One.'"

"You won't take a drug called 'Death.' Okay, I get that. But, Jesus, Doll, you're a linguist. The translation's loose. It's a translation of a translation, anyway. I mean, would you take a drug called 'Go Away Smiling?' Or 'Fucked Herself to Death—?'"

"Alright, already. You have a point. Give it here."

She chewed the mushroom with a delicious grimace, and went to brush her teeth. When she returned her arched lips were etched in a dark red lipstick.

"We're gonna need more tequila, Flan."

We stopped on the far side of Chope's. Chope has an all-night convenience store next to his bar, though I'm probably the only

96

person in the history of the town who's been there after midnight. I think Chope'd like to keep his little bar and luncheonette open all night, but local laws prohibit that kind of civility, so he's stuck with the Pic-Quik, a tiny franchise. Running his two little shops is everything to Chope who's never, to anyone's knowledge, left the premises. Sometimes he takes a short nap on the bench he keeps outside the Pic-Quik.

He was sitting on the bench as we approached, dressed in an undershirt and shorts, smoking a joint and brooding, leaning his elbows on his knees. His meaty arms, covered with crude prison tattoos, were slick with sweat.

"Chope, how's tricks?"

He shook his head and gestured into his Pic-Quik. Chris Johnson, Hezekiah's son, was standing in the far corner of the store, holding a mop and staring at the floor.

"Hezekiah's son, right?" Chope said, letting out a great cloud of marijuana smoke as he sighed. "I take the kid on as a favor, Flan. The Mayor comes by about forty minutes ago, wants some *chicharrones*, I figure what the hell, all this shit about the zoning laws, I may as well be on his good side, so I go open up next door to fry 'em up, and I tell Chris to mop the floor. I get back and he's mopped himself into that corner. He's just standing there, waiting for it to dry. Can you beat that?"

"Yeah, I can. This is my girl, Molly Veeka."

Molly stepped up to Chope who let out a long smoky whistle, and coughing, wiped himself on his shorts before he reached out to kiss her extended hand.

"You datin' chicks with last names now, huh, Flan?"

I'd've been mad but Molly didn't hear him. She'd pushed past us both and was standing in the Pic-Quik, talking to Chris, so I let it go. He didn't mean anything by it, in fact with Chope, who was usually very quiet, flapping his mouth like that was a gesture of friendship. He lay face down on the bench, the joint in the center of his mouth, blowing smoke down through the slats. In the hot air it hung around my ankles.

"I'm gonna go grab a bottle of tequila, how much?"

He raised a hand, five fingers up, and blinked it once. Ten

97

bucks. I left him staring at the ground and went in. Molly'd obviously set Chris straight somehow, and they were whispering as he backed out of the corner, swabbing his footsteps behind him. She kissed him on the cheek and hooked herself under my arm as I flicked a ten on the counter, holding the bottle under my other arm.

Unlike most people in town, I tend to suspect Chris isn't dumb so much as bent inward, and who could blame him, with that fat asshole of a father? He's tall, with long mahogany hair, and his mother's light green eyes. Only in his high hard cheekbones does he take after Hezekiah, or what you might imagine Hezekiah looked like under all that blubber. A combination of his striking good looks and Hezekiah's chokehold over the town council keeps him from being ridiculed as the village idiot; but if only judging by the way he dresses himself—year round he wears a Jack Daniels tank top, green cut-off army pants, and an old Mets cap I gave him when he was a kid—I think he probably has a whole hell of a lot more on the ball than he lets on.

This didn't stop me from taking advantage of his apparent stupidity, as I had with the credit card, travelling under his name for the price of a sack of rotten nuts, but who was I to blow the kid's cover? Also, despite the fact that with his exotic Eastern good looks, Chris has managed to screw every girl in Doña Ana county, he's never gotten one pregnant, which is more than can be said for just about every other kid in town. Molly verified my impression as we climbed into the car.

"He asked me if I thought a crocodile would eat a grizzly bear and when I told him I thought probably, if the croc could catch the bear, he asked me who I thought would win in a fair fight between a croc and grizzly, like in a ring?"

"What did you say?"

"I said I'd ask you."

"They'd probably gang up and eat the referee."

"Not if the ref was Kaspar."

I wanted to sit next to the piranhas, but Molly kept seeing them in top hats. She said fish shouldn't wear clothes and she wanted no part of it, so I steered her past the parrots, to a tiled table for four at the back of the main dining room. I really didn't mind moving. Rosalita, apparently sprung from the hospital, poor flower that she was, had staked out a position by the parrot cage and was immersed in a staring contest with a mean-looking macaw. Her wide brown eyes scared me.

If I'd had my wits about me, I'd've taken the Doll into one of the private back rooms, and thereby avoided all the idiocy that befell us later. But as usual, with Molly, I wasn't thinking straight. I wanted to watch all the flickering motion and light. I discovered long ago that if you take enough drugs, you can pretend El Cabra is a city.

Molly ordered for us both in flawless Mexican Spanish. Her accent was better than mine, which I felt was only right. The tinkling little-girl lilt that marks the dialect only sounds good in a broad's mouth anyway. A Mexican guy could say "let's go rustle up some cooze" and still sound like a drag queen.

The waitress brought our order almost immediately: a pitcher of Tecate, a huge bowl of *chile con queso*, and a pyramid of *flautas* to dip. *Flautas*, tiny rolled tacos, cigarillos almost, haven't hit it big in New York yet. Singularly unglamorous sticks of what is essentially hardened salt custard, they probably never will, and, staring at the food on the ceramic-topped table, I felt flooded with a sense of well-being. Except for *chile con queso*, which provides a velvety coating for anything you might do to your body later, I've always hated Southwestern food, and I thought this might well be the last time I'd ever have to eat it.

As the *Yendo con La Sonrisas* eased into my blood, Molly clicked and flashed before my eyes, back-lit and lovely, jerky like a silent movie, my eyes playing a desperate game of catch-up with my brain. Molly and I were in sync, or as in sync as someone can get with a girl like Molly, so when she spoke, it took me a few seconds to realize she wasn't describing my own hallucination.

"Jesus, Flan, that priest looks just like Buster Keaton."

I turned, moments too late, and Father Burn was pulling up a chair at our table. I could see it her way. The sleazy priest was pale and haggard, agelessly handsome, stone-faced, with thick, black-rimmed glasses and a loping athletic grace.

"Goliath, my son, I haven't seen you at services lately."

"Roberto, you know damn well I haven't set foot in San Arcadio Church in over twenty years."

"And yet neither God nor I have turned our eyes from you, Goliath. Your mother, God rest her soul, said a novena for you every week."

"My mother, God rest her soul, died in a makeshift gambling den that still stank of cows, in fact I understand a cow was present, playing pick-up poker with a bunch of wetbacks."

"Yes, that was unfortunate, but the Lord tests us each."

He turned his attention to Molly, sighing like a phony, and his eyes glittered with frank appreciation. Molly looked beautiful in the changing lights, but that wasn't it. The Padre could smell money clear across ten counties.

"You've brought a young lady with you to El Cabra tonight, Goliath. Perhaps you are considering marriage? I'm having a Fall Special, very cheap."

He leaned his head in close to mine.

"There's been an unusual amount of discretion among the children this year. As a man of business, I'm sure you can appreciate the effect this is having on my calling."

"I'm not that young, Mr. Keaton," Molly said.

He looked up at her briefly but lost interest. There wasn't a percentage in it for him, so he let it go.

"If not marriage, perhaps an engagement? I have a beautiful assortment of rings."

He placed his now-famous pigskin attaché case on the tiled table. It was well known, even to the Arch-Diocese, I think, that Father Burn stole jewelry from the bodies of the dead whose funerals he officiated at, and sold it at the shotgun weddings he performed, but no one did anything about it. The Burns are a powerful family in the Southwest, and Roberto was a well-loved priest, perfectly suited to the repulsive little town that made up his flock.

"No, thanks. I got it under control."

"Suit yourself, Goliath. But premarital involvement is a sin."

"And here comes Fatty Arbuckle."

This from Molly who, tripping wildly, wore a look of panicked delight. I turned immediately, having learned from the brief interlude with Father Burn that the silent movie ran between the two of us only. Just the other side of our joint delusion, the restaurant, I knew, was lurid and garish, proceeding smoothly, with none of the magical jerks and starts of our little world.

I followed her long pointing finger and saw Hezekiah lumbering into the dining room, his short, pudgy arm around Sonia's hips. He wore leather breeches, like old-fashioned cavalry wraps, beneath his somber gray suit, which made him look even more absurd than usual. He didn't see me, luckily, and led Sonia into a private *sala*.

But luck cuts more ways than a fucking traffic rotary. I turned back to the table as Molly clapped her hands together gleefully. Her voice sultry, gothic, letting her mouth hang open slightly as she spoke,

"I like this place."

I saw Father Burn take in the wolf-tooth ring on her hand. He would've said something, I think; tried to sell me some of the garish ice in his pigskin case, but Molly interrupted him, laughing this perfect intoxicated gun-moll laugh, mostly to herself, biting her lip. My heart turned over and she grabbed his arm.

"Look, Mr. Keaton, there's a Keystone Kop making his way toward our table."

At the word cop, which meant only one thing to Father Burn, who probably never heard of silent movies, he jumped. Feck walked up to us, dressed in an oxford shirt and plain blue suit. Blood pounded in my temples. Molly bit her thumbnail, then looked wide-eyed at me. I could see the hallucination drain out of her gray-blue eyes, leaving guilt and a kind of alert horror. As a general rule, I don't just stand still for killjoys, but this was Molly's hand and she had to play it her way.

"Well, well, well. I been looking for you for three hours. See, I was stupid. I figured where would a two-bit con take his girl to dinner? The best place in town, right? Candlelight, monkey-suits with violins, the whole shebang. I drive all the way out to Texas into Sid Dansby's Steak House, push through all these beefy guys eating their fucking steak blue, chowin' down on Rocky Mountain Oysters which are just deep-fried fucking bull balls; and you ain't there. So then I think it over. Maybe a successful con'd go that route, but a sentimental fucking crook like you, Flanagan, you'd take her to some creepy chintz-curtain place like this, a hang-out, show her off. So here you are."

"I never eat with Texans," I said.

Molly drained an entire glass of Tecate before she spoke. She scraped her teeth against her lip and in a weird way I felt sorry for the damn guy. She was furious.

"Have a seat, Special Agent Feck. You look like a fucking corpse," she said quietly.

Father Burn froze in mid-swallow and Feck shrugged. He grabbed the back of the fourth chair and looked at me for permission. I nodded. As he settled in, Father Burn gripped the edge of his attaché case.

"Do I understand correctly that you are a Federal Agent of some kind," he asked.

Feck nodded and Father Burn jumped up, brushing his rings into the case with one swift movement and bowing slightly as he backed away. I'd never seen him move that fast. I had to laugh. It was apparent at a glance that the guy wasn't a G-man and if Father Burn ever left the town square, he'd've recognized Feck, who went slumming in the small towns outside Las Cruces all the time.

"You must excuse me, I think there is a parishioner in need in the next room."

The Padre made a beeline for Hezekiah's *sala*, which meant I could expect a visit from Fatty Arbuckle and Lillian Gish momentarily. Hezekiah, if possible, had even more power in the district than the Burns and it didn't surprise me that they were connected.

The stupidity of it all made me weary. Father Burn was such an idiot. He'd go running to Hezekiah, tell him I was having dinner with a strange woman and a federal agent. Then Hezekiah would have to come check it out for himself, even though if there'd actually been a federal agent in town, the town sheriff would have informed Hezekiah before he even polished his gun.

A comedy of goddamn errors. I'd been hoping to avoid introducing Molly to Hezekiah, and would have dragged her ass out of El Cabra as soon as Father Burn was out of sight. It was the right move. But the Doll had Feck to deal with, and there was no point in queering her deal over a misunderstanding she wasn't even aware of. Plus, there was always the chance that Hezekiah would be so intent on stuffing his fat face and pawing the Totonac girl that he'd write it all off as the priest's paranoia. So I decided to chalk it.

Molly lit a cigarette and looked innocently at her old boyfriend.

"What," she asked him, and I had to laugh. Molly can be a girl when she wants to. Feck was completely taken aback, the wind stolen from his sails. It was the perfect way to handle the situation. That simple flutter-eyed question had squashed him like a bug.

He gestured toward the pitcher and Molly nodded.

"I don't know, Veeka," he said, as he poured, "I guess I'd like to know what the fuck that stunt of yours was about. You oughta know about bureaucracy by now. What the fuck did you expect? You acted like such a—"

"I *am* a girl," Molly interrupted him, finishing his sentence.

"Yeah, okay, Veeka. I guess it doesn't matter. It being me and all, the committee was expecting some kind of temperamental piss-ass hippie anyway. I think they feel justified or something. They're willing to go ahead with the thing and they say you can just give a test in the vocab class. So, it's just the seminar you've got to worry about."

"Kind of them."

Feck snorted and things were cool between them. Just like that. I'd've liked to write the whole thing off as the prof's weakness, his sap's love for my over-determined chick, but I couldn't. I knew it was Molly, that she could tame a fucking Pamplona bull, turn every guy in the ring on as she wept and sucked the blood out of her gored flesh, match anyone stride for stride. It made me uneasy.

The trip had turned on us and I felt that somehow we were melting into each other. Molly's sweet voice was creepily laconic, a sex echo, and I felt a gnawing compulsion to name every thought that passed through my addled skull, a habit of Molly's

103

that normally annoyed me. I wanted to walk away, clear my head, let Molly play out her hand however she had to, but I couldn't tear myself away from the impending sense of merger and doom.

Molly was happy again, her eyes bright, and through sheer force of will, I shoved my rage and jealousy down into my throat. I stared at them, though. I sort of like watching Molly in action and I wasn't about to eat those fucking *flautas* looking down at my plate and letting them pretend I wasn't there.

"I know I acted like a freak, Feck, and I could explain why but you don't really care. You don't care about these people, and you don't care about your reputation per se. You only care about getting to the MLA. So I'm gonna make it up to you in the currency you understand. Go, have a ball, give your little talk, and I'll keep things smooth on this end. I'll even go to church if you want. And I'll go you one better than that. I'll actually teach something in your seminar—even though, near as I can figure, it's really about nothing at all."

"What do you know?"

"Only one thing, Feck. I know how to listen."

"You're gonna teach my class how to listen? Wanna put your money where your mouth is?"

"A hundred bucks?"

"Done. But don't think I don't know you're into this, Molly. I know you got a whiff of it. You *want* to teach my class. You'd've kept grinding it around in your damn pinko brain even if I hadn't interceded on your behalf with the committee."

"Tortured Clods. Don't bet on it."

"Okay, Feck," I said, mustering from nowhere my vocabulary, taking brief comfort in the boundaries of my wrecked desert skin, "you settled your score, now blow."

"Yeah, Flanagan, alright. You got some class for a shitty two-bit con."

We stared at each other, not with recognition, or respect, or even with the revolting knowledge that we loved the same girl, something I didn't want to think about. I'd still've rather seen him rotting in a ditch somewhere, and I knew he felt the same way about me. But we'd each decided to let it go for the moment, and that was something.

"If you guys hurry you could probably still catch Father Keaton. He has a lovely assortment of rings," Molly said.

Feck folded himself out of the chair, stretching his gaunt excuse for a body almost to the tiled ceiling of El Cabra.

"Okay, Dr. Head," he said, "Good luck with the farmers and I'll see you in a week. Be good to my truck."

"You still haven't told me what you're presenting," Molly said, pushing the hair out of her eyes, and I got hard.

I had no idea what they were talking about. Ten-syllable names, sticky on the tongue, pounced between them palpably. But her terse, exaggerated voice was doing funny things to my blood vessels, creating the sensation of jerking-off.

"What's it called," Molly said, as I tuned back in.

"'The Private Language of Grief.'"

"I hate you," she said, laughing.

You'd think that would be the end of it, but it wasn't even close. Fate, that glorious bitch, had given me my big score at the Sunland track, my mushroom deal, and for now anyway, a girl who could turn a guy mad as a fighting cock into a gangling lovesick schmuck. So naturally, there was hell to pay.

Feck nodded grimly and shambled out of my turf in his ugly blue suit. Molly looked down. For a second I thought she was gonna pull some kind of broad number and gush all over me about how damn understanding I'd been, but of course it was Molly, and she handled it perfectly, balling up her left fist and faking a hook to my jaw.

"Thanks, Flan," she said quietly, lit a cigarette and ordered another pitcher.

The table was littered with butts and glasses and the yellow skin on the cold *chile con queso* was flecked with a spray of ash. It didn't really matter. Over the years, I'd eaten *chile con queso* with cigarettes put out in it dozens of times and I knew it didn't mar the flavor. The stuff is so glutinous it can absorb any amount of obscenity. I peeled away the hardened skin and rolled a tortilla.

"Flan?" Molly said, her eyes huge on me.

"Yeah, Doll, what?" She gestured behind me with her chin.

"Looks like it's your turn."

Sonia Totonac slithered into the seat between us. At other times in my life I've sat with two beautiful girls and it's always trouble. They eye each other and they scratch each other, a cat dance of fakes and jabs. But Molly, as I've said, has an instinct for the score, and Sonia, I think, has so perfected her act, blended her delightful dumb innocence with her sex-drenched body and effortless gun-moll ethics, a twisted shadow of Nary's solid goodness, really, that nothing threatens her.

Sonia, giggling and carrying a shopping bag full of bright pink wool from which she was, for chrissakes, knitting, dressed like a damn 10th Avenue hooker, looked briefly at Molly and twisted her wrist quickly back and forth, her thumb erect. It's a gesture that doesn't fly anymore, quaint and almost stylized, having gone out of fashion right around the time Sonia was born in fact, and never having caught on outside the blasted dry moonscape of the Southwest; but on her it looked perfect, her fluttering lacquered nails, and I recognized it immediately. Was Molly with it, she wanted to know? Was it okay to talk?

I nodded but it was too late. Hezekiah bellied up to the table and fell hard into the seat opposite Sonia. For a moment, we were all quiet. Then Sonia giggled and slowly, deliberately, reached out, grabbed my jaw, and reeled me in for a huge kiss. For one surprised moment I returned it, then pushed her away gently.

I stared at her. We all did, I bet. What the hell was she doing? She gazed at me, eyes wide and unblinking. Then she laughed again and went back to her yarn.

Molly's face was clear and bright, tracking all of this with her usual hungry precision. But as I turned to her, her eyes went soft and goofy, following Sonia's lead. I had a flash of remorse, which I know would've made Molly laugh, subjecting the Doll, a straight girl, a citizen, Christ, a *professor*, to this pathetic Southwestern charade; but I knew she could handle it, knew that, at worst, it was a game to her. In the next instant I was furious, looking at my life through her piercing gun-metal eyes.

But Hezekiah's flat, piggy eyes were on me, and I knew that time was up on the moronic self-indulgence. There'd be no more naming my feelings, a bad habit of Molly's I'd apparently acquired in an unmerciful hurry which I didn't care to understand.

"Goliath, my friend, you have something perhaps you wish to discuss with me?"

I shook my head levelly, leading with my freshly grabbed jaw. "Uh-uh."

Sonia undulated in her seat. She'd finished whatever she was knitting and pulled a small pair of brass nail scissors out of her bra. She snipped a few pink threads and held it up. It was a tiny Christmas bell, three inches long and about two inches wide at the base, where the hot pink thread flared. She swung it in a circle from a loop she'd made at the top. It looked more like a cunt than anything and I smiled.

"We are friends, Goliath, and I have done a great deal for you over the years."

A fleck of congealed cheese had caught in the fold between his neck and his pocked, jiggling chin. I kept my eyes on it as he went on.

"I have travelled into Chihuahua and robbed the people of their ancient wisdom for you. I gave you money to travel to New York, when you were but a small boy, still wet behind the ears and with only your man's name to recommend you."

In point of fact he'd charged me twenty percent compounded interest and it'd taken me years of sweat and debilitating boredom in the tiny town to pay him off. And all the time he'd been pressuring me to forget the debt and just do some enforcing for him, which he, sickeningly enough, called "enticing." Had I taken him up on it, I'd've been under the direct authority of his main leg-man, Packy Salvo, the ugly moron I'd trashed in the first place.

Since I'd steadfastly refused to join his chain of command, I'd remained, alone among the players in the county, a free agent. But that required finesse, and kickbacks, and an occasional display of gratitude, which is what he wanted from me now. Gratitude. Which is what I didn't have to give. Now.

"Goliath, you have nothing you wish to discuss with me?"

Molly and Sonia were chattering away in preposterous Chicano Spanglish. Both pretending to be imbeciles. Both succeeding wildly. Molly in that role was an awful thing to see and I decided I had to put a stop to all the idiocy.

"Oh, for chrissakes, Hezekiah. There wasn't a fed at the table. You know Roberto is an idiot. Why do you even listen to him? It was *Feck*. You know Feck. The skinny Anglo teacher? He's here every night, hitting on all the little girls."

"Ah, sí, sí. Enrique Feck. The lecher. Now I understand the little Father's confusion."

"Good."

"But, tell me, Goliath. This I do not understand. Why did you allow Father Burn to believe that your visitor was—"

He paused for the right word, and for the drama of it. Without taking her dumbed-down eyes off Sonia, Molly interjected,

"*Desabrido*? Unsavory? *Un intruso*?"

She proffered her suggestions cheerfully, then turned her attention back to Sonia. Hezekiah's fat-creased eyes widened in insult, and I deliberately looked away from him. I think that was the first time he'd ever been interrupted and I needed time to think before his distrust of me grew to include the Doll.

Sonia and Molly had about forty of those cunt bells piled up on the table. Molly was laughing and twirling them, rubbing them seductively between her fingers. They looked good together, the purple caverns under Molly's eyes, Sonia's ripe, buoyant cleavage, and I immediately felt right, opening myself to fate, to the resolution which would surely come, one way or another. I had a sip of beer.

"Well, Hezekiah," I said, "I let him believe it because it seemed like a funny thing to do at the time. I was fucking with his head, okay? Because I like to do that sometimes. Because I need to do that sometimes. Because I get so sick and tired of all the ass-backwards machinations that pass for brains in this godforsaken shithole nowhere of a town, sometimes I just have to have a little fun. You get me?"

Hezekiah watched me and his face slowly transformed. The blow-up would come later, maybe, his fat head swelling like a puff adder, all pomp and small-town cheesy rage. But that would be later, an afterthought, an act. This was the real thing. He disowned me without words, his face transforming the way a mesa draped in sudden shadow can look like a dead tree stump. But a flicker of light played in the shadow. He was thinking. He still needed me.

"Well, Goliath, my friend, I can see that you are under some duress. And perhaps under the influence of something else as well, hah? Always I have been prepared to make allowances for you. I know it is necessary. You are not of us here in Mapache. Your very name, he tells me this. But to live among us, partake of our ways, you too must be prepared. This is fair, is it not? It is a higher truth."

The truth was—the truth was that my fit of truth-telling had passed as quickly as it came on. My brain hurt and I wanted to bolt. I knew I could be screwing Molly right now, wasted and messy and fused in an easy, conventional way, slick with sweat and spit in that sterile motel room, if it weren't for this passion I'd picked up from her for making things straight as I went along.

I was pretty fed up with Hezekiah. In fact, I found him revolting and I wasn't sure how the dough I'd pull from selling the Smiley to Tom stacked up against looking at his stupid face for another second. But there was a slim chance that if I let the fat slob threaten me, lay out his whole small-town criminal trip, he'd forget what I'd said and even what Sonia had done, which of course was really at the bottom of the whole confrontation. I only needed him to forget long enough for me to score the mushrooms and blow.

True, if it played out that way, he'd hate me, but with any luck I'd be in New York soon and in New York Hezekiah'd just be another fat beaner, drinking beer on stoops, and dreaming not of the cool brutal freedom that New York has to offer, but of his own slimy dictatorship. His power was entirely bound up with the vile red-clay badlands that surrounded his tub of lard. In New York he'd never even find me.

"Alright," I sighed. "What?"

Hezekiah laughed and lit a foul cigar.

"Why don't you join us tonight, Goliath? You can drop the girls off home and we will go into Anthony. Perhaps some, how does it call itself, 'male-bonding,' is just what we need. Sometimes the company of the fairer sex can confuse even a hard man,

Goliath. I have found this myself."

"Tonight? Drop the girls off?"

Maybe he was right. Maybe the company of the fairer sex *had* confused me. Or maybe it was the drugs. Or maybe somewhere between New York and Mapache I'd lost the rhythms of my own hometown. I could barely make out what he was saying. I studied Molly and Sonia out of the corner of my eye, hoping to sharpen my brain with lust.

Hezekiah was still talking, something about loyalty and names, and Packy Salvo's floating crap game which I could attend that night, in a garage in Anthony, a show of fucking faith. That, of course, was something I could not do. I don't take tests of loyalty. I don't ditch my date to gamble in a chicken barn. And I don't hang out with Packy Salvo.

Hezekiah knew full well I'd never agree to his stupid plan. He'd stopped running his mouth and he and I were just looking at each other, his eyes squished down by folds of fat. I still hadn't said anything. There wasn't anything I wanted to say. What I wanted was for a hole of cruel gas flames to open under him. I wanted to watch him burn horribly, the crackling of his melting fat fueling his painful disintegration. But I also wanted the Smiley deal.

Ultimately, it was Molly who clinched it for me, who saved me from my impotent freeze. For someone who'd been told her whole life that she was crazy, the Doll had an odd faith in herself, a kind of wacked moral certainty. Drunk and tripping, higher than a kite, immersed in one damn language role or another, she was likely to say just about anything that came into her head, absolutely solid in the idea that her perception counted and was therefore appropriate.

The girls' voices flickered in and out of our hatred and then, very distinctly, clear and sweet, and out of her pretty skull, I heard Molly say,

"*Se las pones en la pinga?*"

Do you put them on his penis? That flawless accent, perfect Mexican slang, the strangest fucking thing I'd ever heard her utter.

Hezekiah and I turned and Molly was holding one of the bells, smiling and questioning Sonia, who was in a bind. A flush of

incredible mirth passed over her face but she wiped it away quickly. Her proposition with Hezekiah depended entirely on his
believing that he alone, pustular and ruined, was corrupting her,
and she couldn't take any chances. She liked me and I think she
liked Molly too but that wasn't enough. Hezekiah was indignant,
struggling to get his huge body out of the chair. Sonia stood up,
leaving the bells behind, biting the inside of her cheek to get the
tears flowing.

Hezekiah lumbered away from the table, muttering about the
bruja, and as Sonia followed, squealing, she turned and winked at
us. Molly laughed and winged a bell at me and the self-echoes
turned to tremors and I loved her more than ever.

"Well," she said, "we got rid of them."

"That we did, Doll."

"Now, Flan," she started, biting her lip, "about this crap game
you're missing because I'm a *puta bruja*—"

"Don't sweat it, Kid. I wouldn't have gone anyway."

"No, Flan. I think we should sweat it." Her voice, my voice,
dropped a couple of octaves into ricocheting gravel. "I think it's
very serious. I think we better have a little crap game of our own."

"You got dice?"

"I never travel without dice, guy. Language mysteries are
informed by probability."

"You remember how to play?"

"Do you?"

"Of course."

"Then I must too."

"Let's go, then."

"Okay, but, Flan, can I tell you something?"

"Shoot," I said, laying money on the table.

"This place stinks. I hate the Southwest."

12

A Buck for a Fuck, a Fuck for a Buck, and 20 Bucks for Some Fucked-up Luck

"Let's see, what is it, a nine? If I make my point, you suck my cock for ten minutes. Sound fair?"

"No."

"You won't take my bet? Chicken?"

"No. Let's make it if you crap out I suck your cock for ten minutes."

"Why?"

"I think you're gonna lose and, just at this moment, I *want* to suck your cock."

"You do, huh?"

"You wanna roll this week, Flan?"

Flan rolled a nine immediately. He won, so I drank, but he didn't get anything out of it. I had to laugh. The most confusing thing about sex craps, because any bet goes, is whether your aim is to get sex for yourself or to withhold sex, tormenting the other person.

Because Flan and I play pick-up craps, without any House, we tend to use the bottle as our croupier, paying for control of the dice with long pulls of tequila. Sex craps isn't any different from what you might find going in a pay-day latrine. You just bet with body favors instead of money. You roll to make your point. If you come up with snake eyes or boxcars, you drink and the bones pass to the the next guy. If you come up with a seven or eleven, the other guy drinks and the whole thing begins again.

Anything else, and the race is on. You continue to roll until you come up with a seven, in which case you drink, and lose control of the dice, or the number you originally rolled, your point, in which case your opponent drinks, and you begin again. Along the way, any bet about what you might roll is up for grabs. Perusing your chances, maintaining your cool, and bringing your opponent to a kind of bankruptcy of patience and desire are the only requirements.

So, as I say, if you're drunk enough—and if you're not drunk to begin with, you're drunk after a few rolls—it's a pretty easy game. Flan and I have sometimes played a variation in which each player begins with a limited number of moans beyond which he must remain silent, but we were too fucked up to go that route.

He rolled again, this time coming up with boxcars, so he drank and the dice passed to me. My point was four and it was up to me to propose the bet, but I couldn't think straight. The rigid structures of Flan's terse world clamped down cruelly on my head, bits of brain oozing out of the harsh screened grid. I reached out and stroked Flan's hard hand, trying to read his skin. A four is pretty hard to make and I knew Flan wouldn't go for the turn-around twice in a row, getting nothing out of winning.

"Busted, Doll?"

"You know, this game would make more sense if we assigned body parts and actions to numbers. There'd be less control, you know? What might happen next? Something silly? Something sordid? Only the dice would know for sure."

"Quit stalling. We tried that before. You said, if I recall, that you don't believe in the black glamour of fate."

"Tonight I do."

"Tonight you do, swell, Doll, but call the bet."

"Okay, I get the four, I tie you up."

"Kinda of upping the ante, aren't you?"

"Too rich for your blood?"

"Nah. I'll take the bet. It's just, that'd pretty much put an end to the game, won't it? Once you get to roaming all over my body? But it's cool. The game itself has a stake in the bet."

The game, and Flan, lost the bet. Flan ripped his blue shirt into strips, assisting in his own submission. Concentric spirals, yellow phospherenes taunted his ribs. He was silent, grim amusement and fear battling for a front row seat in his green eyes, and that suited me.

I wanted to concentrate, licking salty thresholds, jutting over scratchy edges, pumping myself into the wavering boundaries; and more than that, I didn't want to hear his voice for a while. My head was whirling with his baroque constructs, and I was sick of tripping, sick of the switch, sick of the silent movie. More than that, I wasn't hallucinating. I mean, I was hallucinating, of course, from the hallucinogenic mushrooms. But I wasn't *hallucinating.*

We did look good in the motel mirror though, more like two people having sex than the damned irresolutes of my delusion, thrashing into each other to the slow-cranked slapstick of a bygone era. Flan, bound and silent, grinning beautifully, was a shining prize, but I still had to get there.

It's tough tying someone up. The normal sticky flow of power back and forth melts into nothing you recognize, into a gruff imperative making its home somewhere deep in your gut. You wanna be big enough to contain that power, playing his body like a goddamn pedal steel guitar and you wanna lose yourself, but you're not allowed to; there's a tacit agreement that you'll be there, outside the darkness, to haul him back to ground. You begin with a wild stab toward the middle and the sweaty prerogatives grow out in hideous unpredictable directions. Not hideous, beautiful. Hideous.

The pitfalls are innumerable, salty cold flesh between your teeth, like fat prose in the middle of the night. Half asleep and wasted and terrified that this next edge is the one you'll tumble down. The big spill. Seized balls vie with crippled symmetry and a rippling jaw for your complete attention and you hunker down onto his chest. You deftly skirt your shoulders away from the still desert shadows, stepping over each crack with virginal trepidation, navigating the void for two, your tongue the rudder, knowing that you are not immune.

Tough guys fall in love and get caponed, brilliant chicks fling themselves so deeply into empathy that they lose the way out, people fuck themselves to death in sodden motel rooms. It happens. Squirming maggots eat the trail of bread crumbs, and you're lost in a world where your self-containment quavers wildly. Where is his cock again? For a moment you're not sure. You could easily be somewhere else. These thoughts aren't yours and the lingo you've lived by abandons you in a flash.

It was nearly five and I'd held almost twice that many cigarettes to his yearning lips before we decided he'd had enough. He stumbled into the shower, his body etched with old scars and new red creases. I read his ragged flesh like it was cuneiform, craning my head as he stepped away from me.

We climbed into the other bed. The clammy linen of our used berth gave off a pale stench in the first false light. A coyote, which Flan pronounced "kie-oat," howled against the lightening window. More than we deserved, I thought, but welcome just the same.

It wasn't that we'd fused, I came to think, Flan dead to the world, fit hard against my sore body, so much as that we'd somehow pulled off an elaborate drag-race stunt. We'd switched cars while cruising down the blacktop, clambered and leapt, a speedster's ballet, the Organ Mountains a rushing blur. And so as I struggled into sleep, I had a hard time concentrating on my plans. That fat gangster, the corrupt small-town priest, and even the beautiful Sonia danced around in my brain, making my work the next day seem fuzzy and distant to me. I slept lousy, no foreboding about it; and dreamed I was driving the wrong car.

Academics do a lot of screwy things. This is the way their brains are built. Their schema are thick and clean and their *skandas*, fuck, their *skandas* are lightning bolts. So, you find academics making these distinctions that go down real smooth and only afterward, sitting on the subway, throwing bones at your dog, do you realize that the whole thing was utterly meaningless, or in actuality possessed of a nonsensical meaning. We make a lot of noise, you see. We kind of squawk. But there is a certain unholy logic to the whole sordid mess, the business of academics, the murk of sense-making.

All art, an academic will tell you, goofily stern, can be divided into the seven dwarves, Happy, Dopey, Sleepy, Grumpy,

116

Sneezy, Bashful, and whatever that other poor sucker was called. Or we might get a twist, like, Young's new album is presided over by the three dwarves: Sappy, Gloppy and Maudlin. Lenin was Warner Brothers and Yeltsin is Disney. Harness racing is Lacan writ large. Sid and Johnny as Odysseus. Three Fates: Jonas Mekas, Max Weber, and the bird-faced progeny of the consanguine.

You can't really blame them, or at least I can't. In part because, by default, I'm one of them, and in part because, as I said, there's something wonderful and awe-inspiringly innocent about pattern-hunting. In a way, I'm hooked. I keep looking. Smoldering fool of a drunk that I am, I've been at it for years. I've looked in all the classic places for people like me. I've looked on midnight trains and amid the tobacco crumbs in my leather jacket. I've looked long and hard for the smiling scorpion at the bottom of the tequila bottle. You might call that particular journey an exhaustive search. I've looked into the eyes of a sportswriter looming above me. I've even looked in the Bible.

Of course, all of this is just an elaborate way of saying that I had no idea what the fuck I was doing. The wake-up call startled me into action, that drawn-out nasal twang, and I reached first for the tequila bottle. It helps if you're drunk sometimes. Things come clear in painful white booms, flashes of unattainable comprehension, briefly glimpsed hits of sick true fluid running down motel-room drains.

But as soon as the dregs of the tequila hit my stomach, I knew this wasn't gonna be one of those times. I vomited for easily twenty minutes before I had any real recollection of who I was. Equal parts water, advil, and my favorite blue dress brought me home to myself. Then, listening to Flan retch in the bathroom, I began to get nervous.

I didn't have a plan except to go in cold and listen to the students. Try to talk their bent talk; try to get them to do the same. I mean, with a class like "Metastasizing Praxis," what kind of plan *could* I have? There is, after all, a crippled symmetry to the goofiest array of disorder and it can be almost unbearably beautiful when left alone. Take a gander at Thelonious Monk's delirious seven-note octave, Whitey Ford's curveball, Jack Palance's face.

But if you have to find the axis, you need the heart to go in with a scalpel and eviscerate, plot the spattered blood points along a slope that cuts right through you, swallow the skew in skewer and smile pretty at the acrid taste of the metal.

Flan was hungover, big surprise, and in a rotten mood, muttering to himself about the cheating Mexicans, the Godforsaken chile farms, the fucking tarantulas. While he was in the bathroom, Hezekiah called. He was eerily formal. I passed the phone into the steamy shower and Flan pressed it to his wet ear, grunting "uh-huh" twice into the mouthpiece. He stepped out of the bathroom to hang up the blower.

For a moment he stood stock still, his chest wet, a Quinta towel wrapped around his waist. Then, without a wasted motion, he hurled an empty bottle against the mirror.

The shards of glass didn't so much rain as give way and clatter, falling like a brief silver aftershock around the heavy bottle. It takes more than a little sudden violence to make me start and I turned, smiling. Flan was looking at me nervously, that particular anxious look he has, that one I call: Is she gonna act like a broad?

I didn't, of course, and he matched my smile, a little strained.

"I guess you don't wanna talk to him, huh," I said.

"Let's have breakfast."

We stopped at Chope's and while Flan ordered us steaks and, at the bartender's insistence, green salsa eggs, I went next door to buy cigarettes and a quart of bourbon. When I worked with the Bureau that time, I discovered that easily half the problem they were having communicating with the suspect derived from the fact that the guy had the DT's and was dying for a smoke. Ever since then I've been one of the world's great believers in hair of the dog.

It hadn't been a particularly interesting or important case and seeing as how I was A.B.D. at the time, the only reason they'd fingered me was because I had Feck, their number one civilian fan, in my corner, and I was the handiest person who spoke this mountain dialect of Magyar which the drunk was sputtering in. I guess it's a tricky language, especially if the guy you're talking to is hallucinating, because the severely agglutinating Finno-Ugrian languages bear next to no relationship to any other language group, and because, in the slurred accent of northern Hungary, it's basically impossible to hear the difference between particles and affixes, or even the parts of speech.

The fact that I was down with the fool argot wasn't due to any sterling dedication on my part, though. It wasn't even a test of my peculiar talents. I was a first-generation American and my father, sort of a first-generation hustler, started out as a copper miner in Retsag. My mother was born on the Borzsony Range, near the Czech border. I grew up speaking the garbled patois of Nograd.

The case, as I say, wasn't major by any stretch of the imagination, but working with the Bureau had given me enough glamour, packed enough whump, to get me a tenure-track Assistant Professorship before I'd even finished my dissertation. I felt I owed a psychic debt to poor Tibor, the deranged Hungarian bank robber, whose sole prior accomplishment, before he stumbled across the Pennsylvania state line to pull his second, and final, heist, was, he told me again and again, that he could suck his own penis.

13

Hangover

Looking at Molly stumble into the blinding sun, I felt the crush of the gulf that separated us ram up against the sway of her ass. After all, what was it to the Doll that I was out of the loop, embanked, all these years too late?

Hezekiah had made his pitch. He was sending me into Juarez to pick up the drugs. Sending me with Packy Salvo. Dispatching me to ride shotgun for Packy, the dumbest gunsel in the county, was tantamount to a punishment. I didn't know if I could go through with it.

But if I didn't, it'd be the end of me. I couldn't get a job in the Southwest to save my life. I couldn't even be a fucking pump jockey out on the Corralitos Lateral, surely the lowliest blind worm of a job available. Even poor old Nary Totonac, whose kindness was legendary, couldn't risk his grandchildren's safety by taking me on as a farmhand.

But what did that matter? All I'd ever wanted was to get away from this desiccated hothouse, and the grotesque *lingote* who ran it. I'd always been an outsider and liked it, dreaming of New York, of trading the Land of Enchantment for the land of anonymous freaks. I was just in the habit of feeling somehow subordinate to Hezekiah, jumbled under his threats. More than three decades of pretending to be routed can do that to a man.

Molly had the jakeleg. She fell out of the Pic-Quik, her ragged grace keeping her beautiful as she tumbled. She hit the ground hard, no clemency from the damn New Mexico sun, and as I watched Chope give her a meaty hand up, I thought maybe the comedown, the crash from being soldered to her the night before, was contributing to my mood.

She checked the status of her bottle before she even brushed off her blue dress. I studied her, crumpling the note the hotel clerk had slipped me against the sweaty denim of my pocket. She walked with a sapped swagger, dancing the violent light off her as she started back toward me.

The note, a breathy come-on from Sonia Totonac, almost a summons, annoyed me. I didn't know what Sonia wanted from me. Kiss aside, certainly she had no intention of putting out now, after resisting my advances for three solid years. More than likely she was running some vamp errand for Hezekiah, and I wanted no part of it.

It was no surprise to me that every wailing brat ever born in Mapache was a treacherous guava-gnawing little viper. But Molly, whose hand hit the swinging door with a healthy thud, had a hard day ahead of her. I could tell she was nervous, and I thought the least I could do was spare her the sight of her boyfriend left for the vultures, dead and gutted on some back road in a town that wasn't on any maps.

Molly scraped forkfuls of green chile off her eggs, stoically tucking the food away one grim mouthful at a time. Twice she bolted from the table as if there were a kitten about to fall into a vat of acid across the room. I think she vomited, but with Molly, a lady game to her goddamn fingernails, it's sometimes hard to tell.

She smoked with that charged languor throughout the meal, then spent a good ten minutes replacing her spent coffee and griping under her breath. She was right across the table, but I missed her, my throat tight, and wished there were a drug that would obliterate ol' Evan, that whole crowd, permanently.

Watching her, I popped a thumbnailful of Smiley into my mouth. I had a passing feeling I could join her conversation, see the damn guy, if only I could get exactly where her head was. Not, I knew, that that was possible. Molly seems to be operating on at least three levels of hallucination at once. And even if I could take enough Smiley to penetrate one of those levels, the others would always be hopelessly out of reach.

There are her little perceptual flaws, shadows extended like a proboscis, funny motions half-glimpsed out of the corners of her eyes, tripped-up depth perception, all glitches which I suspected were just a normal part of the average Joe's ordeal while plowing through life. It was only because the rest of her visual field was so inexorably fucked that Molly perceived these things as pathological.

Take the animals. These seem perfectly harmless, if a little on the goofy side. Best as I can tell, from what little Molly's muttered to me, they are almost entirely passive, with no particular interest in interfering in the course of the Doll's life. They don't seem to cause her any undue strife, except perhaps that she feels sorry for the rest of us because we don't see them. It's almost as if Molly gets to spend every day at a private zoo, behind a great stone wall, and salivate though we might, she simply can't let us in.

Thinking about it, I realized it was the ghosts who really pissed me off. Or not even the ghosts. Her father, after all, was just a shrewd old lice-ridden player, and although I'm sure the Doll loves him, she seems to have little or no desire for his approval. And the mother, to hear the Doll tell it, having steered the Doll toward a prospective husband, was borne away on the wings of a fucking song, never to be heard from again.

My problem was with the dead husband himself. Evan, who was realer to her than almost anything, was a nightmare for me. Imagine competing with a dead guy who has absolutely no interests other than the well-being of your girl. The fact that he was generally in my corner when it came to my dealings with Molly was no comfort whatsoever, implying, as it did, that at any moment he might turn against me. And in the face of such a betrayal, I'd be fucking powerless. What could I do, hit the guy?

I was getting annoyed as I sat there, counting off imaginary playmates on my calloused fingers. I felt my own nastiness rising within me, the bitter taste thick against the backs of my eyeteeth. The thing I like best about us together is the way we leave each other alone, but even I was starting to get antsy, forced into my own head. I was just about to say what was probably the worst thing I could say to her, something I'd regret my whole life; not because I believed it, in fact I didn't at all, but just to get her fucking attention.

Did you ever think, Doll, I could almost hear myself saying, the words burning behind my eyes, that Evan did drugs just to keep up with you? I took the freshly rolled cigarette out of her mouth and sucked on it. Molly looked up, genuinely startled, remembering my presence. She smiled and my guts shifted, the black words floating away. Beautiful Molly, who pushed you just that far, to the very brink of silence, before she swooped back in.

"Do you think there's something funny about those mushrooms," she said.

"There's something funny about all drugs. That's the point of drugs."

She looked shocked, then rolled her eyes, making a face of salacious disgust. A knife of recognition went through my gut. Molly could talk any talk with razor-sharp precision, but the flipside of that gift was infuriating. She expected every return sentence to be packed with exact meaning. You couldn't get away with stating the obvious, or even giving what was, ostensibly at least, an appropriate response. She expected you right there in the moment with her, every time; and she used those twin looks, wounded innocence and ironic impatience, to force you there. It pissed me off.

Molly sank nimbly back into herself, content to wait forever in the jammer of her own thoughts until I was ready to come across with a hunk of my heartmeat. She did this casually. It seemed to cost her nothing to be right there in the instant, on the brink of heartbreaking mutual recognition, and then shuttled cozily into the fucking slow simmer of her own brain, blissfully alone.

Molly makes a rotten Catholic. She reviles the way the rest of us muddled along, coating each other with soothing ritual responses. It was enough, she seemed to think, that she could match you memory for memory; speak with your own thick wet tongue, making it hers, tossing off exact poignant references to things you'd mentioned in passing ten years before: your dog, beheaded by a Mack truck out on Salopek Road or Pepe, the drunken Thin Man, who lived in a trailer next to yours in 1955.

Oblivious to my rising fury, Molly carelessly ran her thumb over the slope of her own jaw, a gesture of mine, still waiting for my thoughts on our Smiley trip, and I had to laugh. That was Molly alright, who smoked as well as she fucked, and fucked better than any woman alive. Everything she did she was just pretty enough to get away with.

Of course, as I steadied myself to get down there in the trenches with her, I realized that she was right. There was something funny about the Smiley. It messed up the space between people. My anger at Molly's straight-on talk, stubborn silence and even her zombie entourage proved it. After all, those were the things I normally dug most about her.

"What do you want me to say, Doll? I can't be responsible for the places our sex and drug use take us."

"No, Flan, you can't. But I need my head back, my whole head, soon, any minute now. And I'm thinking you'll probably need yours too."

"Yeah."

Molly laughed.

"Good," she said. "A terse little grunt. Now that sounds like the guy I fell in love with."

"Maybe that's just the way it sounds, Doll."

"Maybe, Flan, but what else is there? That's all I've got to go on, anyway. But, listen, did you have a map of the United States when you were a kid?"

Molly on a tear is marvelous thing to see. Her eyes were bright, their focus manifest, even though she was facing me, if this makes any sense, with her ears. Despite this sudden attention, though, I had to laugh. Terse little grunts, my ass. I had more nuance goin' there than Henry friggin' James.

Still, I found myself resisting having to scour my mind for the memory of some damn map and then, in the same second, realized that that resistance was the very thing the Doll was going for. She was hellbent on proving that we were still disparate.

So I decided to play it out. It was okay with me if Molly wanted to flex her muscles on me. I knew that, whatever she was up to, she'd probably end up making us both feel less on edge. It's just that I didn't think some ritual dance of giving each other back was going to make a fucking difference in the way I felt. We went someplace and something irrevocable happened. Molly, of course, with her stringent belief in "systems of information," or whatever, was incapable of taking it this way.

"Uh-huh. We had one in the trailer."

"Four colors, right?"

"I don't remember."

"Try. What color was New Mexico?"

"Orange."

"What color was New York?"

"Blue."

"Mets colors, huh? But of course, not back then. What about Texas?"

"Blue also."

"That must've driven you crazy."

She was driving me crazy. But as the memories flooded in, they made my head solid somehow, crowding out our little psychic border disputes, and I couldn't help smiling. I remembered painstakingly smearing the tiny picture of Texas with my own shit, coloring it brown instead of blue. I remembered the whack across the head I got with a bottle of mescal for having done it and then, telling Molly about it, I remembered proclaiming the whole thing worth it. It was a huge fuck you to the entire order of the universe to have Texas and New York be the same color. A cut scalp and a few moments of unconsciousness were nothing in comparison.

This little exchange seemed to cheer Molly immensely. She grinned, absently braiding a small lock of hair that had fallen against her neck. But mostly I was still stuck. Molly'd made me feel a little better, it was true, and she'd somehow accomplished this with a series of questions that I found idiotic.

But feeling better was basically irrelevant. Just looking at the Doll made me feel better most of the time, pressing my thumbs into the dark crevices that lived over her cheekbones, parting a mess of hair to reveal her eyes, those two shining beasts. There was a war going on in my brain and I didn't see that feeling better about its existence served any real purpose.

Still, as we made our way out of Chope's toward the NMSU campus, we were quiet and comfortable. Molly drove, fluttering the seat with her imaginary gear changes, her hand curved possessively around a shaft that wasn't there.

Watching her easy motion, I could see it her way. What did it matter if I was suddenly drafting words from all over my head, lining 'em up like fucking soldiers, just praying that one or two might hit home, get drunk and out of hand; or that born of the bottle, a few might light my voice afire, tetched by a true genius for bloodlust? At least I was still talking like the same dumb son of a bitch I'd always been.

She pulled into the campus parking lot, narrowly missing a dead pecan tree, and kissed me, gathering her bottle and papers.

She said, "You okay?"

"Yeah. But what I don't get, Doll, is what possessed you to ask such a moronic question to begin with."

"The map? Or 'you okay?'"

"The map."

I wasn't sure exactly how she'd take my calling her question moronic but for the thousandth time, she was Molly and surprised me. In calling her question moronic, I'd asked *her* a question, and the damn things were so fucking sacred to her that she had bigger fish to fry than quibbling with my words. She smoked quietly, thinking.

"I don't know, Flan. I really don't. It's just I've found through years of battle that the right moronic question will work better than almost anything else to open the right doors. Or, I guess, in this case, shut them. But the map itself just leapt into my head."

She folded herself out of the car and I scooted into the warm driver's seat. Leaning in the window, she said,

"But all that map shit notwithstanding, Flan, do me a favor. If you're gonna go all internal all of a sudden—"

I started the car and, looking away from her, forced my voice into the ribbon of grit I knew made her happiest,

"Don't think before I draw?"

She laughed, reaching in and turning off the ignition, a shooting offense in Mapache, but I guess she'd have no way of knowing that.

"That too. But what I was gonna say was, can it wait 'til after I use you for an exercise? We had a little deal about this, or had you forgotten?"

"You're right," I said. God help me. "We do."

14

No Smoking

I had a huge fight with the English Department secretary, a slab-like woman in a power muu-muu who was way too old, I guess, to be subject to Feck's soothing blandishments. Flan hung around behind me, shifting his weight from one foot to the other, pressing the toes of his dusty boots into the pile of the office carpet.

It was absolutely impossible, the strident hen claimed, to move my class to a room in which smoking was permitted. There were no such classrooms. It was illegal and immoral, to say nothing of unhealthy.

"'Ful," I thought, correcting her, and the notion horrified me. It meant I wasn't really listening, and therefore couldn't, if she ever stopped talking, respond in kind. I stiffened and gripped the edge of her desk. The state of mind, normal, apparently, to everyone else, stopped me in my tracks; the barricade of solitude insoluble as she went on.

"...And simply too late to make any changes in the day's schedule."

I fell into a chair, next to the leaning Flan, my head hard against the wall behind me, trying to hear my request in her vocabulary. I was toying with it, sighing, just getting my mouth around something like "smoke-positive," when Flan's shadow fell into my lap.

"Pardon me, Ma'am, I don' mean to interrupt your conversation with the lady here, but since y'all are talkin' about smoking, I jest thought I might inquire, is there someplace on this here campus where a tired ol' fella like me might have hisself a smoke?

Thet is, without breakin' any rules, of course."

She blinked and the bureaucratic irritation melted out of her face. It was sort of amazing to watch.

"Why, yes, of course. There's a smoking lounge in the Payne building."

"Payne building, thet'd be on Payne Road, out by the Tortugas?"

"Yessir. Right on the arroyo."

"Thank you, Ma'am. I guess I'll jus' drive me over there, grab a couple of puffs on the evil weed."

"You really should quit, you know."

"Don' I know it, little lady. Yessir, don' I jest. Hey, you care to join me, Doc? I couldn' help but overhearin' you got the habit yourself."

This last to me, and I nodded and rose, following him out.

"Now we just put a sign on the door of the real classroom?"

"That's right, Doll. Welcome to the life in the con capital of the Southwest. And don't say I never did anything for you."

We trudged across the sun-blasted campus, our hangovers keeping us company. The adobe buildings struck me as small and scary. The rough pink texture of the bricks made me bilious.

"What's this class about, anyhow?" Flan asked.

"I don't know exactly. It's called 'Phenomenological Vertigo, Metastisizing Praxis, and Other Diseases of Meaning.'"

"Jesus," Flan said.

An hour later, we walked into the smoking lounge, Flan ahead of me. The room was dark and small compared to the rest of the airy campus. There were seven people with notebooks crowded around a short table with only one empty seat. I'd been worried, originally, that the ambient chatter in the smoking lounge would make things hard, but Flan thought I was just being stupid and it turned out he was right. No one else was in the room.

I nodded Flan into the seat at the head of the table and stood near him. Only two of them were smoking. One a long cool Chicana in a kind of suede Clint Eastwood coat and black leggings, the other a dead ringer for ol' Jasper Nitz. This didn't surprise me. They're all over the place, these bastard sons of Iggy

Pop, tiny bodies, nasty wit, dark broody looks. They're like the pre-wagon buffalo. The land is black with them; if you herded'em all together, they'd cover several states. And they wouldn't be what they were without a beautiful girl hanging around. Or, to put it still another way, there's a weasel in every henhouse.

All but one of the rest of Feck's students were girls, one of them thoroughly pregnant, all with big hair and flawless make-up. They looked kind of frizzled and Eastern, perfect candidates for Feck's language study, although not, I would think, his extracurricular ventures. He always insisted on at least three simultaneous forms of birth control anyway. I warmed up to them almost immediately. They looked like a clutch of Mets Ball Girls.

The one closest to Flan was twisting her hair nervously and frowning. Behind her back in the seat on her right, the boy I had fingered for Little Iggy's henchman mocked her actions, ruining the mimicry by glancing for approval across the table at his squire, who wasn't really paying attention. The vassal himself was a trip to look at. He could've replaced The Count on "Sesame Street" without anyone noticing.

"Problem?" I floundered, not knowing the hair-twister's name.

"Cindy. Dr. Veeka, I don't think it's right to have class in this room. It's full of smoke. Secondary smoke like killed my aunt."

Flan erupted into laughter at this, took the toy worm the fat lady'd given him out of his pocket and began chewing on it. The girl looked at him nervously.

"I, I'd rather not participate today if we're going to be working in here."

"Great," I said, "then I can have your seat."

She frowned and started collecting her papers.

"Don't worry about it, Cindy. It's cool. Your objection is totally reasonable. I'm sure Feck won't care. Maybe he can make up an extra assignment for you or something."

The Clint girl let out a little squirt of laughter at this, her voice high and sweet, and I figured she was a sister in Initiation-by-Feck. It made me feel better, actually. Despite all my bravado with Feck the night before, I wasn't really crazy about the idea of teaching the class, and I liked the idea of having the chick there. Hazed by the same goof, I figured we might have something in common that would make this easier.

Of course, the girl was willingly sitting in one of Feck's freestyle seminars, which didn't bode well. Not that I think interdisciplinary classes have no place in academics. Not at all. In fact, in my scant years as a full professor, I've already been criticized dozens of times for being flamboyant, unreliable, over the top, my own freestyle seminars being the least of my problems.

"Okay, thanks," Cindy said.

She dumped all her stuff into a big purple knapsack and left the smoking lounge, sort of mincing her steps. I took her seat and pushed my hair out of my face.

"I guess I didn't handle that too well. Is she gonna be alright?" I turned to her staring companions, fuzzy hair and eyes lined, inside, with a deep cobalt blue.

They looked at each other and nodded.

"Yeah, she'll be fine," one of them said. "She's upset about something, like, personal."

"Okay, then. Here's the deal. I'm Molly Veeka, in case you didn't know. Last night I had a huge fight with Feck and the upshot of it was I bet him a hundred bucks I could teach you guys something. The problem is, I should probably confess to you, I don't have the slightest idea what this class is supposed to be about. And if I know Feck, you don't either. So what I'm gonna do, if it's okay with you guys, is get you rolling on an exercise today and you can, uh, pick up wherever you left off with Feck when he gets back. Is that cool?"

A symphony of shrugs. Motes, light, smoke cleaving the table. I didn't blame Cindy for leaving. Finally, a Ball Girl spoke.

"But what do we, like, call this class on the syllabus?"

"Fair question. Um, how 'bout 'The Dialect in Situ?'"

"Is he the exercise?" A smirk, big surprise, from the weasel-faced kid. Flan stared at him. I was happy, though. At least he hadn't asked why I publish under the name Dr. Silence.

"Yeah. You got a name, smirking kid?"

"Jules Nytown."

"Okay. Now here's what I want to do: we go around the table asking him questions. You can ask whatever you want. No special order. He can answer however it strikes him. Listen carefully. And then everyone writes a profile of our guest. It's easy. Just ask whatever comes into your mind. The trick is, keep the focus on him. Nytown? You wanna start?"

My soul sister shook a Camel out of a wooden case and fit it into a blue ceramic holder.

"But, oh," I said. "Since our guest's a local boy, I guess I should make like a judge and ask if any of you have a prior association with him, and if not, why don't you go ahead and introduce yourselves."

Uncomfortable silence, Evan's calling card, and I thought of him, briefly, laughing uproariously, the morning of the day he died, as he showed me the newest betrayal, the latest parlor trick of his dissipating body. He'd shoved the spring of a Bic pen up his nose, through his deviated septum, poking it through to the other nostril. To the very end he was like that, bawdy, honest. He was a great junkie, no kidding. All those years, and he only hurt *me*.

I thought of him, the memory vivid, saturated. I thought of him, but he didn't come. More silence.

"Alright, I guess you New Mexicans practice a tough, impersonal kind of interrogation," I said. "But for my sake, tell me your names when you think of it. Nytown? I think the ball was in your court."

"Are you now, or have you ever been, a member of the Communist Party?"

Flan snorted.

"No, sir," he said and grinned. The worm made a chinking sound as he tapped it against his teeth.

"Hi, I'm Denise Salvo. I think maybe you know my cousin...um, do you eat meat," this from the first Ball Girl.

Jules Nytown rolled his eyes. The gorgeous Chicana took a long drag, her eyes on Flan, who looked easily at the Ball Girl, pointing with the worm.

"Often as I can."

A second Ball Girl giggled.

"How do you like it cooked?" she said.

"Any way at all, little girl." She blushed and looked down, cutting her eyes up at him like a low-rent Lauren Bacall, whispering, nasally,

"Oh, I'm Kath Van De Water."

"Charmed," Flan said, although by his tone he wasn't at all. But fuck, in for a penny, in for a pound. After all, we had a deal.

"Have you known many chickens?" The Count's contribution.

Great, right? Straight out of the fucking Dadaist handbook. I hadn't counted on the boy/girl thing, to tell the truth, and it annoyed me, watching the unconscious plays for Flan, but I'd had higher hopes than how many fucking chickens have you known. Flan, I guess, saw it differently.

"Yeah, I have. A lot. I was in charge of a mess of hens when I was a kid. They danced some, and played tic tac toe, and for a while I had an aerial fighter, a five-pounder with one eye. I fixed him up a tiny eye patch, looked like a midget pirate, confused his opponents all to hell. Four-time winner he was, too, a real mean sonofabitch. Lost him down in Van Horn. Texas," he said, and shook his head.

"But do you eat," a perfect throaty pause, "chickens? Virgen," she added by way of introduction, turning ever so slightly toward me. Flan looked up and smiled. My heart a little too fast, sweating up into my throat. The Ball Girls hopelessly outclassed, rolling their eyes; a cat fight in the makings.

"Yeah, I do. I even ate Monty, what was left of him anyway."

"Ever cut your tongue on a girl's braces?" I said.

Yeah, well, it wasn't the coolest thing I've ever done but I'm stupid that way. The point of the exercise is to ride the non-sequiturs into Indian Country, grasping at the tumbleweed as you go, at the Russian Thistle, to covertly collect weird information, to push yourself so far down that all that exists is the landscape of the subject's brain. If you use the questions to say anything about yourself you've lost, you've dismounted, you've fallen off the horse. But when a girl that pretty is whispering at your boyfriend, whispering her name, "Virgen," whispering in tones so sweet and soft, you could almost believe she was one, it's kind of hard to stay in the saddle.

Still, if you're stupid enough to use your boyfriend as a listening exercise, if you set him up to be gnawed at by a passel of green kids, it's only natural that they're gonna develop a conception of him. They're gonna have a picture of him in their brains. It's what you deserve.

"No, but a girl cut my cock with her braces one time." He shrugged. "It healed pretty fast."

Jules Nytown laughed and nudged The Count. In the smoky room, The Count's skin did, in fact, look green, but when he opened his mouth, his canines were rounded. I figured there wasn't much hope for the Transylvanian accent.

"Have you ever had unprotected sex?" Flan's eyes widened. His eyes said: Jesus, Doll, just how young *are* these kids? He turned to The Count.

"Hell, yeah."

"So, is it different?" Jules Nytown, weasely earnest.

"Kid, if it isn't different *every* time, you're doing something wrong."

"How big was the fattest girl you ever kissed?" Virgen, coming in fast on the tail of the answer. She was catching on. Flan rubbed his eyes, worm forgotten in one corner of his mouth, cigarette over it: a deformed walrus, Byron hair, bony planes red in his face, green eyes singing to me.

"That'd be my mother, I guess. She weighed in at around 450 on a good day. She was the fat lady at a ten-in-one for a while when I was a kid."

"Did you ever play a professional sport?" A Ball Girl heard from, the one called Kath Van De Water, I think.

"Professional sport," Flan said. "No ma'am. Not unless you count cock fighting."

"She doesn't. She thinks it's mean to the animals." The Count frying some private beef. This wasn't going well. Still, it was interesting. In New York, a guy like that's usually still a virgin.

One thing about Flan, though, and it's not something I'm totally comfortable with, he never gang fights, he never steps on any toes. I could see the little wheels turning in his brain. Even when he was tripping, a time when I'd be intoxicated with the verbal sparring, the textures, the cadence, the glistening blade in the weak soft spot, he wasn't gonna interfere. He's a player, Flan.

On the other hand, if I could see the little wheels turning, maybe someone else could too, Jules Nytown, maybe, or the lovely Virgen; and seeing the little wheels was the point after all. From there, it's just two short hops to really listening.

"Yeah, well, I can see it that way," Flan said. "You just don't know chickens, probably," he said to the Ball Girl.

"Guy's playing a hand, you let him play it, is that it?" Virgen, her voice modulated Hawks.

Flan took the worm out of his mouth and laid it flat on the table. He grinned.

"Call it as you see it, little girl. I think that's what Molly wants."

The Count and Kath Van De Water, oblivious to the breakthrough they'd caused, glared across the table at one another. Nytown stared at Virgen, studying *her* little wheels, I guess. It was what the history books call a pyrrhic victory. At considerable expense to my pride, at least one of them was learning how to listen, catch associations, talk the talk.

Nodding toward Virgen, Nytown questioned Flan.

"Does it bother you any that she's flirting with you in front of your girlfriend?"

Flan laughed. He addressed his answer to Virgen, holding her eyes.

"Nah. She's a pretty intense little girl, and very beautiful, but I figure she knows the score."

"Are you shrooming?" The Count, not be left out, apparently, unzipping his uncircumcised cool.

"If that means what I think it does, yes."

"Any for sale?" Nytown testing the limits. Virgen yawned.

"Skip that for now."

"Why?"

"You're knocking over my lady's proposition. I'll run it by you later if you want."

"I thought we could ask anything we want," he said, his eyes on me, his voice almost a nasal whine, a little gravel in it.

136

"Skip it, Kid," Flan said. "There's an *exercise* in progress."

Virgen stretched luxuriantly, the clotted light catching her incredible face. Bringing her arms down from the stretch, she eyed Nytown.

"You know," she said slowly, "I can't figure out if you look more like a ferret or more like Bob Dylan."

It was a puzzle. Flan says something like "exercise" the way other guys say "take off your shirt," you know, with this low, pained growl as if the words had to climb up miles of ravaged gut in order to drop, ever so softly, out of his mouth. If you're the right kind of girl, a voice like that can inspire undying loyalty. It had with me and it was a pleasure to relive. But on the other hand, the development of loyalty is a complicated thing. Sides are taken. Lines are drawn. And all of this was derailing us, taking us further and further from my purpose. I scanned the table.

"Uh, Kath, you wanna get in on this?" Lost in the fray, I almost called her Ball Girl. The fray was spectacular but I had, well, I had a proposition to run.

"Have you ever been to New York City?"

"You might say I'm on my fifth stab at moving there."

"When was the first?" Virgen asked.

"Let's see, I guess when I was fifteen."

"In tenth grade, then?" A rejoinder from Denise Salvo. Things were picking up. Was there a teeny little television reporter under all that hair?

"If you say so, mamacita. I didn't make it to high school."

"Isn't that illegal?" The Count appalled, about the reaction you'd expect from a puppet whose sole purpose is teaching numbers.

"Why did you go to New York?" Virgen asked evenly.

Flan looked at me, at Packy Salvo's cousin, raised his eyebrows: I can't answer that like this. I shrugged slightly, grimacing: forget it. Virgen followed this, her eyes hard on us, reaching under her cigarette with an elegantly curved hand, flicking ash into her cupped mocha palm.

"Never mind," she said.

"No," Flan said. "Tell you what, if Denise here doesn't mind, I'll tell you."

Denise made a kind of half-shrug which I took to mean: not only do I not mind this, I don't mind anything. She didn't seem like the kind of girl who had passionate feelings about much of anything, although the distended state of her womb probably belied that impression. All in all, I didn't think it was such a hot idea to go on.

The door opened, letting a lot of blinding yellow light into the cramped room, framing the Dane, Lucas Christensen, in the doorway. He smiled at me, at Virgen, lit a cigarette and hunched against the jamb.

I blinked in the light and thought of Flan's face, drawn, behind the bullet-proof screen, and of Feck, who'd found him for me, breathing down my neck, the fat rednecks in uniform sandwiching Flan on either side, the stink of sweat and cigarettes, a young mother wailing on my left: our fucking reunion. Nothing, it seemed, went according to one's own plan in Mapache, a fact that was obvious to me even if Flan didn't accept it.

It was no wonder he kept getting dragged back here. The roots that bound him to the town were dank and gnarled, twisting around him, squeezing him, in such a way that of course a damn fool like Flan would have to think Destiny had a hand in it. But I didn't think so, didn't, as I've said, share Flan's belief in the black glamour of fate. So I was on strike against anything that would further embroil him in the lives of his aberrant jailers.

"Nah," I said, "time's almost up anyway and we've got a full tank of information to play with. In fact, any more we'll have a massive brain spill on our hands. Let's call it quits. Think about all this, though. Over the next couple of days, go over and over every word. Get obsessed with it. Make it give up its secrets. I'll see you on Thursday."

"That wasn't our deal, Molly," Flan said quietly. "We said I'd answer the questions."

I shrugged.

"Go for it, then," I said.

Flan put the worm in his pocket.

"I fucked up a guy, a lunatic, really, almost killed him," he said, without preamble.

"Who?" said Jules Nytown. Right question. Wrong question.

"This young lady's cousin," Flan gestured absently at Denise. "It was getting ugly, a real old-fashioned Southwestern feud. I already had a J.D. card and I didn't want to end up in reform school. A broad I knew had a friend in Hell's Kitchen, said I could come East a while, let things cool down, run with his pack."

"Why couldn't you tell us that?" Jules Nytown asked, distracted, I thought, his mind on the mushrooms.

"Yeah. You're right. I don't know. I didn't want to offend the cousin here. Just careful. I don't know. I guess it's really a matter of what I didn't tell you."

"And what he didn't tell you," I said, awkwardly crimping the edges of the experience, sealing in the juices as best I could, "I want you to hear anyway. And now let's talk about why this worked. Or why it didn't."

Denise Salvo was beaming, weirdly enough, and I could tell it made Flan more uncomfortable than if she'd burst into tears. His jaw was jutted out halfway to Texas.

"Could I perhaps participate? Ask a question or two," Lucas Christensen called from the doorway.

"Sure, Yorick," I said. "But make it snappy. If I'm not mistaken, our guest's already shot his wad."

Christensen addressed Flan with an easy smile.

"Quickly, then. Are your parents living? Do you think Alger Hiss is innocent? Do you experience trouble with your..." he turned to me, "*tandkød*?"

"Gums," I said.

"No. I don't give a shit. And never," said Flan, squinting at the Dane. "Can *I* ask a question," he said to me.

"Why not?"

"Are we square here?"

"You wanna go?"

"Yeah, and I wanna take your truck."

Virgen frowned at that. I shrugged.

"Pick me up at six," I said.

15

The Dumbest Gunsel in the County

Since I was in the city, if you could call Cruces a city, I sat in the car for a few minutes across the street from the jail that had been my home away from home. It looked like a decent place from the outside. The adobe bricks were cleanly weathered. Of course, as you'd expect, the cops wandering in and out weren't weathered at all. But they were coddled and neatly pressed, each with a bushy bandido moustache.

As I drummed my fingers, faking indifference, the car got hot and I pulled out. I shuddered as the faintest whiff of burning mesquite brushed through the front seat.

People say that if you know where you've been, there's no call to ever return. But I know this isn't true. Some roads are endless loops which grow fetid as you circle through them year after year. Some roads are the hot tar of heresy, and you're damned to keep on booking over them no matter how desperately you scuffle away. Some roads suck.

Still, I intended to take the girl and blow as soon as possible. Nothing I could name was binding me here anymore. Just a series of habits I could easily shake: an impending fight with a fat moron, my father's grave out by the Fillmore arroyo, and Arturo, Nary's horse, who on some level I still loved. But if I got all choked up over a fucking horse, my father would probably rise up and haunt me for the rest of my life. He always hated farm animals and ended up killed by one, thrown from a burro and trampled, his head split open. My mother kept the hoof for years.

When I heard she died while I was in the slam, I wondered immediately what became of the damn thing; but it turned out she'd bet it on a pair of sevens and lost to a kid from Austin who was long gone by the time I got out. Probably he threw it onto the highway on his way back to Texas, and I couldn't blame him. I tried to view it philosophically. It was just one more mislaid contrivance, freeing me from all my ties to the goddamn desert.

Anyway, it didn't matter. I was a man with a plan, which included, having made good on my promise to Molly, a few hours fishing out at Burn Lake. Burn Lake, despite its poetic name, is a man-made watering hole, and like everything else worth mentioning in this cursed wasteland, it was an accident. An architect had severed a major aqueduct out on the Burns' massive estate and the water'd apparently seeped through so quickly that the town officials deemed it wisest to make the place into a lake.

Surprisingly, the Burns acquiesced, making a big show of giving the town that part of their property. It turned out they were looking for a suitable occupation for Father Roberto's simpleminded uncle, Chatters, and were just as happy to have the family idiot kept busy, stocking the alluvium reservoir with confused Canadian geese and fish from the Rio Grande, tying "genuine Indian" flies, and baiting hooks for squeamish tourist broads.

Joseph Breem Burn, the family patriarch, cooked up some talk among his old doughboy buddies about taking the architect out by Goering Lateral and flaying him alive in what later became the Mapache drain, but the guy fled into the Navy, and wound up dead when the Nips fucked with the Panay.

Still, it was a quiet place to fish, bound by cement walls, and the stink of the wet '30s concrete blocked out the overpowering smell of pecan trees and cotton that tormented the rest of the area. Old Chatters was still alive, although it took him the better part of every day to hobble the fifth of a mile around Burn Lake.

As I pulled up, I saw him polishing the brass plaque that commemorated the Burns' generosity and I decided to walk the other way. I can't seem to set one foot down without screwing up in the Southwest, and having Molly along seemed to be making matters worse. There would've been no real harm in passing time with old

Chatters for a few minutes, but of course I chose to take the long route toward the tackle shop. Across the lake, there was a little kid throwing a ball for an exhausted greyhound with an engaging snout that I wanted to take a gander at.

Halfway around I stopped short, seeing that I was on a collision course with my sworn enemy, Hezekiah's leg man, Packy Salvo. 6'9" and twitching, with ugly ruined teeth, he trudged toward me, carrying a mangled Canadian goose he'd apparently shot.

As usual he was wearing a creepy Green Beret uniform. I guess he had them made to order. I know that I personally slashed two complete outfits to ribbons the night we had our big fight when I was fifteen. Looking at him heave his inane bulk along the gravel path, I felt a surge of pride that I'd been able to reduce the lumbering moron to a pulp at least once. I was always scrawny, even at fifteen, and it was a testament to my utter loathing for the guy that I'd been able to take him out that night.

Hezekiah had fronted me the scratch to blow town, and then kept us both on short reins when I came back from New York, knowing that sooner or later, the idiot would go for me, and using this knowledge to keep us both under his control. But then, it was Hezekiah's fault to begin with because the reason I hit the guy was because he was bad-mouthing Hezekiah's young Yankee wife, another moron.

I was never totally clear on how it started but from what I put together later, Packy, who claimed to have picked up some undiagnosable stomach ailment he called "the Critter," came into El Cabra that night, complaining about his gut. Norma Jean Johnson, freshly married, who Hezekiah had apparently seduced out of one of those summer camps for the mentally disabled where he was the attending physician, had offered him a back rub. When he responded by pinching her, she left, squealing.

I was late getting to El Cabra that night because we'd buried my father in the morning and I didn't want to leave my mother alone in the trailer, clutching the severed hoof that had killed him. By the time I arrived, Packy was in a black funk, and when Hezekiah left the table he leaned over and whispered, I'll never forget this, "I'd like to Huey that Norma Jean into a pile of pussy juice and bones."

I had mixed feelings about the war, like most kids too young to go, and I knew Packy was obsessed, having been drafted and then summarily rejected, but I didn't really care about his little helicopter fantasy. I know I thought Norma Jean was sort of pretty but I wasn't the kind of kid who went out of his way to be chivalrous. Not then. When you get right down to it, I have no idea why I got so angry.

Maybe I was fucked up on account of my father. I don't really remember. Somehow we started fighting. Hezekiah tried to break it up and got thrown clear across the bar, and at some point we ended up upstairs in Packy's rented room. I swung at him with his own hunting rifle and connected with the ker-chunk of an old-fashioned cash register as his cheekbone smashed. When he went down, I must have started in slashing his stupid Green Beret outfits because that's what I was still doing when Hezekiah and three farmers hauled me away.

Now, as he approached, my bile rose. I considered scaling the cement wall but knew this would make it seem like I was frightened. I was scared, but mostly of myself. I knew that, now that my ties with Hezekiah were practically severed, I was likely to do something stupid, and end up back in jail. Some people just bring out the worst in you, inspiring you to an ever-new eminence of dread and disgust, and Packy was one of these. Everything he touched, it seemed, ended up tainted.

Packy stopped abruptly about twenty feet from me. Swinging his dead goose by its broken neck, he crouched at the side of Burn Lake. I steeled myself to approach him. As I got closer, he started rubbing his green-clad stomach hard, communing with his fucking "Critter," no doubt.

"Salvo," I said.

"Hey, there, Little Flan."

I grimaced, grinding my back teeth hard. The man was an idiot.

"How's the gut? Bad?"

"Rotten. Wanna see?"

Parting his flak jacket, he lifted his shirt and I had to bring my clenched fist up to my jaw and force my averted eyes in his direction. I wasn't worried about this gesture not looking tough, though. Packy wasn't even watching me. He was obsessed with his own stomach. The sight of his bare skin revolted me, but for the hundredth time, I didn't see anything wrong with him. Nothing shooting him in the head wouldn't fix. His stomach was pale, hairless, and rippled with muscles.

"Aw, he ain't moving now. Guess he doesn't like you much, Flan."

He laughed an awful guffaw and I punched my own arm to release some of the pent-up revulsion. Back when I was a kid, and had occasion to pretend that Packy Salvo was my pal—that's how Hezekiah liked it—I spent a few afternoons in El Cabra trying to convince him that there was nothing wrong with him, but I knew it was useless. The man was certain something was moving in his viscera, and had been showing his flawless gut around for years. No one ever saw anything and he was never convinced. At this point I didn't care.

Packy shook his head sadly.

"Between you and me, ol' buddy, I think the Critter's pissed off at me. I ain't had none in more'n a month."

"Uh-huh." I knew what was coming. It was inevitable as the summer drought. Like a kid holding off coming, I silently ticked off Mets statistics, waiting. I was halfway through the all-time game leaders before Packy's tiny brain got a handle on the obvious insult.

"Hear you been busy, though."

...Wilson, 1,116. Mazzilli, 979. Strawberry, 957. Staub, 942. Garrett, 883. Stearns, 809...

"I mean, you been getting it real regular, right?"

...Stolen bases: Wilson, 281. Strawberry, 176. Mazzilli, 152. Dykstra, 116. Harrelson, 115...

"Hear she's a juicy piece of ass, too. Doc Johnson said he ain't seen none finer since he first brought Norma Jean home. Remember that?"

...Backman, 106. Agee, 92. Jones, 91...

"Of course, I'm partial to American girls, myself. A dark cunt like yours probably stinks to high heaven. But I guess that wouldn't bother the Doc."

145

...Stearns, 91. Taveras, 74...

"Hey, Flan, you heard I knocked up Denise, right?"

I knew my eyes were flashing but I kept my face level. He wasn't going to be able to goad me into a fight, no matter what stupid thing he said. He'd effectively blown it, mentioning Norma Jean practically at the outset, as if I still cared one way or the other about the dowdy imbecile's purity. And even if she was about to drop a half-witted foal, I knew his cousin Denise was safely with Molly, the best place she could possibly be.

Fuming, I conjured the Doll, set her to dancing over the endless stream of leaping numbers sprawling from my head. In back of a red haze, I watched her specter quietly, bounding from stat to stat, her eyes alight at Packy's barbed word choices, listening with that hushed awe.

"It wasn't worth it, though," he said.

"No?"

"Nope. She's a lousy lay, still as this dead duck here."

"It's a goose."

"Duck, goose, what's the difference? I use the feathers to keep the Critter warm."

He ripped out a handful of down and shoved it under his shirt, patting his stomach.

"Anyhow, Flan," he paused, seeming to forget what he wanted to say. "Remember when I used to call you 'Trailer Boy?'"

"I remember."

"Yeah."

He scratched his chest, then put the whole slashed-up goose under his coat. I let the "Trailer Boy" go easily. Coming from a man with a dead bird stuffed down his novelty-shop military uniform, it was practically a compliment. Besides, I couldn't help thinking it was a little sad. How could Packy possibly be nostalgic for our scum-scarred youth?

"Uh, Salvo? You wanted to tell me something?"

He beamed at me, his teeth a row of tombstones, cradling his pregnant flak jacket.

"Hold on there, Flan, I'm adjusting the duck, sorry, goose. Now what was it again? Oh yeah, Sonia wants to meet up with you."

146

"I don't want to meet her."

"Yeah, I see your point. With Doc Johnson raking her, it do seem like a waste. But she said if you say no, to meet her at the Whore 'O' Bad 'O.'"

El Jorobado. That made a difference, of course, although I was loath to let Packy see it. *El Jorobado* is a permanent depression in the vast mounds of gypsum deposit out at White Sands. It was typical of the usual half-assed Southwestern logic that a geological depression would be nick-named *Jorobado*, the humpback, even though it is supposedly named for the hunchbacked guy who first hung out there.

It was legend in the Cruces outlaw community that *El Jorobado* was a free zone, kind of like a church. Apparently, after the Civil War, two Texan brothers, who'd fought on different sides and agreed to meet up there, lay siege to one another on sight and both wound up dead. The hunchback was supposedly their grand-nephew. Probably his dumb Southwestern father had taken him there when he was a kid and the romantic story just kept on cooking in the freak's imagination.

Anyway, when he grew up, he used the place as a meeting ground, negotiating a merger there among four gangs of desperados, forging, in effect, a huge ruthless phalanx with which he dominated the entire criminal community. They did big business in bootleg mescal during Prohibition.

The legend had it that no one messed with anyone for any reason out by *El Jorobado.* How Sonia ever heard of the place was a mystery to me. Organization had fallen out of crime in the area long before either of us were born. As much of a vile son of bitch as Hezekiah was, the town wasn't that tough anymore, and there was simply no need for a truce belt.

Knowing Nary as well as I did, though, and the Totonac sensibility in general, I knew that his daughter would buy into all that tender, Old West garbage. If she wanted to meet me there, even if she was stupid enough to send my fucking nemesis to tell me, she meant me no harm.

"Tell her I'll be there by two."

"Alright!"

147

He twisted around, raising his hand to give me a five, and I stepped out of the arc, letting his olive drab arm fall. He laughed.

"You gonna nail her, Flan? The Doc's piece? What is that place, some kind of strip joint?"

"Yeah. Strip. Joint."

I whispered the words, nodding grimly as I turned to walk away from Packy, who seemed to forget about me immediately, clawing at his iron paunch. I needed time to think, to understand why it had taken me more than twenty years, and probably five times that many drug combinations, to realize that the man was not stupid, but insane. Packy Salvo, it now appeared, was just another in the seemingly endless series of grotesqueries that dot my hopeless history.

16

Dukkerer

I hadn't intended to end the class on a rant. I really hadn't. It just, well, it just happened that way. Real shocker there. I mean, man bites dog, that's news.

Lucas Christensen had taken Flan's chair, ostensibly, I assumed, because he was supposed to check me out. Except for that one moment where he bailed me out on interviewing Flan, he hadn't said a word, though. He was just sitting there, eyeing Virgen with the crinkly slit eyes of a pudgy shark. And Jules Nytown was eyeing him. The Count was eyeing Nytown with a panicked fascination.

The guy's sycophant demeanor was starting to get on my nerves, and the exercise had more or less dissolved. The taste of Flan's voice had disappeared from the room. There was so much poorly directed energy, so many little internecine skirmishes, I figured the only hope for the experiment lay, ironically enough, with the Ball Girls, all of whom were staring at me blankly.

"But I don't understand what we're supposed to do," Kath Van De Water whined.

"Okay. What you're supposed to do is sink irrevocably into our guest's idiolect. And don't come up for air until the way he talked has told you something intensely personal about the way he is. Then write that down."

"What's an idiolect?"

"Fair question." I turned to the room at large. "What's an idiolect?"

No answer, and no effort. Virgen's perfect rose-brown lips twitched once. Nytown rolled his eyes. Ball Girls stared, unblinking. The Count sank in his seat.

"Okay. What does it sound like?"

"Um, like 'idiot?'" Denise Salvo said.

"Yo. They're cognates. So what do you think it means?"

No answer. Lucas Christensen looked up and shrugged, smiled. Bastard. Then again, his English wasn't perfect. Maybe he really didn't know.

"Alright," I sighed, taking Jules Nytown's pointy white face gently in my two palms like the gypsy I thought I wasn't.

"I know you know what idiolect means, kid, and you're just pretending you don't because that's what you're in the habit of doing, which is something I can understand better than you could probably imagine. And there's a word for feigning ignorance like that, too. Aporia. But I don't have time or patience for it right now. So, spill it."

He wriggled out of my hands and smirked. Virgen's eyes widened.

"It's a kind of private dialect of a language, right? Like an idiot mutters to himself," she whispered, her voice sexy enough to fell a ponderosa pine.

"Right. So, what do you think the experience of mucking about in an idiolect will be like?"

"A maze." Jules Nytown, precipitating a juicy burst of ah-hah endorphins in my brain. As the chick goes, so go the smart boys.

"That's a good analogy, Nytown. It goes down real smooth. Of course, in an academic setting, just about any myth metaphor does. But, speaking personally, I have a hard time viewing myself as a trumped-up Ariadne. I think you'll find the experience lonelier than that, and more interesting. To me, an idiolect is more of a stygian pit. You descend on spring ladders. Up above they hear your feet clomp the floor, catch the ladder as it bounces out of your reach, and tactfully retreat. An idiolect is between you and your demons. Never mind skirting the minotaur, you are alone, and without the sounds that shape your thoughts."

They checked their watches en masse, as if responding to an

invisible prompter. I laughed and waved a hand at the door. Kath Van De Water blinked at me.

"So, like, we're supposed to describe that guy, right?"

"Right," I said, and sighed.

"What happens at the MLA, Dr. Veeka?" Virgen asked, with sublime disinterest. I looked at her, my vision impeded by Lucas Christensen's pleading ice-pick eyes, the real question entrenched less in their idiolects than their careless gestures: is Feck gonna get any? And what will that mean for me?

"Oh, you know. Charts and graphs, men in white suits clocking the incidence of the schwa sound in children with red hair, dull-eyed nose-ring girls exposing their dugs in mass protestation of sexist pronouns, that kind of thing."

"Oh," she said.

Christensen raised his eyebrows and opened his mouth. Jules Nytown paused, holding the door for the mincing Ball Girls, calibrating.

"Don't," I said, holding my hand up flat against the Dane's face.

"I was only going to ask if you would care to join me for a drink."

"Can I smoke?"

"Of course."

Nytown banged out, his sneer in place. Virgen turned away from us, taking a textbook out of her bag. Evan pulled up a chair next to her. He craned his head back against crossed arms and stared at me.

"Never known you to break up someone else's tableau," he said.

"There's a first time for everything."

"Yeah, Chica. But why?"

"Why what, Evan?"

"Why not let the Prince here say that people go at it like rabbits at the MLA? Break the girl's heart? What's it to you? Who cares which chicken-hawk she ends up with?"

"Can't you see that if we continue this conversation the way it's going, you're going to say something so stupid, so glib and facile, so utterly inane about my relationship with Feck that I'll be totally disillusioned and miserable?"

"Of course."

"Then why do it?"

"I think it's cute that you have illusions about me."

"Idiot."

He smiled crookedly, blowing a jet of smoke out the open side of his mouth even though he had no cigarette, just the kind of parlor trick I hate (just the kind of only-Evan gesture that fluttered my guts.)

"Intercession, Chica," he said, blinking out, "it's the watch-word for the nineties."

Christensen's face was bland.

"Are you ready, Dr. Veeka?"

"Yeah. I guess."

We drove in silence through Las Cruces, a real miracle-mile town, parked in the "Papa Pawn Pawn Shop" lot, and marched into a sleazy roadside motel bar called Fat Eddy's. I didn't know or care what he made of the lack of talk, but maybe my reputation really had preceded me. He went up to the bar and brought back two martinis.

"I hope these are okay."

"Fine."

"Tell me, Dr. Veeka—"

"Molly."

"Molly, then. And I am Lucas. Why do you interfere with my little romances?"

The way he said "interfere," I could tell he really relished the sound of it. But I couldn't tell whether the Dane knew that was a line from the most famous movie in American history, or, if he did, what he hoped to accomplish by quoting it. The danger, because I'm a world class sucker for that kind of thing, lay in taking the smarmy throwaway remark as a gesture of genuine friendship.

I sighed, looked around the room. The guy who had to be Fat Eddy smiled from behind the bar, holding up a vermouth bottle, shrugging his shoulders, questioning his recipe. I smiled and gave him a thumbs-up gesture. The drink was revolting, actually, the proportions absurd, a tumbler of gin-scented cough medicine, but what difference did it make? The prevailing wind was blowing from Vichy. I turned to the Dane.

"Look, if it's okay with you, I've already had this conversation."

"Indeed. We'll say no more about it, unless of course you would care to make a small wager on which of us will earn the young lady's favor."

"I wouldn't. But if I did, my money'd be on Nytown."

"The boy?"

"She's a girl."

"Certainly."

"Look, you're just bored. Feck's a tired old lech. The kid's the only one with any real passion, so he's the only one with a legitimate claim."

"You speak from experience?"

I snorted.

"Hardly. In my case, Feck had a real claim."

"I see. This was some years ago, I take it."

"You take it correctly."

"And when you say you've already had this conversation, you mean what, precisely?"

"I mean I've been over this whole story a million times but most recently not twenty minutes ago with my dead husband. Precisely."

"You're a fascinating woman."

"You think so?"

"Tell me—"

"Do I think I actually see the Dead? Have I ever sought professional help? Is there a name for my condition?"

"Do you always know what people are going to say?"

"Usually. It's easier when people are speaking their own language, though."

"*Vil du heller at vi taler Dansk?*"

"No. I don't especially want to know what you're going to say. And it's fucking impossible to bluster tough in Danish which is how I prefer to converse with new friends. But, Lucas?"

"Hmmm?"

"This is more than a one-martini kind of story."

"I'll have a word with Eddy."

He rose gracefully and walked toward the bar. A dapper lummox. The room was cool and empty, the quiet accentuated by the tinkling chink-chink of day-bar glasses.

153

I thought about what I wanted to tell him. People who believe in mental health are so strange. It's hard to imagine what they want to hear. Almost anything but the truth seems to work. And once you codify your memories into the sweet clean lines of a psychological profile, the truth simply melts away.

My mother was two weeks dead the first time it happened. I awoke to find her sitting cross-legged on the edge of my *perrinas*, frowning at a hole in the top quilt, fingering the puckered fabric, and finally plucking out a small piece of feather.

"You should sew this, Little One."

"Yes," I said. "I know. Why are you dressed up as a *dukkerer*?"

She wore a blue and orange silk *diklo* wrapped around her head, several skirts, a ton of copper jewelry she'd never owned in life. To my little kid mind it was more incongruous that she was dressed up in full gypsy regalia than that she was dead and talking to me.

"With you, always questions. Sometimes, Molly, it's better just not to think."

"Can I tell Pappa you were here?"

She laughed.

"Tell him, don't tell him. That black-hearted goat, what do I care?"

Her laugh lingered in the room, riffed a paprika beat against the Pitt Street noise, smoothed the lumpy places in the goose down *perrinas*.

I told Pappa in the morning, asked him if he thought it was weird. He said what did he know from weird but that I was certainly lucky and if she came again would I tell her he loved her and that my Aunt Persie's stew was a curse?

Lucas Christensen returned with a martini pitcher.

"Just gin and ice this time," he said. "I am not so polite as you in these matters."

"Maybe you're just used to better service."

"You think I am well-off?"

"I'm a gypsy. I know money when I see it. Besides, my mother was a tailor."

"I would have thought perhaps a coppersmith."

"That's a myth."

"Ah."

He poured us each a glass and we gulped the gin in a reasonably companionable silence.

"So you wanna know, did I ever seek professional help? The answer to that is yeah, a couple of times. Because Feck thought it was a good idea and I thought the sun shined out his asshole. Also I kind of liked it that he wanted to expunge my craziness. I was sick of to death of guys who thought it was sexy."

I caught his eye and he nodded.

"And what happened?"

"They kept me up all night, drinking coffee, smoking cigarettes, trying to induce a seizure. That part was fun. Then they hooked me up to an EEG and aimed a flashing light in my direction. A photic stimulator. Do you know how that works?"

"No."

"Okay. Well say you're hooked up and you're looking at that light."

I gestured behind me at the sun streaming in the door, picking up the flaws in his sculpted pumpkin head, the intricate weave of his million dollar suit.

"All right."

"Now, your looking at that unobstructed light produces a specific pattern in your brain waves, one that can be read on the EEG. But if I lean this way," I shifted in the seat until I was directly in front of him, "I block the light and that also creates a recognizable pattern."

"Okay."

"Okay," I said, siphoning another two glasses, pressing my wrists against the sweating pitcher. "So they try to fuck me up, set me off balance by keeping me up all night. Of course staying up all night drinking coffee is not exactly much of a stress on a twenty-year-old girl, even if she is crazy, but that didn't matter because I didn't need to be tired or hungry or freaked out to be open to visitation. The point is, the big thing they discovered was that when I was, as they said, hallucinating, the pattern of blocked light appeared in the waves."

"So your brain believed something was there."

"Well, that's what they said. But as far as I'm concerned, if you have to bend the language around so much to make it jibe with the truth, you're looking too hard. What they proved was not that my brain believed something was there, but that something *was* there."

"So they couldn't help you?"

The cold gin felt like a slug running down my throat.

"No. I didn't say that. They *could* help me. But not the kind of help I needed. My disease is for the most part treatable. But in treating it, I not only obliterate my father, my best friend, and enough animals to get me locked up for wholesale slaughter, I lose my facility with language. Those drugs are only useful for people whose 'hallucinations' make them miserable, terrified, or dangerous. Or unable to deal with the living."

"So, then, you have chosen simply to live with this disorder."

"No, Christensen. You don't get it. This disorder has chosen to live with me. But I'm comfortable in my craziness, which is more than most people can say about their sanity, don't you think?"

"I see. I think. It is...*tvetydig*?"

"Ambiguous? I guess so, but what isn't?"

He smiled and poured the last of the watery gin down his throat directly from the pitcher.

"Would you like for me to tell you the truth?"

I sighed.

"Why not, Lucas? Everyone else does."

"Because you are such a gifted listener."

"You think so? Or is it because I'm not really there? Wait! Don't answer that. The truth about what?"

"About what I am doing in this, as you call it, 'godforsaken burg.'"

"Yeah. I wouldn't mind knowing the truth about that. But I'm drunk and I still have to give a vocabulary test. And I don't know where the hell we are. Why don't you make with the mysterious European chivalry and drive me back to the campus. We can talk about it on the way. Or after the class. Truth always sounds hollow in a motel bar, anyway."

He stood, doing something elegant with his eyebrows.

"Certainly, if you like. But 'hollow,' I don't know this word."

"*Hul.*"

17

El Jorobado

The road out to White Sands is wide and desolate, flat despite the twisting mountains. The air was that awful pre-windstorm pink that Easterners are always raving about. It's pink, alright, but not the pink of a baby girl's nursery. It's the cloying, ominous pink of a daylight-strewn nightmare.

Once you cross the Roadrunner Parkway out on 70, there's just a whole lot of nothing. Across an expanse of desert shrubs is Mexico, its border towns pulsing with small city slime. You can't feel it from Highway 70, though. No people, just the land's dry desperation born out of millions of years of baking sun.

Twenty miles short of Las Colonias, a town even smaller and more pathetic than Mapache, the highway was diverted by a long rattlesnake of orange cones. I moved among the cones, pulling over at a slapped-together roadside booth made of corrugated tin. A highway patrolman, a kid with a pinched handsome face, not quite old enough to shave every day, knocked at the window. He rolled his wrist.

I lit a cigarette as I let the window down.

"Afternoon, sir."

"Yeah."

"Where are you coming from?"

"Las Cruces."

"I see. And where are you headed?"

"White Sands."

"What's your business there, sir?"

"Sightseeing," I said, and laughed.

The kid looked at me funny, but he nodded me through. For half a second I was pissed off, wishing I'd actually been harboring a wetback in the trunk and gotten away with it; or something, anything, to get at the kid's exaggerated sense of importance before he got comfortable enough in that uniform to actually hurt someone, to catch a young Mexican girl fleeing into this country with big useless dreams and toss her back on her ass into the rat-infested factory town that spawned her, imagining he was doing something worthwhile.

But I let it go. The highway, when I rejoined it, was completely forsaken, and I raced along at 75, which was as fast as the truck would go, emptying my head of everything I could. My sole purpose was to hear Sonia out, put whatever scheme she had out of her head, and get back to town in time to take Molly out to dinner. I didn't need any distraction.

White Sands has an official demarcation, of course, but the gypsum moves where it damn well pleases, filtering down into the surrounding ranches slowly and imperceptibly until, suddenly, you find yourself surrounded by nothing but the massive ivory dunes.

I drove ten minutes past the *Jorobado* to get to the official entrance, then I had to stash my car someplace inconspicuous and hike back through the sand for more than two hours. As a kid I'd tried more than once to pull over on the highway, bypassing the three dollar fee and cutting the traveling time by hoofing it over on the direct latitude of the *Jorobado*.

There wasn't much point to that, I guess. Even as the crow flies, it's probably a long, miserable hike, and once you swallow the awe, painfully boring, trudging through the unrelenting glare. Apparently there are sufficient markers, placed by generations of small-time criminals, to navigate you through, but I'd never gotten the chance to try it out. Highway patrolmen stopped me every single time, and once even held me for questioning, suspecting me, I guess, of being a Ruskie spy. Only a place like New Mexico could dream up something as contradictory and stupid as a combination state park and missile range.

Sonia Totonac was hunched in the *Jorobado*, looking more or less normal for the first time in what seemed years, dressed in jeans and a red and black flannel shirt, and consequently more beautiful than ever. Cross-legged beside her was Chris Johnson, also looking normal. He was looking at a book, but as I approached Sonia nudged him, and he snapped it shut, hiding it down under his tank top.

We could see each other long before there was any point in speaking, three lurid bugs, preposterous against the forlorn chalky knolls. When I was within twenty feet, Sonia started to wave, as if I might miss her. I wouldn't have minded waving back but Chris's presence there made me wary. I compromised, nodding grimly as I trudged the last few feet down into the depression.

"Hey."

"Hey."

"Alright, Kid. I'm here. What do you want?"

"*Ojalá que—*"

"Give it a rest, Kid. The show's over. Speak English. And as for you," I said, nodding at Chris, "I know you know how to read."

I hadn't really known it, but there was no harm in pretending. I hadn't known he was with Sonia either.

Chris shrugged and Sonia sat up straight.

"It's for true, Goliath? You join us here? You will be on our side? It's very important."

"I have no idea. Your side about what?"

"My father," Chris said.

I had to play this carefully. I had no idea whether Chris knew his father was nailing his girlfriend, just one of many things I was apparently in the dark about. In any case, I didn't want to be the one to spill it to him.

"What about him?"

"*Chocha apolillado,*" Sonia squealed, and I had to laugh. The pretty Mexican girl sounded so absurd calling her boyfriend's father a moth-eaten cunt.

"No kidding. What the hell do you want me to do about it?"

"We want you to kill him, Goliath."

"What?" I exploded. Chris's face was unreadable.

"I think you heard me."

159

"Yeah, Sonia. I heard you. I just don't know what the hell you're talking about."

She fell backwards in the white sand, her breasts riding up under the lumberjack shirt. Chris lay his hand flat against her stomach.

"He won't let us marry, Goliath, and he won't let my father sell his land, that fat slob. I hate him," Sonia said, her voice tired.

"Yeah, okay, Sonia. You hate him."

"It's okay, Flan," Chris said, kneading Sonia's belly, pressing one slow finger at a time into her flesh. "I don't mind talking about it. You don't have to protect me. I know Sonia's slept with him. That's totally beside the point. She's right. He deserves to die."

"He deserves to die? I don't have to protect you? Since fucking when? I can't believe this shit. You got me out here for this? And you," I said, bending over Sonia, "you set this up. You set me up. What the hell were you thinking kissing me at the table?"

"Goliath, I—"

"You? You wanna get married? Fucking elope. Shit, man, I need this like a hole in the head. Hezekiah's a goddamn freak. I wouldn't mind taking a poke at him myself. But 'deserves to die?' Are you guys fucking crazy? And I can't believe you'd drag Nary into this. You think he can't take care of himself? Jesus, your father'd love to see you married. You think he wouldn't sell the land at a loss if he knew you were safe and happy?"

"He shouldn't have to."

"No, Kid. He shouldn't have to. And it's Hezekiah's fault he does have to. What's that got to do with you?"

"You know we can't elope."

"Why the hell not?"

Sonia turned and spat in the direction of Mapache.

"No one ever escapes from this town."

"Bullshit," I said, reflexively, although in some ways she was right. I had to hand it to the kid. She was sharp, needling me right at my own weakest point. But Sonia and Chris, although obviously much smarter than they appeared, were still at heart the spawn of this rotten town, failed small-time criminals, like me, plotting and thrashing, groping uselessly toward the faintest glimmer of

160

escape. Left to their own devices they'd seal their fate permanently, ending up in jail, inside the town limits, or dead and buried, inside the town limits. I didn't really care, except that they reminded me of myself, but, fuck, I could get over that. The problem was Nary. I couldn't let his daughter throw away her whole life over something that was essentially stupid.

They looked at one another. Chris shrugged and they went into a kind of lover's huddle, whispering. Chris's long body looked like a viper wrapped around the rounded Sonia. I lit a cigarette, trying not listen.

I heard Sonia say "*no sirve pa' na'*," calling someone, probably me, a good-for-nothing, and I laughed out loud. It was a decent description. My laugh sounded strange even to my own ears, gruff and obtuse, like a seal's bark, the edges of the rough sound breaking up, floating off into the barren landscape.

I walked to the top of one of the hills while I waited. In the deep distance, at the periphery of the range, I saw a herd of cattle grazing and got annoyed. The government leases all the land around the missile range to ranchers who pay a nominal grazing fee, as little as 5,000 dollars a year. They also pay the ranchers a daily rate for the inconvenience of running a ranch near a missile range, and then when they actually clear the area, which happens all the time, they pay the ranchers an additional evacuation fee. Even minus the grazing fees, the ranchers were pulling in some 50,000 dollars a year, gravy from the Army.

It was a choice scam, if you were willing to live your life as a corporate cowboy, and since I don't pay taxes myself, I didn't particularly care that the money came out of the people's pockets, but the stupidity of it enraged me. There hadn't been a missile accident in more than five years, nine-tenths of the time there weren't even any missiles anymore. Yet the Army just keeps doling out those checks. They'd spent more than three million since the end of the Cold War.

I felt Chris's hand on my shoulder. I turned and we started back down the hill.

"Well?"

"Will you take care of Packy so Sonia can—"

"No."

"Why not? Everyone knows you hate him and once Hezekiah's out of the picture, you won't get in trouble. Everyone hates Packy."

I sighed and fell silent. Chris sat down next to Sonia and I looked down at them.

"You really want an answer to that?"

"Yes."

"Okay. I won't, as you put it, 'take care of' Packy because he needs to be alive to support Denise and their cretin issue when it arrives. Denise is in college, God knows how, and she deserves a chance to get away same as you. To say nothing of the fact that I don't trust you two clowns to 'take care of' Hezekiah even if I did hold up my end of a deal like that. And what gave you the idea that I hate that son of a bitch Packy Salvo?"

"Well, I just thought, I mean—"

"Yeah. You thought."

"Will you do anything to help us, Goliath?" Sonia said, dead earnest this time, her erratic voice empty of squeals, empty of flirtation, empty of everything except honest hunger and desperation. It was the kind of voice I like.

I sat down next to them, feeling the gypsum make a leap for my boots, the crunch of pale sand against my back teeth.

"Probably," I said, and waited.

Chris flicked his long hair out of his face like a girl.

"Maybe you could talk to Mr. Totonac, ask him to talk to my father directly?"

I liked the simple respect in his voice, the way he called Nary "Mister," the hopelessly naive notion that Nary's decency awarded him any clout with Hezekiah.

"No," I said.

"Why not?"

"Well, it's probably not my place to tell you this, but Nary's tried that. A lot of times. He's been hammering at Hezekiah and the town council for years to let him sell off parts of his land, in lots smaller than five acres so he could make a profit. That farm's much too big for him to handle alone. Don't you think he knows that?"

"I guess," Sonia said.

"Have you told Nary you want to get married?"

"No, we're afraid he'll say no."

"You're not planning to kill *him*, are you?"

"No."

"Okay, then. Assuming you can get Hezekiah to roll over on the land thing, what makes you think you'll get Nary's blessing?"

Chris grabbed a handful of the white sand and let it run through his fist.

"We thought if we were all out of here, with a little money, maybe Mr. Totonac could see that we're really in love."

"You're probably right about that."

"Will you talk to him, Flan?"

"To Nary?"

He nodded.

"Yeah, I will. But you'd do better going over there yourself, maybe offering your services as a farmhand, getting to know the guy, for chrissakes, before you rope him into an elaborate game of town politics and make off with his youngest daughter."

"But what about—"

"Your stupid fucking charade?"

He nodded again, glumly. Sonia was looking back and forth at us, exaggerating her motions as if she were watching a tennis match.

"Chris, half the time I think you're really as stupid as you pretend to be. It doesn't take any brains to work a farm. And if you can pull it off, fine. But if you think Nary's gonna let his daughter run off with a nitwit, a nitwit, mind you with the worst blood in town running in his veins, you really are an idiot. Just go to him honestly, let Sonia work on your father."

Sonia sat up.

"What should I do, though?" she whined.

"I guess you have to convince Hezekiah that it's good for the town to break the zoning laws, that he'll be a hero. It's not gonna be easy, though. Hezekiah moved here and drew a line in the sand. He wanted it developed enough so he could be comfortable, but he doesn't want a lot of Eastern money around here. He needs to be the boss. Damn, he used to kick the chickens outside my grandmother's whorehouse, disgusted with all that rural crap. You gotta tap into that big-city kingpin thing of his."

"But how do I do that?" she asked.

"Shit, Kid. I don't know. Maybe I can talk to Packy, feel him out."

"Packy?" Sonia said, her eyes wide with a freaked-out mixture of horror, frustration, and disappointment. "You're not planning on going on that trip with him, are you?"

"Yeah. Why not?"

Sonia freaked, beating her fists into the sand. I was her last hope I guess, and I turned out to be a disappointment. No surprise there. Chris patted her on the back, looking up at me.

"You're on the outs with Dad. We thought you knew."

"I knew. Thanks to your girlfriend."

"Don't you know he wants Packy to dump you in Juarez?"

I felt dizzy and dug my front heel into the sand, grinding down, my knees bent, a batter at the plate. It was hard for me to accept that Hezekiah, a man I'd worked for since I was a kid, would have me killed over—over nothing. A drunken kiss and a fake G-man. It was absurd. Hezekiah had taken plenty of people out before. But always outsiders. If he sensed in me that I was no longer part of the town, it meant that, at the very least, I was on my way to making something of myself for once. Pride and confidence flooded my veins. Sonia and Chris stood, looking at me.

"Doesn't surprise me," I said.

Sonia's voice climbed in hysteria, until, at the end, it was nothing but a little squeak.

"And you're still going? Just for *los champs*? Travelling with Packy? Why?"

"*Si me han de matar mañana, que me maten de una vez,*" I sang, hoping to cheer her up with the revolution-era ditty. If they're gonna kill me tomorrow, they may as well kill me now. Sonia and Chris looked at each other, rolling their eyes. But I didn't mind. I was perfectly at home playing the quaint cowboy clown for the two kids. Good old-fashioned white hats were so rare in their puny lives, and anyhow, it was Halloween.

"Just because Packy intends to take me down to Juarez and slit my throat in an alley, doesn't mean he can pull it off. Don't forget, he couldn't even get rid of that lady developer."

"She left."

"Yeah, Kid, she left. She left Mapache. But where do you think she went? And who'd she report to? And who's coming next? Jesus, you guys. You'll never get out of this town if you think like that. She ain't here, so she's disappeared entirely, right? Because that's all there is, huh? Mapache and then Not Mapache? Even a fucking simpleton like Denise Salvo knows more about the real world than you two."

"You're right, Goliath." She nodded.

"Yeah," I said, hopelessly, "I'm right. Listen, Sonia, are you gonna be at your mother's shindig tonight?"

"Of course. We build the *ofrenda* tonight. But she is such a fool. Last night, Vulf he jumped up on the counter, ate a whole package of frozen spinach she left out to defrost, and my mother she says it is *los infantos limbos*, that they eat the food."

"Kid, when you're around me, don't call Mrs. Totonac a fool. How do you know it wasn't the *infantos limbos*? Just 'cause you saw a hunk of frozen green hanging out of the dog's mouth? Lots of kids in every family die before getting baptized. Rosalita might die. She looks half-dead now. Or maybe your mother had an abortion when she was young."

"Oh, you're disgusting."

"Uh-huh. I'm disgusting. But I respect your parents. And the Day of the Dead."

"*Todos Santos*," she corrected, automatically, and I grinned.

"See? You are a bead-rattler, for all your hip talk. But okay. You two come up with a plan that's a little bit less fucking insane and we'll talk it out tonight, you and me and Molly, over a jug of aguardiente."

"Your girlfriend? *La gringa*? What does she have to do with all this?"

"Nothing, Kid. But you might say tonight's her special night. She's got a private line to Quetzalcóatl."

18

I Am a Gypsy

Feck hadn't given me a word-list or anything, but I did the best I could with the test. I started off with "tirade" and "encumber," quickly enough moving down the scale a bit to "fortitude" and "tranquil." Just for the hell of it, I threw in "*piropo*," cat-call. No one's gonna accuse me of cultural bias, anyway.

Once that ordeal was over, I waited on a stone bench under a statue of Billy the Kid while Lucas went off to do whatever it is that Visiting Vice Secretaries do. Someone had put a cigarette between the statue's onyx fingers and I swiped it to smoke while I rolled my own. I didn't particularly care about Lucas's real reason for accepting a moronic job in such an awful town. But I knew Feck was curious and I had time to kill and plenty on my mind.

I was excited about the Smiley, the way it fortified my head, posting a sentry at every entrance point, sealing me in. I was planning on becoming a goddamn Leary for it, making the TV rounds with a leather satchel of the stuff, saintly, mysterious, ghost-proofing the world.

Of course, I hadn't talked to Evan about it yet. He'd been too busy harassing me about Feck that morning to complain. But if, during the thirteen some hours of his abatement, he'd passed the time being flayed by malefic gnarled minions or something, I guessed I'd have to give the cure a miss. My parents, I knew, could out-curse Ol' Nick himself. They'd take oblivion by storm. But Evan was a coward.

And I could already see another problem with the lovely little drug. A massive headache was coming at me like the charge of the fucking light brigade, hopelessly, stoically, marching its way along my nerves, blissfully unaware that my brain could eat anything it served up. My field of vision fogged over with the red of a barely remembered thunderstorm. Loosely tatted black lace, shadows of blood vessels on my retina, fractured the campus into a cloisonné ball.

What the men in white coats call an entopic event, a hallucination based on actual structures in the brain. I laughed. Headaches are so cute. Like a little black kitten with its claws out, they think they're tough. If your synapses are fucked up enough, though, you can beat pain at its own game every time.

I closed my eyes, blinking repeatedly without opening them, tilting the latticework into right angles, forcing it deep into the musky corridors of my own private hagiography, spinning it, cross-hook turn by cross-hook turn, into cool sweet memory.

Boiling hot Summer, 1979, the night I first met Evan. Midweek around eleven o'clock my mother appeared in the living room ensconced in a stinky beaver coat, little beaver heads chattering endlessly up and down the lapels. She sneered at her nodding husband and insisted I take her dancing. Around her like a funky kaleidoscope, the zoo concurred. I didn't think it was such a hot idea. The clubs would be empty and there was only one boring party I could think of.

Mamma tapped her foot. I rolled my eyes. I paced the small room, elbowing my way through an increasing throng of animals. Pappa looked up through lizard eyes.

"Better for you should take yourself for a walk, Little One," he murmured. "Not to stay here jumping so like a frog."

Still alive that year, he had a tendency to treat me like the goddamn guy from Porlock. Normally I just ignored it, but I could actually see how a whole room full of writhing parasites led by his deranged dead wife might well clot the milk of paradise. So dancing it was. I guess you could say my will wasn't particularly strong back then. I had, well, you can imagine, I had kind of a herd mentality.

The party was on Attorney Street. We moved in a pack along the molasses summer streets, taking up the whole sidewalk. We laughed as passers-by scurried through my mother's body, cursing the infernal heat, unaware they were standing in a gypsy.

Of course, the party sucked. I suppose from this distance you could call it a growth problem or something, although at the time it seemed like a soul betrayal of the deepest magnitude. Anyhow, most of my friends from the neighborhood had disappeared into the bowels of top 40 radio by the time I was 19.

It seemed to make no difference that the music I tried to get them interested in was coming out of bars in our own neighborhood, dives we'd had staked out for years. And even though I openly confessed to a fondness for "Heart of Glass" and even some of *Live at Budokan*, they were frankly suspicious of the stuff I countered with, of me, of everything my traitorous trek up to Columbia each morning represented.

I couldn't really blame them, but my mother could blame me, and did so, in scalding language, drowning out the ambient party noise. She left the party within the hour, in search of real music, she said. Cursing the Doobie Brothers with a spate of boils as she lingered, translucent, in the party's smog, she whistled loudly for the specters. She did a kind of cheshire cat number, which wasn't like her at all, and, before disappearing entirely, solemnly announced that the rise of Supertramp was all my father's fault. I can only imagine she found for herself the greatest fucking dance club in all of eternity, though, because that's the last I ever saw of her.

I drank for an hour or two more, sweating alcohol into a white T-shirt. I'm not sure when I started to cry. Silent tears filled my eyes and tracked down my face to an awful E.L.O. beat. I was still fucked up when Evan walked up to me, though, that much I'm sure of, because as he bent his long body beside me, he asked, the faintest twang of bay leaves in his voice,

"Why is it that the most beautiful girl at every party is always sitting by herself crying?"

"Probably because the music sucks."

"You think?"

I nodded, looking down at him, crouched too near me, taking in the hard sway of cheekbone, the lanky guitar arms, the primordial bog eyes. He knocked time to "Turning Japanese" on my knee, then laughed and nodded assent.

"Damn," he said, "I wish I'd known that last week. There was this girl even more gorgeous than you. The music, huh?"

Nodding again, I rolled a cigarette in a lightning flash.

"Well, hell," he said, eyes tracking me, "that I can fix. C'mon."

"Where?"

"I live upstairs. Don't you trust me?"

"Not at all."

"You will."

I trudged after him, up the dank tenement stairs, stood behind him shifting my weight from one foot to another, as he unlocked the four locks to my first taste of paradise.

Evan's Attorney Street apartment consisted of a bed and hundreds of records. But when you say that you have to curtsey as if you've just encountered a goddamn queen, or break down into sheer sobs of gratitude as if you've been given a cigarette after being trapped in a well for two weeks. Let's try again. Evan's Attorney Street apartment consisted of a bed and records.

He slipped me out of my clothes with sad compassion on his pale Southern face, a look that seemed for all the world to mix pity and world-weariness with a kind of desperate inevitability. With that same gentle sorrow he lead me to the bed, tied me to it, and paced over to the stereo console.

(It was two years later almost to the night that he pawned the stereo. He dragged the components down the stairs, one by one, trailed by a detachment of mocking snakes who hissed cruelly, nonsensically, "sub woof nyx, sub woof nyx," as my eyes turned into wells.)

Late into the morning he hovered over the turntable, playing one perfectly lethal punk ballad after another, each a flawless surprise, each somehow setting a dark dream stage for its successor. The shimmery feedback blew a soft breeze across my sweating body. The room breathed itself smaller to expiated lullabies. The rushing harmonies cloaked me in goose down, which stuck to my wet skin, as the ever-branching dissonance danced arson along my exposed nerves.

The Dolls themselves mopped my brow. The Voidoids rico-cheted over me, chucking beer cans around with graceless gallows splatter. Nepenthe Diner played ghoulishly with my eyelids while PT109 ran knife-blade tongues along my thighs. The Stooges danced in my stomach, the Dead Boys in my spleen, and once, I was sure, egged on by Wayne County and the drummer from Thalidomide, Darby Crash knelt below me, tying little knots in my tampon string. His grayish tongue stuck out between his teeth with little-boy concentration.

Periodically Evan would amble over to me, lean down, and with a soft plosive, fill my mouth with icy bourbon from his; or bring a salty lit cigarette, sloppily rolled, to my grinding teeth. Phased in counterpoint and deliverance, the hours crashed around me. After dawn I skated along the surface of sleep, dip-ping in and out, dreaming, when I did, that I was craned into the bright city sky, bound by three steel braids.

I awoke to quiet in a dismal studio apartment that stank of sweat and smoke. I awoke to quiet in the holiest place on Earth. Evan was rubbing my hands between his, blowing on them, trying to get the circulation going.

"It's almost noon, mystery girl," he said, handing me clothes. "Do you need to be anywhere?"

Dumbly, I nodded, started dressing. After a performance like that, I couldn't very well say I had to be at Columbia University two hours ago. We'd both look like fools. At the door I bit down hard, searching for words. He laughed and laid his huge hand on top of my head.

"Don't worry," he said. "I'll find you again."

He was good as his word, although it took him three weeks. Within two months we were married. Not wanting to be overly possessive or traditional, we nipped the "until death do us part" thing neatly out of the ceremony. We were young and modern, moronically hip, and as easygoing as the relentlessly damned ever get. We didn't know then that the phrase was designed as an indemnity clause.

I don't know, Evan. So much has happened. I guess it bothers me that you don't get any less dead as time wears on. You said:

The millionth time through a memory like that, the edges don't get frayed so much as spiky. It gets harder and harder to filter out the background noise. To the clackety-clack of the world rushing back in, I picture you spinning in your grave, Evan. Because you wrote those words, your version, in a love letter, because you never intended that image to be used this way, blaming you, shaming you, for kicking off when I needed you most.

That's a fair enough criticism, I guess, except that at the moment I'm engaged in blaming myself, not you. You were young and didn't believe in your own death. Besides, even if my knowledge of such things hasn't yet reached the legendary proportions of, say, Dante, I'm still what you might call an expert and I feel perfectly at liberty to borrow the image. Because grave-robbing assuages grief in a way that you, with your vague ghost burdens, couldn't even imagine.

"Grief, shmief," he said, and I opened my eyes to see him bleeding and crucified against a dying pecan tree, a crown of worms around his head. "Get a load of these wounds."

"Jesus, Evan."

"Hey, you really are smart."

"Fuck you. What happened?"

"Nothing at all, Chica."

"Then why all the stigmata?"

"To reduce your guilt to absurdity."

"But those are your symbols, not mine."

"Hey, mea culpa. But since when do you make a distinction between other people's crap and your own? First time, right? How's it feel?"

"I'm a gypsy."

"Yeah, you're a gypsy, Girl. No argument here. Listen, you really wanna go into a whole thing about whether I'm real or you make me up?"

"Not really."

"Good. Me neither. Now what's the problem?"

"I guess I wanna know—should I use the Smiley to control my craziness or is that stupid? After all this time, I mean, is there any point?"

"What am I? A fucking pharmacist?"

"Practically."

"Shit, Girl, I don't know. You seem a little more boring and obsessive than usual but probably it's nothing your admirers can't handle."

"But what about—"

"Little ol' me? What do I care? Look, Chica, you're just gonna have to accept that I can't explain how I experience all this. You wouldn't understand. I'm dead. You're alive. The gap is uncrossable. Whaddaya want me to say? 'I went away smiling?'"

"Yes."

He strained his neck on the cross, like a shrug without shoulders.

"Okay," he said. "I went away smiling. Speaking of which, your pal is upon us."

In pink dusk light, beyond the splayed specter of Evan, Lucas was ambling toward me. Around him, across manicured fields, kids with books milled. Some scurried across campus carrying candles and paper bags filled with sand. Others hefted pumpkins, decked out like Dracula, Mexican wrestlers, Raggedy Ann. Nuns and revenants in high tops laughed, pouring out of buildings. In all the turmoil, I'd sort of forgotten it was the end of October. My favorite holiday, the one day a year I'm not a freak.

"Didn't you ever love me enough, Evan?"

"Whaddaya think I'm doing here?"

"You're. Not. Here."

"Uh-huh. Don't you think I'd rather be cruisin' around with a harp, jammin' with Gabriel?"

"No."

"Yeah, well. I'm gonna make myself scarce, Chica. That guy stinks like an A & R exec."

"First time you ever announced you were gonna split."

"Hey," he said, "looks like maybe it's a week for first times."

"And that's absolutely the first time I've ever heard you utter a word of poetic bullshit."

"Uh-oh," he said, invisible, his voice mocking faint, "you don't think maybe I'm getting a little...intangible, do you?"

I grunted.

"Well, hey, consider it a Halloween present, then. You love Halloween."

Then Lucas was kneeling in front of me, peering into my face, and there was no time to digest it all.

"Are you quite all right," he said.

"Fine." I smiled. "Now."

He took a seat next to me on the bench. He was quiet, nervous, unsure of how to proceed with his confessional. We watched the kids light candles in the weighted paper bags, creating the simple magic of *luminarias* out of kindergarten supplies. The light that flowed out of the brown paper was the soft taupe of ritual. They placed the *luminarias* methodically, goofily, spacing them into a tightrope of fire.

"So?" I prompted.

"So."

"C'mon, Lucas. Say what you've gotta say."

"What do you think about NAFTA?"

I laughed.

"You really wanna know, or are you just asking to fill up the time?"

"Really."

"I don't know, man. I'm a gypsy. And a street rat. The little foibles of nationalism don't interest me."

"Meaning you have not, that is, do not have, rather, don't have an opinion?"

"Not exactly. Meaning, I guess, fuck the unions; they voted for Reagan. Why so careful with the verbs?"

"I am a little nervous."

I suppose I could have said "You don't have to tell me anything." Or "We're strangers." Or even "How 'bout them Aggies?" But I didn't. Those facile fragments hung in the air between us. He'd talk if he felt like it.

"Do you know Kroystag Ale," he said, finally.

"A dauntless brew, if you go for all that rich, nutty flavor stuff. I'm a watery swill by the gallon girl myself. Why do you ask?"

"I am its—"

"Biggest fan?"

"No. How do you say?"

"CEO?"

"No."

"Second Executive Vice Warlord in charge of mergers and acquisition and Chief Barbarian?"

He laughed.

"Chief Barbarian. Yes. That would describe it."

"You are? Undercover as a university gnome? Cool. You really must be loaded. Will you buy me something expensive?"

"If you like. I would anyway as your company is so pleasant, but I would with special relish if you could arrange an introduction to your boyfriend."

"I was kidding. Why do you wanna meet Flan?"

"You don't play the market, I trust?"

"Me? Are you kidding? Yeah, I've got a million shares in Lithium."

"Well, Dr. Veeka—"

"Back to that, are we?"

"Molly. Listen. We are diversifying. We already have an ancient fishing village in Hokkaido. We are prepared to buy up a good portion of this town. Make it, how do you say, viable—"

"Put it on the map?"

"Exactly. Mapache will make an ideal bedroom community once the trade agreement truly gets underway. We have bought a sample ranch, built a model home. We are ready to proceed, but we cannot seem to get through to the town council. The meetings are closed to outsiders, guarded with shotguns, even. Our plan is useless unless we can subdivide the properties."

"What's any of this got to do with Flan? He wouldn't care if you blew the town sky high."

"Yes. Exactly. I'm so glad that you have verified my impression. I am thinking perhaps your friend is the loose rock in the political structure. With his help perhaps we could, how do you say, 'take down' this Dr. Johnson, make him see reason at least."

"Okay, yeah, the course of progress, the town must enter the modern era and all that, but I still don't see why you need Flan. Guys like you eat guys like Hezekiah for breakfast."

He sighed.

"In a way, you are right. But we are proceeding cautiously. My assistant was dispatched here last year. She was as a, how do you call it, it swims with teeth like so? *Haj*?"

"A shark."

"Yes."

"And she returned to Denmark a beaten fish?"

"She retired without pension and would make no report. So, you see, if I could gain a better understanding of this Doctor Johnson, a mystery too would be solved."

"You know my soft spots well for a guy who just met me."

"I, too, am a shark. Could you see your way to clear to making the introduction?"

"Yeah, I can do that. But just so you know, if any shit comes down, I'm gonna do whatever Flan wants."

"Because your loyalty, it cannot be purchased?"

"No, Lucas. Because that's the kind of guy Flan is."

19

The Story of the Pig

A Danish beer company? In some ways I liked the way Molly repeated the story, her almost total obliviousness to the absurdity. At times she seems to view the vagaries of life as simple problems in transportation, in getting from one moment to the next. In response to the goings-on of my afternoon she said only, "I think I brought a marigold scarf I could wear."

It's true that yellow is the ancestral color of death in Mexico, required attire at traditional Day of the Dead functions, and of course it didn't surprise me that Molly knew this. I knew she'd spent some time in Vera Cruz as a college kid, and anyway, Molly always knows everything.

But her lack of connection to the boiling, ridiculous events of the town also frightened me. She didn't seem to notice that I felt like ten miles of bad road, or that I already had one foot on a path which would lead me, inexorably, into hopeless disaster.

Of course, if she'd fluttered her hand to her breast and cried out, her voice wet, "Oh, Flan, darling, you mustn't. It's too, too dangerous," I probably would've slugged her, so I knew I wasn't being fair. No question about it. I had myself a situation. I was fucked up.

Parking the truck on the road behind Nary's farm, I turned and kissed her.

"Careful you don't start talking like Nary, Doll. You're gonna fall for his accent like cowboys fall for Swedes. But if you do your number, he might think you're making fun of him."

"Say what you mean, Flan."

"Why the hell should I? Don't you already know? You're the expert, right? Can't you hear it in my pauses, in the 'shape of my words?'"

She shrugged, sighed, rolled a cigarette, lit it with one hand, dragged deeply, ran her hand through her hair. Weary, sarcastic tropes, all adding up to a body posture which said, in no uncertain terms, that she was prepared to face the inevitable. It was an attitude I kicked against, despised with all my being. And envied.

"It's not that I don't care, Flan. It's just that I don't have an angle on it. I don't have the words. Why?"

"Why what?"

"Why is Nary sensitive about his accent?"

"I don't know, Doll. It's something to do with his parents. His mother was some kind of fussy Kraut, didn't want the kid to be an Indian. God knows why she got involved with a New Mexico boy."

"Probably not even God knows why someone would do something *that* stupid."

"Cunt," I said, laughing, and felt better.

We trudged along the long pecan shell and gravel path to the Totonac house. The ancient *hacienda* was decked out with *luminarias* and Christmas lights in the shape of chile peppers. The tiled doorway, lit by a garden flood, was nearly hidden under a bower of marigold chains. As we got closer, the smell of boiling sugar wrapped itself around us. Molly laughed and grabbed both my hands, spinning me around and around.

"Flan?"

"Doll?"

"Please don't go. I don't think I could stand it if you got killed," she said in a dead monotone.

I growled and picked her up.

"You're a laugh riot, Doll."

"How do you know I don't mean it?"

"Because I know that's the one thing you *could* handle."

"I guess," she said, ramming her knees into my gut, knocking us both off balance, kissing me as we rolled over the gravel, crushing pecan fragments, laughing and swaying, yelping right through the boneyard that surrounded us; and as we turned, I thought I saw her mouth form the words: No. I mean it. Please don't go.

As if by mutual consent, we ignored this, sealing our fate by being chicken, backing away from honesty, and opting instead for a kind of cowardice disguised as decisive action. Anyhow, right there, right then, we blew it.

Sonia met us at the door with a tray full of *calaveras*. I took one and put it in my pocket. I'm sure those grinning skull sugar candies are partially responsible for all the awful teeth and botched bridgework for which our community is justly famous and I wanted no part of it. On the coasts, teeth matter, and at that point I was still planning my great escape.

Besides, when I was kid, *Calavera*, which has also come to mean something between henchman and bandito, was my nickname. I hadn't really liked it. It lacked class, I thought, and I didn't want anyone to be reminded of the moniker and start it up again, especially in front of Molly.

I made the appropriate introductions and let Molly slip into the crowd. I knew that despite her own almost grotesque awkwardness, she was absolutely at home in any situation. In some ways, travelling with Molly was like travelling with a funhouse mirror.

Chris and Nary were standing next to the *ofrenda*, which was littered with food and drink for the Dead. In the center of the table was a roast suckling pig, with a fucking apple in its mouth. This was a tradition at the Totonac house. When I first start celebrating the Day of the Dead with them, I thought it was strange, to say nothing of revolting; but apparently the dish was a favorite of Nary's classy European mother, and even though she herself had detested the Day of the Dead, he honored her with the treat.

As I approached Nary and Chris, I saw that they were bombed on aguardiente, which is a kind of distended Mexican rum. It was a good sign for the impending nuptials, as Nary never drank with anyone he was upset with. We'd argued about this several times over the years, me insisting that alcohol was a lubricant, as good a way as any to smooth ruffled feathers, and Nary insisting that alcohol was some kind of sacrament that shouldn't be messed with unless the heart was pure.

I was glad to see them drinking, and just as glad, as I got closer, to see that they were in a heated argument. It was apparent that, for whatever obscure reason, Nary was willing to consider Chris' proposal seriously. I hadn't relished the thought of getting in their way. Also, if Chris was arguing, it meant he wasn't in his slow-witted down-mode. I knew Nary cared more about brains than just about anything except common decency. He'd never let his daughter marry a simpleton.

I took a long pull on my beer as I came up to them, less for fortification than to prevent them from offering me the cane spirit they were swilling. I didn't drink the stuff on general principle. Behind me, I heard Molly chatting in Spanish with Nary's oldest grandson Ireneo about the Civil War, which I guessed he was studying in school. Ireneo was sort of a revelation among the Totonac clan, to say nothing of the district in general. He always did his homework.

"Goliath," Nary said, "I'm so glad you are here. But what are you drinking? Put down that beer and have a real drink with us."

I grimaced and accepted the hand-blown bottle. I knocked back a deep draught, letting the aguardiente rest on my tongue, diluting the horrible sweet taste with as much spit as I could muster before I swallowed. Chris caught my expression and gave me a sly look.

"Yeah, Flan," he said. "What are you doing drinking beer? Don't you have any respect for Mr. and Mrs. Tontonac's dead relatives? What you drink, they drink vicariously. You'd deny them aguardiente?"

"Af," Nary said, smiling. "Goliath, this young man is a heathen, just like you. Worse than you. He think my people eat and drink through us. He don't believe in the spirit of things, food, people, animals. For this heathen, only the flesh."

Chris laughed and Nary shook his head.

"It's sad, very sad."

"Yeah," I said. "The kid's a smart-ass, no doubt about that. But, he's young, Nary. Maybe he'll wise up."

"Maybe my Sonia will wise him, hah? Maybe," Nary said, and his voice changed. "You know about this, Goliath?"

"Uh-huh."

"'Uh-huh' you say, like a goat. Always you are careful. I tell you often enough I think that the time come in every man's life when he must to pick a side."

Chris looked back and forth between us, the drunk smirk fading slowly off his face. The mood had changed quickly.

"I'm on your side, Nary," I said quietly. "What side *is* that?"

"Enough," Nary said, and passed me the aguardiente again. "Tonight is for fun, for crying. You tell this young man the story of the pig, hah? Maybe this will change his heathen mind."

"Okay," I said, shuddering as the rancid liquor ran over my tongue.

"What pig," Chris said, and in creepy acid stereo, I heard Molly cry out from the kitchen, laughing,

"*Cuál cerdo?*"

The folk tale was a favorite one in the Totonac household. I'd heard it at least a dozen times myself; but I'd never had to tell it before. I hoped I was up to the task.

"Once upon a time, Chris," I said, "there was a young man, who was married to the most beautiful girl in the village. Her parents weren't very rich, and he had to travel across quite a few towns to make enough money to support all of them. His own parents were drunks, unable to help, and eventually they just wasted away.

"Meanwhile, the son, selling pottery and blankets within several hundred miles of the American border most of the year, began to get some fancy notions. He wasn't a bad man, Chris. He went to church while he was away, and sent every peso he made home to his poor extended family by pack train. The church he attended was relatively close to the border, though, and had more of a gringo flavor than the thatched altar his home village used."

I looked over at Nary, as I paused dramatically, and he was grinning from ear to ear. I knew I was taking some liberties with the old tale. The story was certainly older than any border dispute except that psychic kind that plagued Molly. But Nary seemed pleased, and Chris, well, who knew what went on in his half-smart head, but he was wearing a riveted, almost vapid stare on his face, so I went on.

"Well, one year, as the young man was preparing to travel home to be with his family on All Saints Day, he came to a decision. The way his village celebrated the serious Catholic holiday was primitive, he thought. He sent word to his wife that she was not to build an *ofrenda*, or attempt to talk to the Dead, or prepare a picnic at the graves of their relatives. He informed her that they would say a simple prayer when he got home, and that if she had any wishes for her people in heaven, she was to address them directly to Jesus.

"The thing is, Chris, in his travels away from the village, the kid had somehow become afraid of death. This wasn't something that had ever happened to anyone in the village before, and he didn't know what to make of it, so, instead of appealing to his dead relatives for help, he tried to cover it up with a bunch of anglo mumbo-jumbo about intercession.

"Anyway, his wife worried, but she did as she was told. And on his way home, the young man ran into a black dust storm. Then a freak hail storm joined the dust. He could hardly see, and his horse began to whinny and buck. The young man had to dismount. As he tried to calm his horse, he began to shudder. He heard strange singing and chanting, and all at once, he was knocked down and trampled nearly half to death by a great parade of the Dead. He recognized several of the elders from his village."

At this, Nary coughed and raised his eyebrows and I realized I was probably laying it on a little too thick. The whole idea of village elders was one I had from television, and it had no place in the tale. I realized I was getting further and further away from the pig. But I went on, the aguardiente making treacle out of my bloodstream.

"They were all wildly drunk and out of control, dressed in fabulous clothes, and they'd stop, now and again, to upchuck wondrous, multi-colored puke. They'd all obviously overeaten.

"Needless to say, the young man was now doubly frightened. He remounted his horse, shuddering mightily. He was afraid of the Dead, of course, because he had become afraid of death; but he was also afraid of the retribution of the Dead, because now he realized that he was wrong.

"Just as he was about to ride off through the black hail and dust, pale and shaken, he saw his parents struggling up the hill in front of him. They were weak and almost translucent, tattered black and white skeletons. He hoped they wouldn't notice him. But his mother's head turned, hollow-eyed, and looked right at him.

"'How could you do this to us,' her voice cried on the wind.

"Well, now the young man became terrified and began to gallop at full speed toward his village. He felt sicker and sicker. He could barely hang on to his horse's mane, but he knew he had to get home in time to tell his wife to build an *ofrenda* for his parents.

"Although he was half dead himself by the time he arrived, he was able to tell his wife about his change of heart. Greatly relieved, she borrowed a pig from a neighbor and the man fell into bed, exhausted. As his wife prepared the pig for slaughter and cooking, he grew weaker and weaker. He was feverish, and, after a night of deranged screeching about his parents, he woke up dead. The pig was served at his funeral, and his children ate it with great abandon."

"I wish that would happen to my father," Chris said, deadpan.

Nary looked back and forth between us.

"Af," he said, and walked away.

Chris looked stricken. He'd picked a bad time to remind Nary that he was Hezekiah's son. But Nary was a fair man, and there was still hope that he'd learn to judge Chris on his own merits. Just at that moment, though, the kid didn't seem to *have* any merits. He stood alone. I watched him try to think of some face-saving thing to say. After an eternity, he settled on

"It's time for the dinner, anyway."

Poor bastard.

Molly walked up to us and pulled me aside. I saw Chris start to trail after Nary.

"Do you have anything, I mean, that we could put on the table for Evan," she said.

I sighed and tucked a couple of mushrooms behind a blue glass plate of bone-white tortillas, where the kids couldn't get at them. I reached up and kissed the top of her head.

"I don't have anything stronger," I said. "My girlfriend won't let me deal that stuff."

"What a bitch," Molly said, and slipped her arm into my elbow, leading me to the tiny dining room.

Nary sat at the head of about five tiled tables which were rammed together and covered with an inconceivable spread of food. Of course I knew that Nary was famous for his expansive holiday hospitality. He is known, all over the county, to really throw his house out the window on such occasions, which is how they describe such largesse in Mapache. His entire extended family, living and dead, I supposed, was crammed into the small room, but Mrs. Totonac had managed to make room for Chris, Molly, and me. Molly and I were the last to take our seats and the whole dark-eyed clan stared at us.

We sat, and bowed our heads slightly, waiting for Nary or Mrs. Totonac to make some kind of speech. Then Nary shocked us. He looked from Chris to Molly and back again.

"Welcome," he said.

Molly smiled and Chris muttered something that might have been "thanks," and looked down.

"Would one of you like to say grace? It is the tradition in my family that the guest speak first."

This was not, as far as I could remember, any kind of real ritual in Nary's house, although maybe since I was his farmhand, he hadn't considered me a guest. It was puzzling, because it was totally unlike Nary to lie, but I figured maybe this was just his way of drawing Chris out. A little white lie in the service of making his table comfortable was certainly Nary's style. Chris just sat there, though, staring at his feet, and eventually, in a hypnotic, singsong voice, Molly began to speak.

"With humility," she said, "we proffer this spread; we wait at peace, day and night; here we sing and speak. When you grace us with your presence, we have fun, dancing to the music that danced in your ears. We meet here with tremendous happiness because you have made things right between us and our gods, who are neither sad nor angry, who are also at peace; our greatest fear is to cause anger or jealousy or irritation."

I have to say, the Totonac family more or less took all this in stride. They watched her with a rapt attention which grew as she went on.

"Look at this spread, what we proffer from what we've gathered, all to symbolize your kindness, the trouble you've taken to join us here from your intangible home. To you, gods, makers, ancestors, who have given us everything important we know, and, most of all, memory, we wish to exchange the sweet scent of marigolds, the music which dances in our ears. Here you'll be at peace. We have made it so, here, in *kantinyán*, the place holy to you, our home. Join us in this feast of *wati*, of flesh and skeleton, for your nourishment. Tonight, accept our apologies for calling you here. And tomorrow you can return home."

By the end, everyone, except the very smallest children, stared at her. Nary caught his wife's eye and across the makeshift banquet table they smiled in tandem.

"Beautiful," Nary said. "I have not heard it since my father died. My mother, she did not like this prayer. But how did you know?"

Molly looked uncomfortable. At times, she gets sickened by the effect she has on people. I was worried she might feel that way now and I kicked her under the table, which set Tita, Yesenia's daughter who had slipped her high-chair and was giggling at her mother's feet, to slapping at people's toes with her chubby fist.

"It seemed like a nice way to open a feast in a house named Totonac."

Sonia translated for her mother, who smiled and said,

"*Melindroso, sí*," nice, yes, although I doubted she understood any of what Molly said, only the deep pleasure in her husband's eyes. For me, I was happy Sonia had translated the simple remark. I knew having to do it herself would have put Molly over the edge. She hates to be the center of attention.

We fell to eating, everyone talking at the same time. Every once in a while, I felt Nary's curious stare hit our corner of the table like a rockslide. I looked up once and caught him moving his eyes back and forth between Molly and me like a gila monster. He gave the thumbs-up sign and I smiled at him. I pointed at Chris, and then Sonia. I shrugged, asking, and he shrugged in return. I guessed he hadn't made up his mind, and I didn't really blame him.

We were finished with all five desserts and well into the alcohol when the door to the *hacienda* shook with a loud knock. The children, most of them tipsy and half-asleep, lying on the floor under the table, woke up and scrambled onto their parents' laps.

Mrs. Totonac got up, opened the back door, and Hezekiah pushed past her, into the crowded room, pulling Rosalita by the hand. Leading the list of things I hated about Hezekiah at that moment was the way he used his bastard daughter as a scary little monkey. He was pretty creepy-looking himself, and it wasn't as if his entrance really needed any bolstering. Nonetheless, his late-show ingress had the desired effect. All eyes swiveled to the unhappy girl and Nary stood.

"*Buenas noches*, Señor Johnson," he said.

Hezekiah surveyed the room until his gaze, at last, fell on Nary.

"Ah, my little friend Nary. So formal, you are. Why don't you join us at the town council one of these nights, my little friend? You will learn, perhaps, to, what do the kids say, Chris? loosen up."

He didn't mention me, although I knew he'd seen me. Nary's expression didn't change and Chris, who I guessed was hoping to blend into the scenery, blanched. The open end of a roast turkey carcass was butted-up against my plate and I had a fleeting desire to fist it, cracking my knuckles instead, as Nary spoke.

"What can we do for you, Señor Johnson? I regret to be so rude, but we are, as you see, eating. You would join us maybe?"

"No, thank you, Nary. It pleases me to stop by on the people in my town now and again, enjoy the quaint old customs. I thought, perhaps, I could have a word with Sonia."

"Now is not a right time, Señor Johnson, for to talk alone. But join us, please."

"Daddy, please," Sonia said, and I noticed her four older sisters looking nervously at their husbands. Hezekiah laughed and squeezed out from in front of Rosalita who, I could now see, had been staring, unblinking, at Molly.

"Yes," Hezekiah said. "'Daddy, please.'"

As he said this odd thing, his fat eyes seemed to trail away from Nary. He looked at Molly and shuddered, whether involuntarily or not, I didn't know. But I didn't want to stick around to find out. Something odd had been going on between them ever since they spoke on the phone about Rosalita and I was sorry I had ever introduced them.

I simply hadn't counted on the Doll's ferocity once she got involved. Or maybe I had, and that was the problem. I would've excused myself and Molly and left right then, but it was up to Nary to respond, and I knew I couldn't rob him of the opportunity.

"Fine," he said. "You may speak together on the porch. Maybe Rosalita would like a *calavera*? Of course she would. Every good girl wants a *calavera*. Mrs. Totonac, get a sweet, for our little guest."

"No, no," Hezekiah said, waving his short arms. "Rosalita does not need this. Instead, she wishes to recite a poem. Go on, little flower. And come, Sonia. Let us chat."

Somehow, in the minute space available, everyone managed to squeeze to the place Hezekiah had assigned them. Several of the children had begun to cry. Rosalita started to speak in a monotonous voice, but at first I didn't pay attention. I was looking at Nary, who was still standing at the head of his table, expressionless, and at Molly, who watched Rosalita fixedly, her face alarmed. I thought I better get the Doll out of there fast.

"...On February 20th," Rosalita was droning, "a mail carrier was attacked and wounded at Cooke's Canyon. Horse killed. March 2nd. Indians cut and parted the ferry cable at Fort Selden and shot a cow belonging to Lieutenant Conner. November 14. Indians killed a herder and drove off 1200 sheep from John Lemon of Mapache. Posse of citizens gave pursuit and recovered part of the sheep and killed three Indians..."

"That's not a poem," Ireneo said, "It's part of a filthy, Indian-hating speech Colonel Ryerson made to the Territorial Senate after the Civil War."

I guessed the kid really knew his local history, but I had no time to be surprised. Just as Ireneo spoke, Rosalita still hissing on in that monotonous voice, Molly said, to no one in particular, "*Esa muchacha tiene autismo.*"

That girl's autistic. No one responded and Rosalita kept talking, repeating the unbelievably boring statistics, and staring at Molly. I made up my mind, as I heard the little girl say, from a great distance,

"...August 15th. Train of Martin Amador attacked near Burro mountains, Grant County, by 60 Indians. Teamster Esquino Lazo killed..."

I stood and got Nary's attention.

"Molly and I are a little tired, Nary. Could we crash in the shack?"

"Flanagan, of course. This you do not need to ask. Would you see that our little guest Chris also finds his way home?"

"Sure."

I put my hand on Molly's shoulder. She seemed made of lead. I had to knead my fingers into her collarbone to get her attention. We all thanked Mrs. Totonac profusely and edged away from the crowded tables as best we could. At the door Nary called Molly's name and spoke in what I assumed was some Indian language.

The air outside was crisp and stank of mesquite fire. We could hear Sonia sobbing on the porch as we lead Chris out. We made our way across Nary's land to the crumbling adobe shack I'd lived longer in than anywhere else except the slam.

"What was that all about," I asked Molly. We were stretched out on my old bed. It was weird seeing her next to me there, just as I'd imagined all those months, manifest and relentless, her head bobbing with emphasis as she rocked on certain words.

"You tell me."

"No, I mean that part at the end."

"This is rough, mind you," she said, "but I think he said something like 'tell your good man my daughter will never join a family with such a roof.'"

"I thought it was something like that."

She laughed, pulling a pack of cards out of her pocket. We played Hollywood gin for a few hours, at one body part a box, sitting cross-legged on an old Indian blanket, and in that way managed to avoid talking about anything important at all.

20

Que Bonito Es El Mundo—Lastima Es Que Yo Me Muera

Morning broke clearly in my dreams, finding me suddenly exposed, mucking about in the halls of let's call it *unter*space, pumping my ass in tandem with some borrowed alphabet shape. There's stuff to fuck down there, tentacled, wrong; it just doesn't bear close inspection. So when I opened my eyes, it wasn't with that usual sick thud, the realization that sunrise, this cataclysmic event, had once again passed me by.

Flan was nowhere to be seen. He'd left me the *Las Cruces Sun-News*, a paper cup of black gas-station coffee and a cloud of dank sour gloom swathed like a firmament across the adobe ceiling.

I put on his shirt, wondering briefly what he was wearing. It smelled like him, that unmistakable mix of cigarettes, corn husks, whiskey, and sweat, a smell, well, if you could bottle it, you'd be rich. He has that over Evan, you had to admit it. He has a body.

I thumbed desultorily through the paper, my head returning again and again to the little girl's found poem. I guess it was my first experience with really identifying with someone and I wasn't particularly enjoying it. I mean, look who I picked.

I came at last to an article Flan had circled in red wax crayon. The night before, 71 head of black cattle had apparently been set loose and were roaming all over the highway system, freaked out beyond belief, and causing countless accidents as drivers, unable to see them in the dark, plowed right into the terrified heifers. A kid had been scalded by spurting anti-freeze when a cow shattered, on impact, his father's radiator.

189

Only five of the cows were still at large and it was assumed they would eventually find their way to some grazing area or another, joining up with another herd. Below the circle Flan had scrawled, "Packy's War Cry." I was just wondering what the hell that meant when Flan came in, shirtless and sweaty, followed by a blast of cold air.

"I knew you'd want my shirt," he said.

"Why didn't you need it?"

"I was exercising Arturo."

"What about this," I said, flourishing the paper.

"Every time Packy's jazzed about something, he sneaks out in the middle of the night and lets somebody's livestock loose."

"And last night he was jazzed about slitting your throat?"

"I never thought I'd say this about you, Doll, but you seem to be losing your sense of humor. Don't you get it? He's such an idiot, he can't contain his excitement. He gets drunk and out of hand, and what does he do? Lets cows loose, rounds up a bunch of goats, drives a family of pigs to the town square. And not just once, a long time ago, when he was a kid. This is something he does every fucking time he's excited. For years he's been doing this."

I slithered out of the shirt and handed it over. Flan took it absently, weaving the flannel through his fingers, cackling to himself about the IQ of his appointed executioner. I was annoyed, so I kissed him.

I ran my lips over a long raised scar on his upper arm. It seemed exotic, suddenly. Flan's skin dips and buckles with scar tissue, rising pink and sinking white. I scar in one dimension only; a bad cut leeched of pigment as it heals, a minor one leaving a chicken scratch of red lines. But if you were blind, or even color-blind, you'd never know I'd been around the block.

"Where'd you get that scar?" I asked, and Flan laughed.

"Whaddaya wanna know for? After all these years? My gravestone?"

"Serious? Or bullshit?"

"You'd lie for me? This I gotta hear. Bullshit."

"I'm worried about—"

"Go on."

190

"I never noticed before."

"Fair enough. Your first lie?"

"Flan?"

"What, Doll?"

"Where'd you get the scar?"

"Bullshit? Or serious?"

"Whichever," I sighed.

"My mother was really fat, right? And she had to wear this special kind of truss. So one Friday when I was a kid my father hauled me out of school and we drove out to El Paso to this strip of surgical supply places over on Sun Street to order her one. While they were making it up, he went into a bar and left me outside.

"So I wandered around for a while, getting bored, and finally I went into an orthopedic shoe store and asked the Jewish guy who ran it if he carried the 'Round Robin' shoe and he said something like, 'Vat is zis, the Round Robin?' and I went like this, holding my hands apart like I was cradling a softball, and said 'it's a round shoe for people with round feet.' The guy got pissed, started screaming to wake up the dead and flung some kind of leather cutting device at me."

"Did you cry?"

"Sure. Wouldn't you?"

"What did your father do?"

"My father beat the crap out of the guy and they both got hauled off by the cops. I had to hitch a ride home."

"Who picked you up?"

"I don't remember, Doll. No, wait, I do. A Connecticut broad in a yellow bug. She'd split on her old man and was gonna start a new life as a weaver or something. You wanna wear that shirt, I can borrow something from Nary."

"Okay," I said, laughing.

"What's funny about it?"

"It's just, all these years you talking about this stupid place, the last thing I ever imagined was that you were right."

"Meaning what, Doll?"

"Meaning, I guess, this town is destroying us."

"Yeah, Doll. But you gotta remember, we're destroying it too.

That's what this meet with the Dane's all about, right?"

"I don't know."

"Get dressed. I'll meet you in the truck."

In the bar in San Miguel, Flan looked like a grinning skull, like one of those sugar candies he despised. We waited for Lucas, Flan's lips drawn back over a shot glass. I couldn't tell what disgusted him, exactly, since he wouldn't say anything. Honestly, I hoped it wasn't me.

The tiny bar was unquestionably what it was; and it wasn't quaint. The warped wood floor was covered with sawdust and there were cow skulls over the filthy windows. Middle-aged Mexican men slumped on tables, cow shit on their feet, feet on the chairs opposite them, chairs rocking on rotten boards, boards squeaking against the backbeat of a tinny jukebox. And all for the want of a nail.

I wanted to stop him, but I couldn't. I wanted to help him, but I couldn't. It was an Evan-lesson, really: some demons can't be bridled; but I didn't think of that 'til later. I also wanted to understand, but I couldn't even do that. Nothing had ever imploded on me. My reality just expands to absorb each new indignity. Everything was caving in on Flan.

"Tell me a story," I said.

"What the hell for?"

"We don't have anything else to say to each other."

"Since when does that bother you?"

"I don't know."

"Can't you talk to Evan?"

"No. He doesn't know any stories."

"If you're so pissed I'm going with Packy, why are we meeting with this guy? Let's just split right now, hop on a plane. We could be at Fee's by happy hour."

"It's too late."

"Yeah," he said. "So, leave me alone."

"I can't."

He sighed mightily.

"What do you want to know?"

"Why do they have to break the five-acre law?"

"You can make at least 20 times more money selling the land off in quarter-acre lots. A lot of the farmers around here aren't exactly what you'd call die-hard traditionalists. They know the money's all in real estate. And they know if they stick to rotating cotton and peppers year after year, they're gonna ruin the topsoil."

"Which means what?"

"It means, sooner or later, they'll have themselves a nice, tidy little dust-bowl."

"So why don't the land-owners wanna do it?"

"I don't know, Doll. Some of them don't want the town to change. Some don't have any interest in selling to anyone. But most of them are just afraid of Hezekiah."

"And without Packy, they wouldn't be?"

"No, there's a dozen guys who could take Packy's place. Hell, *I* could take Packy's place. But with Packy gone, there'll be a window of opportunity, some way to get Hezekiah out of the picture. I could set him up with the drugs, for example. Or somebody could. People disappear in Juarez all the time."

"If it's you who comes back."

"Right. If."

"But what will happen then?"

"Precisely what I wish to know," Lucas said, joining us at last, too late.

"When I was a kid," Flan said, unwilling to be interrupted, or maybe as a parting gift to me, "my grandmother used to claim that she was descended from a monk."

"What kind of monk?"

"I don't know, Doll. She said the guy was a hotshot from someplace in Italy. Lombardy, I think. One day in the 1820's he'd seen the Virgin Mary wandering around his garden, pointing West. So, she said, he gave his purple robe to the gardener, got a brown one, and started traveling West. First he tried South America. He stopped in Brazil, Venezuela, Columbia, Ecuador; but always the damned Virgin kept appearing, pointing West.

"When he ran out of frontier, he hiked up the Isthmus, hung out in Rizaba, teaching Indians about Jesus. I guess he was some kind of revolutionary, though, because my grandmother insisted that he'd been thrown out of Mexico on a trumped-up charge. He kept on moving, though, staying in one place only as long as he could withstand the constant taunting from the blessed mother.

"I remember my Grandmother used to say that the longest he lasted anywhere was up in the Raton Mountains and that's 'cause he kept the delusion at bay by building fourteen crosses on top of Old Baldy. He finally ended up in a cave in the Organ Mountains. My grandmother insisted that he was released from the Virgin's service only after he fucked my great-great grandmother. According to my grandmother, that's what the Virgin'd wanted all along. Anyhow, the guy died on April 17, 1868. They thought Indians had poisoned him, probably, and every year on that day grandma paid her girls double for every trick."

Lucas' moon-shaped face rose and set a dozen times as he nodded.

"*Har din historie en moral?*" he said when his head finally stopped bobbing.

I translated for Flan, who blinked once, knocked back a shot and stormed over to the bar, kicking over a table as he blazed by. Alone among the people in the room, Lucas flinched, and I felt sorry for him. Guys like Lucas always wanna know if a story has a moral.

The way I figured it, if someone's just spilled their guts, the only respectful reaction is to get down on your knees and start lapping. If you have to say something, it should be something like "what kind of dog was it?" or "what color was the dumpster?" or "what was playing on the radio?" Something to take you in. Asking if the story has a moral is just a way of distancing yourself. It's the equivalent of saying, "This viscera's a little bland; got any hot sauce?"

"You tell him," Flan said, returning to the table with a label-less bottle of clear liquor and three glasses.

I turned to Lucas.

"Flan and I, we're the same, is what he means."

"How?"

"We both inhabit ghost towns."

"I don't, how do you say, get it?"

"No," said Flan, "You don't. But I'm leaving tonight, anyway."

"So, we understand each other, then?"

"No," Flan said. "We don't understand each other. A guy like you could never understand me."

Flan ran his hand through his blood-red hair and sucked in a lot of air.

"Tell me something, Christensen," he said. "What does a Danish beer company want with this town, anyway?"

Lucas shrugged slightly.

"As I told Dr. Veeka, we are diversifying. We have acquired a number of charming and unusual properties around the globe."

"Yeah," Flan said. "What else?"

Lucas paused for a moment.

"I won't deny that there are other considerations as well. Kroystag Ale has long been concerned with our rivals' successful ventures in the Mexican market. Our interest in Mapache is linked to our desire to rectify this situation."

"Christ," Flan sighed, shaking his head. "You want Mapache as a beachhead. You're gonna flood Mexico with that perfumed pisswater you call beer."

Lucas gazed calmly at Flan.

"Kroystag Ale remembers its friends. There will be a place at our table for whomever helps us now."

"Thus speaks the Danish Mafiosi," I said.

Flan slapped both his palms on the table. He bared his teeth.

"No," he said. "I don't care about that. I won't be needing friends. I'm doing this one thing, live or die. And then I'm out of it. The fuck out of it. I don't care what happens, I'm going to New York. Let the whole town to turn to shit."

"But what about Rosalita," I said. "What about Chris and Sonia? Denise Salvo? What happens to them?"

"What happens to them? I don't know. They get squashed. I don't care about that either, Doll. They've been tying me down to this town with one goddamned weak person after another for years now. Always some new half-wit to watch out for. Fuck Rosalita. Fuck Chris. Fuck Denise. I mean, God bless them. I wish

195

them the best, but I don't care. I do this one thing, and I blow. I don't ever wanna hear about it again, whether the beer industry flourishes or not."

Flan looked ugly. Lucas looked mad. At least his eyes flashed, though. Flan's were empty.

"Can you tell him for me, '*Du taler som om du er i en stilling til og slås om detaljerne?*'"

"I don't think you wanna say that to Flan."

"What," Flan said, through gritted teeth.

I sighed.

"He says you're talking like you're in a position to bargain."

"Well, shit, Doll," Flan said almost sadly after a moment, stroking my jaw with coarse fighter's knuckles, "isn't my life worth something?"

21

Juarez

You have to drive out to El Paso in order to cross the bridge into Juarez, and on the way there, it snowed for just a minute or two. Packy was excited about it, even though he was too stupid to think of the snow as any kind of omen. I could understand the thrill; after all, once upon a time I was a guy who'd only seen snow five or six times in my entire life, too.

I let him whoop and holler and whistle Johnny Reb. I wanted him set off balance, but not over the edge, at least not until he'd introduced me to the connect, so I had to keep my irritation to myself. I kept my eyes on the road, both hands on the wheel, driving like a granny.

"Guess you get lotsa snow up in New York," he said, after a particularly grueling rendition of Dixie to which I showed no outward reaction.

"Not really, Packy. In New York, the snow melts, or dogs piss in it, or someone comes along and snorts the stuff up."

"What do you mean?"

"Nothing."

"Damn, man. My Critter's better company than you. You never did know how to have a good time. We're on the road. Hey, you wanna cut loose a while, get a little nookie? Oh, I forget, you don' go to whores. Damn."

I wasn't really averse to talking to him. I knew one of us was probably going to have to take the other one out and so it seemed only civilized to make conversation on the way to our showdown, but I was concentrating on sealing my goddamn doom and didn't want to lose my temper.

"Know what, Packy?"

"What's that, Trailer Boy?"

He guffawed and my stomach turned over.

"What about if we leave the truck in 'Paso?"

"And walk over the bridge? Geez, Flan. Ain't you got no class? The Customs guys'll think we're no better than a buncha wetbacks."

"What do you care what those asshole Texans think?"

"My momma was from Texas."

"Uh-huh. I wasn't thinking about walking, though, Packy. I thought maybe we'd take the trolley."

The El Paso-Juarez Trolley was the biggest tourist shunt around. They charged you an arm and a leg, sat you onto this idiotic Disneyland cart, and loaded you up with coupons for free 16-ounce margaritas at every fucking rat-trap joint along the path. The trolleys circled Juarez for hours, stopping every two blocks, and the goddamn marks would get on and off, collecting stupid souvenirs and strapping on the old feed bag at every shop on the market.

"What for?"

"Well, you know, Packy. All them stupid drunk Texans packed on the cart, vomiting burritos and watered-down tequila, the Customs officials never even go on board. They just shout out, 'Anyone got anything to declare,' and all the ugly Americans shout 'No,' and that's it. The trolley just glides on through."

"So what?"

"What do you mean, so what? So, we'll be carrying on the way back. If we're tucked in among all those puking women with frosted hair, no one'll hassle us."

"But we won't—"

"Uh-huh, Packy. Go on."

"Anyway, I think it's stupid."

"Yeah? Well, I think you're stupid. You and your Critter. Can't you rub your two fucking brain cells together and see the wisdom of this? Christ, Packy. We can't cross the border in this ratty old truck."

"Well, why'd we take the truck, then," he whined. "We coulda took my Caddy."

I snorted. Packy's car was a jacked-up two-ton monstrosity covered with crude paintings of skulls, tanks and barbarian blondes with enormous tits. About the only stencil it did not have was a flaming asshole, which of course was the only image appropriately symbolic of the guy's vehicle.

"You ever hear the word *discreet*, Packy? Christ. If we're driving that thing, we may as well hang a sign on the bumper that says 'Shoot Us, We're Idiots.'"

He was quiet after this, and I saw him trying to think. He didn't want to deviate too far from Hezekiah's instructions. It was kind of sad, really. But I was ready to take full advantage. I wanted to throw as many variables at him as possible. I knew he was especially worried about getting home after he'd railroaded me. The trolleys stopped running at sundown. I thought I'd let him stew a little. I had to take this one step at a time.

"Say, Packy, your momma really from Texas?"

"You bet."

"Know what Sherman used to say about Texas?"

"Who's that?"

"A general in that war you're so into."

"No shit?"

"No shit."

"A good ol' boy? Wha'd he say?"

"Not a good ol' boy. An Ohio boy."

"Oh."

I waited a full five minutes, turning off the highway into downtown El Paso before I said anything else. Even knowing him as I did, it was incomprehensible to me that Packy could be as stupid as he was acting. I figured he had to be lost in his own dim thoughts. It's not an easy thing to kill someone you've known all your life and I struggled to give him the space he needed, keeping my nasty remarks about the space in his head to myself.

I pulled into the garage at the civic center, paid for trolley tickets which included parking in the underground government lot. Packy didn't object, so I figured he had given in on the idea of the trolley. It did make sense. If the buy had been on the up and up, I'd have suggested it to Hezekiah in the first place. After all, one of us—we just each had a different notion about who—would be weighed down with enough contraband to get us put away for life on the way home.

My next step was to get Packy fucked up. I led him up to the plaza on the government center. All the tourists were crowded around a murky chlorine wishing well, painted in those ugly patches of turquoise and black favored by people who want a fake Old-West feel.

A little blond kid had jumped into the filthy water and was splashing around. The mother was screeching from the side, wanting the kid out but not wanting to go into the water herself. I stepped in, catching the kid and lifting him out to his squawking mother, who gushed her thanks all over me. A cute trolley attendant handed me a towel and I ran it over my neck. The sky was clearing, but I felt a little cold.

Packy followed me dumbly to a fake marble bench and we sat down. I took a little Smiley out of the chaw pouch in my shirt pocket and started chewing.

"What's that?" Packy asked.

"Nothing. Don't you wanna know what Sherman said?"

"Who?"

"The general."

"Oh, yeah. 'Bout Texas. What?"

"He said if he owned Texas and he owned hell, he'd rent out Texas and live in hell."

"Texas is in the South."

I was momentarily stunned, then worried. I could see I was beginning to develop a perverse fascination with the depths of Packy's stupidity, something I'd been peaceably raving about, without giving it a second thought, since I was a kid. I cursed the Doll, knowing I'd picked up this particular plague from her. I was on a job, though, and I didn't have time to think about shit like that. But I couldn't help myself.

"You don't know anything about the Civil War, do you, Packy?"

"I know we coulda licked those boys if I'd been there, me an' my Critter."

He commenced to singing "The South Will Rise Again," and I

refrained from saying anything about his 4-F status. We boarded the trolley, and were issued little paper ID bracelets that branded us as soft-touch tourists. I thought I'd save mine. Molly had a collection from the various hospitals she's been to. But I was betting she didn't have one that recalled this breadth of madness.

We clacked through the streets of modern El Paso on the kitschy wagon train. At the border the driver gave us each a packet of coupons for free drinks and a canned lecture about the customs procedure. I guess they wanted us drunk so we'd buy more little painted animals and shitty, factory-produced Indian blankets.

One woman wearing a T-shirt imprinted with a fluorescent crucifixion scene managed to get a hold of two books of coupons and she was smiling from ear to ear. She elbowed Packy, calling him "officer," I guess because of the Green Beret costume, and he reached over and tweaked her nipple. She squealed but remained seated and I set my teeth hard, waiting.

I repeated my own instructions silently, trying to will myself into a kind of tunnel-vision: my next step was to get Packy fucked up. Nothing else mattered. Nothing else existed. He looked almost pensive, and I had to admit, my heart went out to him. I was in trouble.

"Flan?"

"What?"

"Was there any generals from Texas?"

"In the Civil War?"

"Yeah."

We were across the border now, flanked on either side by little begging Mexican kids. The deep distance was all mesas and shanty towns. Packy leaned out the window and spit on a young guy carrying a tray of poorly thrown clay pots.

"John Bell Hood," I said.

"I bet he was a good ol' boy."

"His men called him 'Old Wooden Head.'"

"How come? He was brave, right?"

"He mangled an arm at Gettysburg, lost a leg at Chickamauga. They had to strap him on his horse every morning. Yeah, I guess he was brave."

"Me an' the Critter, we coulda fought wit' him, maybe."

I didn't see any point in telling him the war was Hood's procrustean bed, that they'd cut him down to fit it. I knew that particular tidbit would just puzzle someone like Packy, who dwelt in a land of Critter-infested certitude.

"At Antietam, he lost more than half his men in the corn around Dunker Church," I said. "And when they asked him, 'Hey, John, where are your men,' know what he said?"

"What?"

"'Dead on the field.'"

"No shit? Dead on the field? He was a tough son of a bitch, huh?"

"He cried in the lines at Nashville," I said, cruelly, even though I knew most people would consider that a poignant detail.

I ate another pinch of the drug watching the wannabe confederate watch me. Maybe Packy would've been better off back then. A luckless bastard like John Hood probably would've leapt at the chance to send Packy to his death. It wouldn't have mattered one good goddamn that he was crazy. Hood could've used the Critter to bolster his lines at Franklin. Besides, Hezekiah paled in comparison as a boss. True, he had all his limbs, but he lacked style.

I took a third hit, the bitter mushroom dropping with a thud into the mixture of grain alcohol and bile collecting in my gut. Maybe I should have eaten something, but it seemed like bad luck.

"You samplin' the merchandise there, Flan? I wouldna thought it."

I grinned.

"I need something to fortify me, Packy. After that act of heroism."

"You mean fishing out that kid? Shit, I coulda done that."

"But you didn't."

"Naw, I don' wanna get all wet. Maybe we'll meet some girls or something."

He elbowed the girl with the coupons and she giggled. The Jesus on her shirt was a blond, lurid mess.

"You oughta try some of this stuff in the rack, Packy. Makes your dick feel ten feet long."

He held out his hand and I gave him enough to give a

mastodon a decent ride. It was that easy. Like most small-town blowhards, Packy didn't have much experience with drugs. After he swallowed, I felt the sting of a minor penitence. The guilt flowed gracefully through my bloodstream, feeding every cell, and passed quietly out with my next breath. Then I felt nothing.

The trolley made its first stop, at the museum. I thought I wouldn't mind staying on all day, just circling the garish city, but I knew that sooner or later, I'd make a move.

Outside the old market, the coupon girl asked us to join her for a drink, on her, at Pepe's. Packy roared, picking her up like a kitten, banging her head against the plastic ceiling of the trolley. The drinks, paid for with the coupons, would seal his fate. Now, all I needed was to find out where we were meeting the Indian, if there was one. God bless free trade.

By his third 16-ounce margarita, Packy was wide-eyed. He'd showed Annabelle Lee the Critter five or six times. She said she thought maybe she saw something and his smile lit up the grotesque salon.

When he went to the bathroom, needing to squeeze out a loaf I think he said, I had my inspiration. I had no remorse about pimping. It was a family trade, after all, and there was no one I admired more than my grandmother.

The building above the brightly lit tourist trap was fairly large and I knew it must be filled with trick pads. A tiny Mexican waiter came by and I flagged him. He looked exactly like Pedro Gonzales-Gonzales, the guy who plays the hotel owner in all the old oaters. I knew, by then, that this was a minor side-effect of the Smiley and I paid it no mind. After all, if this was a movie, I was the hero.

"Unless I miss my guess," I said gravely, "my friends aren't feeling well. Is there someplace they could lie down?"

Annabelle Lee giggled, then fake-coughed and I felt a rush of zen confidence, empty of any affect. I slipped the waiter a fifty. One thing you gotta say for Juarez, and I don't mean that anything can be bought or that life is cheap there, although these things certainly are true. But it's the perfect place to be high.

I asked Gonzales-Gonzales to bring Annabelle Lee a pack of

condoms, tipped him mightily, and sat back, nursing an icy, old-formula coke. Morricone soundtracks played thrills against my pulse. Gonzales-Gonzales came back with a key to the ten-and-two, saying I had to pay the whore who was giving up the room. I gave him a twenty.

"Why are you being so nice to us," Annabelle asked, her tits heaving under Jesus.

"Packy's going into the Marines tomorrow," I said. "I just want to show him a good time."

"Ain't he a little old?"

"He is, yeah. You're a smart girl, you know that? But they want him special. 'Cause of how good he was in 'Nam."

"Wow."

"You'll be kind to him, Annabelle, won't you?"

"What about you, though? You got a girl?"

"Uh-huh."

"Wanna know a secret about women?"

"Sure."

"Anytime you wanna get laid, all you gotta do, see, is find out what a girl wants to do next, like with her life? At work or, like, whatever?"

"Yeah?"

"Then you just advise her to do it."

"What about what I want?"

This puzzled her. Her freckled brow furrowed and I could see she was becoming uncomfortable with me. Packy was ambling back to the table, massaging his stomach.

"Well, all you want's to get laid, right?"

"Right," I said, thinking, trying not to think, thinking fuck I wish, the Smiley working as a pitchback in my brain, lobbing my thoughts around. Out of the corner of my eye, through the reverberating haze, I saw her relax.

"Hey, there," Packy said, cuffing his conquest on the back of the head.

"Hiya, honey. Guess what? Your friend here, he arranged everythang for us."

She dangled the key in front of his face and he caught it in his teeth, growling. I had to get away. I thought I might start to feel something at any minute.

"Say, Packy?"

He had his face buried in her chest.

"Wha?"

"Where we meeting that guy?"

"What guy? Oh, yeah. I'll tell you later."

"Why not tell me now?"

"Whuffor?"

"Christ, I don't know, say you and Annabelle are having a good time and you don't show? Or say she rolls you and you end up dead? I still gotta make the connect, don't I?"

Annabelle winged a chip at me.

"Oh, you," she said.

"In the church," he said, his voice muffled by a mouthful of Texan breast.

"Which church?"

"Whaddaya mean?"

"The one they use, or the old one?"

"One they use."

It was priceless. The big Juarez church was only half a mile into the city from Pepe's. It was practically on the trolley route.

"What time?"

"Around five."

"I'll meet you in the alley behind the old one at four, huh? We got that thing we gotta do, remember?"

"Flan, I—"

"Sure, you remember, Packy. We gotta stop at the church, pin a little silver leg on the St. Anthony post, for Norma Jean. You wouldn't want her gout to get any worse. I just know you wouldn't."

"Flan, I—"

"You only got the room 'til then anyway, Packy."

"You go on, honey. Go to church with your friend. I can make you real happy 'til then," Annabelle Lee said, stroking the monster's head, and I fell in love with her a little.

I had to get out of there. I'd lost most of my peripheral vision and my heart was pounding. I braced Gonzales-Gonzales on the way out and passed him a C-note.

"You know, I was thinking."

"Yes, Señor?"

"I don't know that girl from Adam. What if something happened to my buddy? I wouldn't even remember what she looked like. I might not even remember which joint we stopped at, you know?"

"Sì, Señor. Remembering can be hard sometimes, especially here at Pepe's, for some reason."

He shook his head sadly.

"How are you in that line, Señor," I said, and he smiled. "You got a good memory?"

"Sadly, no. Mine, it is very bad. All the time my wife she yell about it."

"Damn shame."

"It is, yes. But then we all have our cross, is it not so?"

I wandered around the city for two hours. Every fifteen minutes like clockwork I bought a coffee and sucked a few Smiley crumbs off my thumbnail. Twice I stopped and pointlessly replaced the flint in my Zippo. I was on automatic, my focus indisputable. A grey mist hung around me, blurring the edges of the bustling city.

Every once in a while, the wail of a kid or a laughing woman would pierce my wacked seclusion and on one of these occasions I stumbled into a clip joint and bought two stuffed frogs, one playing a set of bongos and one in little nun clothes. This, I felt, was sufficient ammunition to protect me from the unhappiness that swirled around me.

I killed time as carefully as I could, trying to prepare myself, but the begging children, stinking alleys, and toxic limestone grit were scant distraction. The church reared up like an ugly old bull at the bottom of a slum street. Past a certain point, I figured I may as well just go for it.

I left the frogs under St. Anthony's altar before I settled into my crouch in the alley, and it was only when I took my Zippo out, disinfecting the blade on my father's knife as if I was worried about Packy getting blood poisoning, that I realized I wasn't ready.

I don't know how long I crouched like that, staring at the knife blade. I was still doing it when Packy showed up. He made a lot of noise coming toward me with scary eyes and then, at the perfect moment, he tripped and fell at my feet like a fucking rag doll. His head banged against the bricks. There was an incredible amount of blood. I'd schemed with absolute precision to bring myself to this moment and it wasn't even that I hadn't figured in how awful I'd feel, or even how easy it would all be. I simply wasn't prepared for the absurdity. He grinned at me.

"I don't suppose you lied about where we were supposed to meet the guy, did you, Packy?"

"Naw. I shoulda, though. You woulda thought of that, I bet."

"Maybe. You have a good time with Annabelle?"

"Yeah. She sucked my ruby raw."

"Good."

I felt dizzy and leaned against the wall, praying no one would come by, praying anyone would. I didn't want to draw it out, torment him, but I was momentarily paralyzed. I thought if I wasn't so fucked up myself, maybe I could think of some other way. My eyes filled and I wanted to say something like "if I let you go, you'd just come after me," but the words braced against my teeth. I leaned down and vomited, then wiped my mouth.

"How's your Critter, Packy?"

"Happy as a scorpion at a sock hop. He do love a hose job."

"I can't do it, Packy."

"Sure you can, Flan. You're a Mapache boy. Shit, I done it 13 times already. Wanna know something? I always thought this'd happen. Since we was kids. All I ask is you look after the Doc. He ain't tough like us. He needs someone, you know?"

"Packy, I—"

I suppose he was already half dead when he shifted for me into taunt mode. Not that that's much comfort. Anyway, he stank, and his blood looked like jello.

"Listen here, Trailer Boy. You're a fucking pussy, you know that? You let me go, I'll come after you. I'll carry your goddamn ears around wit' me as a trophy. That ain't all, neither. Me an' my

Critter, we'll travel on up to New York City and stick it to that brunette a yours. I always wanted to try a box like that."

"Packy, I—"

"I won't have to rape her, neither. I'll get her good an' wet telling 'bout the time you an' me watched your Momma go at it wit' Hezekiah. Shit, Flan. 'Member that? Us on tiptoe, peeping through the trailer window? She was so fat, the Doc looked like a raisin floating in a toilet bowl fulla vanilla pudding. Know what I woulda liked to see before I went, though? I mean, besides some real combat?"

"What," I said, through gritted teeth, then laughing like a kid at the miracle of my rising fury, my eyes streaming.

"Norma Jean and another big fat gal like your Momma, you know, eatin' each other out."

He played me like a violin, and as I cradled his bloody head in my hands, raising it to smash to the pavement, I whispered,

"Thanks."

"Shoot. We Mapache boys gotta stick together."

When he was dying, before I killed him, it was unmistakable, but once he was dead, he didn't look dead. He just looked stupid. I took his wallet, his fake dog tags, and his trolley ID and walked quietly over to the church. I collapsed in a pew and bent my head. My ears were clogged up with the sound of his cracking skull. The echo was awful.

I was slapping my own face, enjoying the fireworks, trying to stop thinking, hearing only godspeedgodspeedgodspeed, when the dealer slid in next to me. I took my own head in my hands and forced myself to look over. I could only see him in flashes. He was tall, with a sloping hat. He was Geronimo, Peter Lorre, Satan. He was green, short with an eye patch and endless spider legs. He was fat and skinny in places, chiseled out of ice. He was...talking.

"I thought I was supposed to meet two men," he said. "What happened to the other?"

"Dead on the field," I said.

22

Like a Bat out of Hell

I was proud and I didn't cry out: Evan where are you? Down that road, I knew, lay madness, lay a deranged widow, a crone out of Grimm, waiting with sharpened clutches. I sat in the motel room, still except for my fingers, caressing the keyboard of my lap-top, trying to hide, trying to, I don't know, jack myself into cyber-space. God only knew what I was hoping to find there. Jimmy Hoffa, maybe, or a used William Gibson condom.

I tried to think about practical people, typing their names. Truman, Florence Nightingale, Margaret Sanger, bleaching them, silently, of any romance. I rearranged the letters into ingestible bits, rooting around in the sounds for edible pragmatism, coming up with more and more complication, endless layers bespeaking a genuine mortal populace.

Under the starched uniform of the Crimean War nurse, beneath the ice glare of her famous goddamn camp lantern, lay a whole awful human drama. I moved the tracking ball with one finger, gently nudging the fragile letters, snuffling around for pro-saic secrets in their rearrangement.

Wanna know what I found? *Lice range the long fin. Legit change for Lenin. Fellatio, I cringe, hen. Nothing fecal leering. Nice frontal leg hinge. Lecithin on green flag. Hence, in telling a frog.*

Pay dirt. And then I made the lunatic's greatest mistake. I allowed myself to believe that there was meaning in the random assortment of letters. The exercise in calm depersonalization fell away and I picked through the chaos of tones, looking for groupings which were germane to my terror.

Wanna know what I found? *Filling the anger cone. Conning hellfire gate. Fleeting choir angel. Fence not, healing girl.*

Of course they started to leap out at me. Of course they did. Shouting their names as they pounced, barbed with specifics, depicting me into a smaller and smaller place until I was crouched under the Quinta desk, unbound from my torso's netherworld, quivering like a storm-soaked tree mammal. *Nil tang of green chile. Grafting hell on niece. C, elegant heroin fling. Lone fighter, in glance. Nee frightening local. If conning leather leg. I feel cretin hang long.*

Until finally, absurdly, under the awful pelting rain of *in line for the egg clan*, the Pocket Lady's *raison d'être*, absolute verification, to my mind, that we never should have come to this place, Evan's soft voice brushed past my shoulder and I emerged to find him, grinning on the bed, wrapped in the piss-drenched hounds-tooth coat he'd died in, the piss-drenched houndstooth coat that smelt like home.

"How 'bout *o', flinging clean ether*," he said.

"Evan, I'm lost."

He laughed.

"You? Never."

He looked at me, cocked his head, nodded to himself. I crawled out a little further.

"Long past time you had a TKO, though, Chica," he said. "And what're you acting so worshipful for? Sit up here with me. You're giving me the creeps."

I collapsed on the bed across from him. I rolled a cigarette, lit it, brushed the stray tobacco off my shirt.

"Take a blind leap toward lucidity, Molly. Wipe your fucking nose. Good. Now, if I were you, I'd lay off those buttons for a spell. They're making you goofy."

"No," I croaked. "If you were me, you wouldn't."

I snuffled like a baby, great gasps up into my red streaked face. He laughed again, shaking the room down to size.

"Okay, I wouldn't. But that was me, right? I had no reason to guard my sanity."

"And then what?"

"And then maybe go get something to eat?"

"Why?"

"You want a Veeka why or an everyone else why?"

"Do you listen in on every conversation I have?"

"Most."

"Bullshit, then. I already know why everyone else goes to get something to eat."

"You do?"

"Hey, I know everything, right? *Sult, honger, la faim, el hambre, Der hunger, a fome, la fame, kufuku—*"

"You could find out why they call that joint 'The Goat.' You wanna know that, right? And—"

"Uh-oh. And what?"

"There's something you gotta do."

I shook my head.

"Aw, Christ, Evan. I hope you're not telling me there's no free will. I couldn't handle that right now. Wait! Don't even answer. Just tell me this: where are the animals?"

"What animals, Chica?"

"Evan."

"Okay, okay. I didn't wanna tell you this 'til after. There's been a kind of *coup d'etat* among your guides, Chica. It's nothing to worry about. You know how these banana republic are. It'll shake down. Any minute now, you'll be hearing the pitty-pat of little furry feet."

"You didn't want to tell me 'til after what?"

"I'm insulted. Shocked. I thought you hate predestination like poison. 'Take-it-as-it-comes Veeka,' and all that. That's what we call you upstairs."

"Can't you drop the Loki act for just a second?"

"Shit, Chica. You think it's easy to gambol and scamper around like a fucking idiot, *tricking* someone into staying on the right track? You're getting to be a world-class bore, you know that? You're fucking occluded. What happened to the girl I picked out of the crowd? The girl who viewed salvation as one long, bloody toss in the hay?"

I hid my face in my hands and he burst into song.

"Rosalita jump a little higher. Rosalita come stand here by my fire."

"Come on, Evan. Which is it? You wanna misquote the Boss or you wanna taunt me about good works?"

"There's a difference?"

"I really have to go to dinner right now?"

"Speaking with the authority of a hallucination of your dead husband, I strongly recommend it, yes."

"Will you go with me, Evan?"

"I can't."

"Why the hell not?"

"I got something else I gotta do."

I plodded slowly along the Avenida de Mapache, watching it turn from Highway 28 into a tiny rural street. The setting sun expelled horrific crayon-box colors all around me. I wasn't thinking. I said it like a mantra: I'm not thinking. I passed hitchhikers and a woman with silver hair walking a goat.

I didn't care about their plight, or my own. I was engaged in an off-key simultaneous translation of "Bat out of Hell," sending Meatloaf, one tank too many, to Beijing. I brought all my forces to bear on the simple exercise, singing *gen yi bianfu cong diyu yiyang*, then taking out the *yi* and its partner *yiyang* to make it scan, singing, in effect, like bat out of hell, which is more or less allowed in Beijing *Huar*, the article being optional at best.

I perused the song's ticker-tape behind my eyes, trying to, I don't know, grasp the gestalt of the next line: I'll be gone when the morning comes. I puzzled over various pictograms, seeing with sudden laser clarity how I could do it, singing, *wo bu zai zaoshan laide shriho*, then laughing because I couldn't remember the next line in English, taking it from the top.

At that pace, the miles fell away like daydreams. I banged into the restaurant with all the false assurance of a local and seranaded the parrots with my new repertoire while I waited for a table.

It seemed obscene to eat, but I ordered green goat chile, a specialty of the house, and spooned it slowly, barely monitoring the

212

waitress's answer to my question about the restaurant's name. I listened with maybe half an ear, which, I suppose, is twenty ears at least more than most people. I wasn't paying any attention, but I could repeat the story verbatim even now is what I mean, and maybe I will. Maybe I will. I don't like to talk about what happened next.

On February 29, 1908, a leap year, almost thirty years after Pat Garrett might've hanged Billy the Kid, if the Kid hadn't escaped from Lincoln jail, a rancher named Wayne Brazel had apparently braced the sheriff on this very spot, which was, at the time, a post office.

"Lock me up," Brazel wailed. "I've just killed Pat Garrett."

Brazel, it seemed, had leased Garrett's Bear Canyon Ranch in the Organ Mountains, a verbal agreement which included the clause that Brazel would never bring a goat onto the property. Pat Garrett, the waitress informed me, for a reason which is now obscure, detested goats.

Brazel ignored the clause, sensibly, I thought, and raised himself up a whole passel of goats. The two fell to arguing about it when Garrett found out. Guns were drawn. The hero's death ensued, and was thus commemorated.

It wasn't exactly what I wanted to hear right about then, but I supposed it made about as much sense as everything else I'd heard about Mapache. I bluffed it through, laughing for the waitress, ordering another beer.

One thing I'd learned, in no uncertain terms, from years of protecting my wits with a linebacker's tenacity, was that you could innocently turn a corner, and be lost for years. Or you could spend all your time debating each corner before you turned it, and be lost for years. Or else you could calmly order another drink.

I was okay with that system, I had to be, byzantine as it was. But looking back on the whole thing now, my fondest wish in rewriting that moment isn't that I'd never met Flan, or never gone with him to Mapache, or even that I'd ignored Evan and stayed out of El Cabra. No, my fondest wish is that I'd never calmly ordered that beer.

It came, icy cold, in a sweating glass, carried by Hezekiah Johnson, who proffered Rosalita in his other hand.

"May we join you," he said and I remember the weird calm in which I thought one block-letter metal sentence only before nodding, thought: this is happening now.

Hezekiah sat across from me. Rosalita stood by his side, staring at the empty chair to my left. But of course it wasn't empty. Her eyes, black holes burned in brown cloth, told me that. I didn't want to see. I didn't want to turn and see. But of course I did. And there was Cump, in the chair, whittling at a corn chip.

"I wish to speak with you," the fat man said, and I laughed a laugh which sounded hollow even to me.

"Can't it wait for the funeral?"

"Ah, I see you haven't much faith in your man, little witch."

"He thinks I'm a witch," I said to Cump, who shrugged elaborately.

"So go for it," he squeaked, borrowing Mel Blanc's voice.

Rosalita shrank back.

I forced myself to look again at the fat man.

"Is everyone in this town on a Smiley jag, or is it just an elite few?"

"You recognize the effects, hah? Good, I knew you would. No, *brujita*. Is not everyone."

"Your daughter there's autistic," I said.

"*Sí, sí, sí.* That is what they tell me at the hospital."

"Shouldn't you do something about it? She's got a high function index."

"What is to do, evil one? It is God's will."

"God's will?"

"*Sí.* My little flower, she come with me everywhere. It is like a gift, no? She is special, and maybe ignorant people, they are a little frightened. She helps me, you see? And in return I take very good care of her. Still, is not the same as if she were having a mama. Rosalita's mama, she died in the travail. When we spoke on the phone, I thought perhaps you could be her mama, but Rosalita tell me no, that you scare her."

"*I* scare her?"

I'll tell you the truth, I envied him then, my heart groping toward the little girl. He saw her lost and had no intention of helping her get found. It was a system I could almost imagine, the opposite of my own, in which each skewed charge I guide to his purpose leaves me more alone.

I almost admired him, that ever-widening circle of human wreckage he left in his wake, never looking back, except to enjoy what he had wrought. I envied it, but it was too late for me. I'd already made my choice. And he'd made his.

"You really think I'm a witch," I said.

"It is something I know, not think. You are accompanied, hah? My little flower has told me. And so, as I tell my wife, you must leave this place."

I suppose even then I could've said "your little flower is nuts." But I couldn't change horses. I did what I'd always done. I backed silence, rooting around in the iced butter dish for my answer. And, sure, I found it. What did you think? Tiny, five inches maybe, he gripped my fork like a rafter. My father.

Rosalita burst into tears, covering her ears rather than her eyes with her free hand, as if something irrevocable had been said. Nothing had been said. Hezekiah crossed himself, his pudgy eyes on the fork between us. I was terrified.

"*Madre de Dios.* Make this stop, now," Hezekiah said.

"I, I can't," I cried, and then I really cried. Worse by far than not sharing my perceptions, I learned with an awful clang, nerves lighting up all over my skull like a pinball machine, tilting from girl to tormentor and back again, was sharing them with someone who wasn't playing for your team.

I ran my index finger over my father's head, his pockets, stroking him. No, not stroking him. Let's face it. I was patting him down. And, yes, he had it in his possession. Hell's puniest opium softball.

Hezekiah dropped the girl's hand and started backing away from the table. His hideous face was unreadable. Rosalita let her hand fall hard against her hip.

"*Evék óta várom, hogy védjelek a szörnyüségtöl,*" my father said, his little voice booming.

215

"What does he say," asked Rosalita in her robot voice as Hezekiah began to weep.

"For years I've been waiting to protect you from evil," I said, just as flatly.

My father leapt tremendously, from the fork to Hezekiah's loudly flowered tie, clinging there.

"Yes," Pappa continued. "For years I wait for this thing and what do I find? Nothing. *Édesem*, your life for you is too easy. A *patchiv*, a cakewalk. Finally, I get my chance. What for to cry, Little One? This Pappa can fix. Easy. Is what I wait for. You see, Pappa can fix."

"And, boy, can he. Fix, I mean," said Cump as Hezekiah fled from the room, my father swinging against his protruding gut, mountaineering ever upward.

He fled from the room and he fled from the restaurant. My father took him. He fled from the town, I guess, maybe the country, maybe the hemisphere. My father took him. He fled from accompaniment he couldn't control. He fled from the damned. My father took him. He fled from me. He fled from me. He fled from me.

Rosalita ran after him and I wanted to stop her, but it seemed I couldn't stop anyone. As Flan had predicted, the innocent were going down with everyone else. Still, I felt I should say something, save someone. I mean, something was definitely called for, so I cried after her:

"Tell my father goodbye."

"He left in a hurry," the waitress said. "Another beer?"

"He did. Please," I said, slumping in my chair, "and a taco."

I was hungry beyond description.

23

Billy the Kid

I walked over the bridge to El Paso carrying the drugs in a god-damned papoose. I wouldn't have cared if they stopped me, tossed me in the *calabozo*, threw away the key, and maybe that's why they didn't. I guess I looked like I couldn't be hurt any worse than I already was. I said I had Sauza Blanco tequila in the sack, paid the duty for it, and, as they say, walked on down the hall.

Once on Sun Street, I rented a car in my own name, and head-ed out. The visuals in the city were stunning, all those melting faces and monster angles. I knew I was in no condition to spring Feck's truck from the government center, and didn't want to try.

The driving was rough. I had white line fever in reverse. I was aware of every freeze-frame of the car's motion. I pulled off the highway in the lot next to Tita's Trousseau House and crashed for about an hour. The trajectory of the cars whizzing past me pene-trated my sleep, appearing in my dreams as all this awful foreign geometry. When I was fully under I wept, smashing my hand against the glove compartment repeatedly, parsing unknown num-bers according to the terrifying new math of Packy Salvo's face.

When I woke up, I saw I had sprained my left wrist and I was thirsty as the damned, but I laughed. I had a plan. The Trousseau House was flanked by a dog-wagon and a Salvation Army outlet. I sauntered into the outlet and bought a sleeping bag, thumbing through my wallet as I paid.

Following the wishes of my father, who'd been a consummate outdoorsman, I had an up-to-date license for every activity that the state sanctioned. I could fish, hunt, camp, even go clam-raking any place in New Mexico. I used to kid my father about the clam-raking. It was, after all, a useless thing to be allowed to do in a desert community. But now I thanked him. In a kind of a way, clam-raking was just what I had in mind.

I ate three burgers, drank five jumbo cokes, and I was ready. I couldn't face Hezekiah, or Denise's orphan fetus. I couldn't listen to the Denmark fat cat bluster about progress as he played footsy with my girl. And I certainly couldn't lay out the bail for that bastard's Ford Custom Deluxe, or allow my hollowed eyes to graze over Molly's face, surf those ivory planes of honesty unchecked. But I was amply prepared to do exactly what I had to do next. I was going camping.

I told the ranger-attendant at White Sands that I was going clam-raking and she didn't bat a fucking eye. I guess a lot of weirdos come through there. She actually asked to see both licenses, and I proffered them seriously. The thing was, and this came to me clearly as I tossed my sleeping bag under the dimming sky, I was home.

I slept hard, dreaming only once, and that a jokey dream, full of titters and canned light. I was Billy the Kid, hiding in a flour barrel at Dowlin's Mill in Ruidoso. The flour made me sneeze and the sneeze blew Captain Dowlin into the star-littered sky, laughing Packy's grisly laugh as the pursuing gunmen fled.

Round about three in the morning I thought by the moon's light reflected off the gypsum, just really coming down for the first time from the Smiley, I opened my eyes. My head was still with the Kid, his stupid enduring legend. You should have stayed back East, Bonney, I thought, been a shopkeeper, a munitions clerk, a priest.

"Or an anti-mayor," said a voice next to me and I didn't even have to turn. I knew it was Evan.

"Hey," was all I said.

"You off the oaf?"

"Sort of. He committed suicide," I said, trying, weakly, for gruff.

"Offed himself, huh? Know what Molly would ask?"

"Uh-huh."

"Well, what?"

"This a test?"

"Oh, I forget. You don't take tests. No, man, this ain't a test."

"She'd wanna know how."

"Right. Only what's really true is she'd need to know how. You got an answer prepared for that?"

"I'll think of something."

"She inspires great dialogue, doesn't she?"

I sighed. I lit a cigarette. I closed my eyes and found him again, pasted against the brown sky inside my eyelids, a long skinny thing in tight girl's jeans and a ripped-up pajama top.

Molly'd prepared me for this in some ways. After all, she more or less dressed that way herself. On him it looked absurd, though; a goofy oversized rag, held together by safety pins. My parents would have tanned me raw if I wore something like that. I would've liked to write him off as a sissy shitbird right there. But how could I? It was the Doll's husband.

"What do you want?" I said.

"Cold, here," he said, huddled tiny in my mind's eye. "Go on, unclench the peepers. First time, it's easier that way."

"You wanna make things easy for me?" I asked, genuinely amazed.

"'Course. What else? What did you think?"

"I thought you wanted the girl."

"What, Molly? Shit, man. Don't be stupid. She's yours already. That is, if you can keep her."

"But you mean I can't."

"I don't know yet. Go on, open your eyes."

I did and he lay next to me, fishing-buddy close, his eyes flashing. Miserable knowing eyes. Old eyes which reflected a national mood hearkening back to, say, 1931, eyes which were maddeningly never quite green.

I kept waiting for him to disappear, waiting to shake my head like Nary, waiting for that one delicious moment when I could smack my forehead in comic wonder like the movie drug addict and say, as he so often must have, "Oh wow, man, musta been the drugs." But he didn't budge. I heaved myself up on my elbows.

"Molly says you always blow after you make your point."

"That's my M.O., yes."

"So?"

"You're gonna stay here, Flanagan. I can just feel it."

"No," I said, and it sounded ridiculous, childlike.

"You won't want to, but you'll have to. There'll be a power vacuum, and you'll just get sucked in. What the hell, right? It's what you've been waiting for all these years."

"No."

"Yeah, man, I can see you out here, bare-chested in the moonlight, surrounded by your army of motorcycle goons, renegade scalpers, chickenshit pirates."

"Bullshit."

"Sure, the West will ride again. See, you're the only one with any brains in this town—"

"That's why I get to leave."

"No, man. That's why you have to stay."

The sand felt like a rack beneath me.

"But I love her."

"Sure you do, man. I love her too. But we're dealing with monumental forces here. The ghost of the fucking *Jorobado* gang. Lineage. Fate. Love is nothing stacked up against all that."

"If you had it to do over again, would you have cleaned up?"

"If I had it to do over again, I would follow her to the ends of the Earth—"

"So, can't you see—"

"But it isn't good for her to know that. And, anyway, I don't have it to do over again."

"But—"

"And neither, my sorry cowboy, do you."

He stretched and hung over me, leaning in with an irrefutable pre-kiss posture I usually associate with myself. Myself, that is, the guy. Myself, that is, in the clinch. I wrenched away. Still he hovered.

"Don't kiss me," I said. "For Christ's sake. You're a guy."

He laughed.

"I'm dead."

"You wouldn't know it by me."

I sat up and felt around in my pockets.

"Can't you do anything useful," I asked.

He rubbed his hairless chin, scratched his head.

"Lemmee see now. I never could when I was alive. Useful like what?"

"Like turn gypsum into cigarettes?"

"Sure. That I can do, if you really need convincing. But cop to Ockham's razor, Dad. What's the point? You believe in me now."

"I feel like smoking."

"I see why you and Molly get along. She'd rather smoke than just about anything. I guess that doesn't bother you, though."

"Can you do it, or can't you," I said, and he laughed.

"Man, you're a sulky son-of-a-bitch, huh? I'll tell you the truth, Flanagan, I wish it was you I was bound to for all eternity. My wife's so, I don't know, there's, like, a relentlessly sunny, plump-cheeked little kid inside that long sad body, you know? You're, well, you know what you are—"

"The cigarettes?"

"If I remember right, you left a butt in your shoe before you crashed."

I had and he lit it for me, swooping in with my Zippo like Cary fucking Grant.

"I don't understand you, cowboy. I don't really want to, either. I mean, you're a bloody cartoon. Look at you, you're threatened 'cause your hallucination isn't butch enough. But I have to understand you because Molly wants to. So, now, what's the problem here? You been telling her for years you're stuck to this town. She sure as hell believes it. She's cryin' her eyes out over you right now. So, why can't you believe it?"

"I don't want to."

"Not good enough."

"What about Hezekiah?"

"The fat guy? Molly took care of him."

"The Doll?"

"Look, there's something maybe you don't understand about Molly. She doesn't really dig it herself, come to think of it."

"What's that?"

He blew then, too soon, too late, who fucking knew? He left his voice as a creepy after-shock. I rolled over, pounding the sand into a pillow, listening to the words toll through the desert howl, rasp against my tired ears. I awoke just at sunrise, springing to my feet then falling to my knees. Crying, I raised my snout like Kaspar and repeated the snide punk's mantra, screaming it to the world: The kid's a powerhouse.

Wouldn't you know it? A goddamned coyote answered, and for me, the cock crowed.

24

Still Alive, Still Awake, Still a Fraud

I was still awake when Flan knocked on the door and I didn't
bother asking him where he'd found a bouquet of chicory blossoms in the middle of a desert in November. I couldn't have been
happier if he'd knocked over every greenhouse from here to
Amarillo. Or sadder.

Did we fall into each other's arms? Well, yes and no. We fell
to the dice table, the bedspread, really, playing in the morning
light a ludicrously complicated game with the fervor of the con-
verted. How much easier than authentic reflection was the simple
act of bringing all our faculties to bear on the convoluted ins and
outs of an unexpected roll.

For myself, I had room in the ol' noggin for what seemed like
endless variables. Considering all I had on my mind, the game
was almost too easy. But Flan's head was such that he had to reason the possibilities out loud, and part of me monitored the
words, marking the sorry silliness and socking it away for later. I
thought maybe, if I was lucky, there'd be a later, some time in the
still-veiled future when I'd need something of Flan to subsist on.

"Hang on, hang on," he said. "That's a jackrabbit and three
pigs in a blanket. A mixed combo. So I could take my 25 points
and fade, take them and roll, or not take them and sell my accu-
mulated points to you for half their value. Which would mean
you'd take 36 and a half points into your zoo and any time you roll
a scored double, you'll have to pass and use those points on me. Is
that right?"

"That's right, boss."

"But what does my 36 and a half buy me?"

"Mouth anywhere."

"Do it."

"You're easy to please. What makes you think I'll roll a double?"

He blew smoke in my face, laughing as I winced.

"Doll, I don't care what you roll."

"Just playing the percentages?"

"That's right...boss."

The very next turn I shook a scored double out of my clasped fingers, two fours in fact, the roll we called "Ol' Valentino." I never said fate didn't have a hand in the game. Or maybe I did. Probably I did. But all I meant was, the game served to make fate look silly, which is what we needed right about then.

Mouth anywhere quickly turned into mouth everywhere which more or less put the game behind us, too far behind us, if you ask me. Because when we stopped playing, we fucked. And when we stopped fucking, we'd have to talk.

So we fucked for a very long time. And after, I dressed slowly, listening to the cars on 28 lap and crash outside the window, pretending the highway was a lake, banishing the desert, stitching my brains together. I watched Flan pace shirtless until, suddenly, I snuck up on myself, finding the presence of mind to bark out, simply,

"What happened to Packy."

"He committed suicide."

"How?"

"He used me. What happened to Hezekiah?"

"Same."

"And Rosalita?"

"She went with him, I think."

"Oh. Will you come with me to meet that beer guy, Doll?"

"Okay. Yeah. If you'll come with me to the class."

He sat hard on the bed, his lower jar banging shut.

"Oh, Molly. We're fucked. What are we negotiating now? I'm sick of negotiating. You realize we're bargaining with chips we don't care about?"

I sat at his feet, rubbing my knuckles along his boots.

"Yeah, Flan. I realize that. But what should we gamble with, our souls? I mean, it's good, right? Otherwise we'd be degraded. We don't want to be degraded, do we?"

"No, I guess not," he said quietly. " Hey, did you see Evan last night?"

"No. Why?"

"No reason."

On that raw note we went off to meet Lucas. It didn't work out very well. Lucas was gloating, packing up his ersatz office, braying about the town meeting the next night, how he had everyone in his pocket, how he was drafting plans for a miniature golf course out by the municipal office complex. Flan stood for it until Lucas offered him a sizeable bribe, a consulting fee he called it. Kroystag Ale remembers its friends, all that.

Flan blew sky high, all arage about what shit it was and how he almost preferred the evil he knew to the faceless anonymity of some corporation. He ended with his face up against Lucas', that weird animal challenge thing men do, talking through his teeth.

"You think you got this sewed up, asshole? Well, you're wrong. You'll get your development, sure. But this is Mapache. Things happen differently here. Things get resolved in the desert. You're from Denmark. What do a bunch of goddamn Danes know about the desert?"

Lucas stood up to him. He was used to small-town resistance. And he clearly saw in Flan's tirade a chance to say "interfere," his favorite word. I could see it in the shape of his mouth as he inhaled to speak.

"Frankly, I cannot see how that matters in the least, although I do hope you realize that I appreciate your concern. But tell me, what could happen to interfere with our little, as you say, 'beachhead,' now?"

"I don't know, Christensen. But I'd watch out, is all I'm saying."

"I'm late," I said, at last, "can't you resolve this tomorrow?"

"Of course," said Lucas.

"No," said Flan, but he left with me anyway.

When we walked into the smoking lounge, Feck was there, leaning over Virgen, smelling her hair. I was disappointed to see that he wasn't wearing the MLA fez. I'd been looking forward to seeing him in it, a buzzard in a chicken bucket. The class had dissipated down to the chick, the Count, Jules Nytown, Denise Salvo, and her dead cousin's unborn spawn. Everyone looked unhappy.

"Well, well, well. Joined at the hip are you?"

"Hey, Feck. How'd you do?"

"Ah, they ate me alive. They're all hot for those other voices up there, you know, cunnilinguists, and klingons of color. And what do they get? Me."

"A bald white lecher."

"Yeah. Hey, what did you do to my class, Dr. Veeka? I would've sworn I had a whole heap of students when I left."

"I don't know yet."

"Yeah," he said. "You never know, do you? That's the problem with you, Veeka. I keep telling you. You don't have a master plan."

Feck sat and Flan leaned against the door. I collected myself with a deep breath. Notice how men always "keep telling" me stuff?

"Anyone wanna read," I said.

"I will," Denise said.

"I hate this," muttered the minute Iggy Pop. "Who cares about good listening? It just makes people confessional. What about secrets? Lies? Remember those?"

"Keep your bullshit to yourself, Nytown," I said. "That's what you got a fly for."

"Why should I? No one else is. This one's got a crush on the teacher. This one's diddling the other. This one's got a problem with what the fags call chicken. You're a freak. Your boyfriend's a two-bit drug dealer. That one's pregnant with her first cousin's kid. It's a freak show."

Feck surveyed the blustering kid.

"Want me to throw him out?"

"No, Feck. I want you to stop flirting with his girlfriend. Because that's what's going on here. The kid's furious. And I want him to understand that even if he thinks we're all bliss ninnies, he still has to listen. Authentically listen. Because at least that's something."

226

"All I'm saying is some ears still thrill to loneliness," Jules whined.

"And all I'm saying is button your fucking lip."

There was quiet and the kid rolled his eyes. I saw Virgen's hand grasp his knee. Flan leaned, Feck grinned, and I grimaced inside. I hate when people I've slept with are proud of me.

Denise Salvo was waving her hand.

"Can I, I mean, read now?"

"Please."

She stood up, clutching her papers, not looking at Flan.

"He is not real tall but he is uquibitous," she began. I saw Virgen's mouth form the right pronunciation and I put a finger to my lips, pointing, then mouthing myself: listen.

"That means, I looked it up, he is always there. One time when Aunt Bianca was in the hospital with her bladder, me and my cousin got to horsing around and I got caught behind a chest of drawers when Packy went off to go hunting with Mark from up the street. I cried and cried and who do you think came along to rescue me? I'll give you one guess.

"His hair is red and brown like a calf's and another time he stopped me before I squashed an ugly frog that had scared me in the porch. He explained why it wasn't right and when I said to him that I had to do it because I was scared he told me being scared wasn't a good reason for anything. Only after he went on his way, I wondered to myself how come was it that he happened to be there just when I was right about to flatten that frog.

"I think he works for the town doctor like my cousin. Sometimes when you see them all out together, it looks more like they work for him. The doctor pretends he's just a doctor and my cousin pretends he is a soldier. But if Goliath is pretending too, I can't figure it out.

"He went away a lot of times when I was real little. He always come back, though, and when I heard it from my girlfriend at Fajitas restaurant, I was really happy. I don't want you to get the wrong idea. I didn't like him for a husband, nothing like that. I guess I should add the part from class about how he eats meat and all that but I'm not sure how it fits in."

She made a big show of putting her paper carefully back in its crinkly cellophane package. I didn't look at Flan, but I felt him deflate behind me.

"I like it," I said.

"If he's a dark magician, what's that make you?"

This from Nytown. I was freaked and refrained from pointing out that the answer was obvious. Hadn't I made his fondest wish come true? Didn't he, at this very moment, have the much-coveted hand of Virgen Santísima Blanco resting on his very own black-clad thigh? Of course, all that begged the question: just where the hell was *my* fairy godmother, and who would do the same for me?

"I gotta get out of here," I said, imploring Feck.

"Well, I'd say your work is done. Go on. I'll send you a check. I gotta tell you, Kid. This is way more than I expected. Maybe you'll be a teacher after all."

"You mean I win the bet?"

"What do you think, Kid Gloves?"

25

The Desert

Outside the smoking lounge Molly fell against me. For a moment, I held her in my arms, felt that steady twisting weight, stroked those sweet tendrils of smoke-scented hair. I breathed evenly in and out. I was okay. I knew just about anyone else would ask me how I felt about the kid's report just as I knew the Doll wouldn't bother. She never sweats the small stuff.

"We got a problem," she said.

"Yeah. We do."

The Doll stood and pondered this for maybe half a second. The stripes under her eyes darkened and she grinned. At that moment, maybe the last chance I'd ever have, I loved her perfectly, and I was grateful. She's a trooper, my Molly.

"All that stuff you said to Lucas, about how things get resolved in Mapache? That was bullshit, right?"

"Yes and no, Doll. More yes, I guess. Why? You wanna try it?"

"Yeah. It's worth a shot, right?"

"To the desert, then."

As improbably gorgeous as an impulsive move like that can be, especially for a tourist, we took our time getting ready. I didn't want anything to fuck it up for her. There was a lot that needed to get done.

We drove the rented car out to El Paso, turning in the keys to a young woman at the rental agency. Molly wanted to know if it was the same Sun Street where I'd had the incident with the corrective shoe guy and I didn't bother reminding her that the story was bullshit. I was determined to protect her as long as I could.

When we went to spring the truck, the attendant remembered me from getting the kid out of the fountain the day before. She told Molly her husband was a hero, meaning me. Molly smiled but muttered under her breath "you couldn't be more wrong," meaning Evan. I thought. I hoped.

I thought we'd head straight out from there, but Molly shook her head, her long hair swishing around the cab of the truck.

"If we're doing this, we do it right," she said.

"Meaning what, Doll? Oh, no. Come on. You've got be kidding."

"On a horse," she said, "or not at all."

"My father wouldn't approve."

"Neither would mine."

It was almost sundown when we set out from Nary's farm. The Totonacs had long insisted that I feel free to take Arturo out anytime I want, and for once I fully appreciated the scope of their generosity.

When we snuck past the *hacienda*, we saw that Nary was holding court on the porch, engaged in elaborate negotiations with Chris, Sonia, and what looked like half the county's farmers. They were citizens to a man, and I felt I had nothing to contribute.

It's a two or three mile ride from Nary's to the open desert, straight out toward Picacho Peak. Molly laughed for what seemed like the whole trip. She clung to me as if we were on a motorcycle, which, come to think of it, is probably as close as she had ever come to riding a sixteen-hand appaloosa.

I tried to keep her happy, pointing out jack rabbits fleeing with their radar dish ears, and imitating the roadrunners, whose real call is something like a strangled eeeeeeaaughk. Molly joined in with the classic meep-meep, though, and I didn't correct her. Her arms felt like bliss clasped around my waist.

We set up a makeshift camp between a pair of those giant testicle cactuses. Cross-legged across from one another, we shared a cigarette, hot-boxing in the trailing light. I put the butt in my shoe. How could I tell her?

We fucked then, al fresco, a first for Molly if you didn't count tenement roofs which, I told her sternly, crushing her under me, I certainly didn't. She called me provincial and I called her provincial, familiar easy patter, staked out over years.

"Flan? Explain something to me?" she said quietly and my heart dropped. I wasn't ready to talk about it. But it wasn't me that was bothering her. I should've known better. Molly had me pegged.

"What?"

"Why do you think Evan took the acid that time?"

"Why would anyone take acid?"

"I don't know. To see more."

"Uh-huh."

"But, then, why did he go out?"

"Why would anyone go outside, Doll?"

"To see more."

"Uh-huh."

"But why did he walk under the bus," she cried, sitting up abruptly, hugging her arms over bare breasts.

I could see where this was going and I didn't think it was something we ought to kid about. I mean, it didn't strike me as particularly funny. But if the Doll had proved anything to me, it was that she could take care of herself, so I played it out. And with Molly, who ever knows? Maybe that realization was what she had in mind all along.

"Why would anyone walk under a bus," I said, going for gruff, and she laughed with delight, clapping her long arms together like a seal.

"To see more."

"Is that all you're worried about, Doll?"

"What?"

"Whether Evan did himself in?"

"That's some of what I worry about, Flan. When I'm in the mood to worry. Why?"

"I guess I just don't think it's any of your business."

"No, huh?"

"Not really. Does that make you mad?"

"When I'm mad, you'll know it."

231

I stood up, tossed Molly a shirt. That much of what you've heard is true. It gets cold in the desert at night.

"I don't know, Doll. Even given that every word spoken in every tongue is your responsibility—"

"Which I am not entirely prepared to grant, but never mind," she said, in perfect imitation of what I planned to say next.

I leaned down and took her chin in my right hand, then switched, balancing it on the ace bandage wrapped around my left as I knelt before her.

"Right, Doll," I said, "even so. I guess what I mean is, that doesn't—"

"The only soul I'm responsible for is my own. Is that what you mean?"

"Yes," I said, relieved.

But only for a second. We lay side by side, staring into all the speckled night space. That much is also true. The Southwestern sky is unimaginably huge.

"That being the case, Flan, go ahead and scar it. I think I'm ready."

"Your soul?"

"Right. Shoot."

I didn't say, although I could've, if you already know, why do I have to say it? It was Molly, and I knew for sure she'd have a damn good reason, one that would put me to shame if I asked.

Still, I waited, staring up into all the endless patterns of tiny flaring suns. You miss that in the big Eastern cities. Or at least I do.

"I can't go back with you, not yet. I have to see this thing through, make sure about the transition."

Silence.

"And I've got to solidify my connection with the harvesters. I don't have Hezekiah as a middle man anymore. Thanks to you."

Silence.

"I'll come, though, as soon as I'm sure everything's gonna run smoothly. I mean, all those fucking illiterates who worked for Hezekiah, what are they gonna do now? Someone's gotta work that out. Nary'll split. And what does a commie beer executive understand about real people? These people need me."

Silence, and then she dropped her head and cried, her shoulders shaking. It went on and on, unlike anything I'd ever heard. I was worried, my heart clenched tight.

I'd expected any number of things, her slugging me, hating me, arguing me out of it. I never expected her to act like a girl. But Arturo whinnied, breaking the spell, and when she picked up her head, she was laughing, her eyes glowing like embers of a blue cigarette.

"That's the stupidest thing I've ever heard. When will you visit?"

"Soon," I said, and we laughed together.

"Soon as I can," I said, and cribbed her head in my bent elbow. She ran a finger along my nose.

"You look like you've seen a ghost."

"Great, Doll. For a genius, you've got kind of a low sense of humor, you know that?"

"I know. But what were you so scared of?"

"I guess I thought you'd want to get hitched, make things certain somehow, something like that."

"I'm already married, Flan," she said. "Didn't you know?"

26

This Visitation is but to
Whet Thy Almost Blunted Purpose

New York greeted me with its usual elegant sinkhole, all steely gray sky, skeletal leaves, shining lights. Kaspar leapt into my arms, his wide white paws on my shoulders, knocking me to the filthy welcome mat. It was only after disentangling from my dog that I noticed Jasper Nitz was in my apartment.

He spared me barely a nod. He was frantically running from one end of the loft to the other, filling a tiny Hungarian tea cup with water, dumping it on the blissed-out Nell, refilling it. I was calm, petting my dog, looking at the girl's sleepy half-smile, her familiar pin eyes. Her own dog, who'd know better than anyone if she was in trouble, was snuffling peacefully in its sleep. This was old hat.

I caught Jasper in mid-skid and held him to me.

"She's okay," I said. "Shhh," I said. "She's okay, Little One. *Nyugi, nyugi, édesem,*" I said.

"But—"

"There's nothing you can do, Nitz. Just let her enjoy the ride."

"But—"

"You can worry about that tomorrow. I'll tell you what to do. Just get some sleep now. It's out of your hands."

"But—"

"Isn't that great, Nitz? Think about it. It's out of your hands."

"But I—"

"But you love her?"

He nodded, and sank, catching his breath.

235

"Doesn't matter. Still out of your hands."

I made a bed for him on the couch, walked Kaspar and Mary along the river, and fell into bed. I didn't bother telling him that if she'd really been o.d.ing, a tea cup of water wouldn't have done jack shit. It seemed mean. There'd be time enough for him to learn. Or else he wouldn't need to. Or something.

Home, in bed, pressed against the snorting malamute, I felt short of breath.

"Maybe I'll quit smoking," I muttered.

"Maybe you'll quit breathing," Evan said, lying next to me, his long arm half over Kaspar.

"Could we be together then?"

"No, Chica," he said, his bony hand half-buried in the furrows of Kaspar's undercoat, "not even then."

Jasper took Nell over to a lab on the East Side for a urine test a couple of days later. I guess those puny snide bastards have their uses, after all. It was certainly more than I'd ever done. I didn't have much faith in methadone, thought it was an even stranger animal than dope, but I figured I might as well hold out hope. I mean, what else was there?

She blew off classes, but, like Feck before me, I arranged for her to keep her funding by demanding her as a research assistant. Actually, I did need her, at least someone. Sharon was moping around with the ol' Feck-jilt written all over her tough puss. Of course, she probably wouldn't show up. But then I could get someone else and her funding would still be in the bag. I'd never thrown my tenure around before and I was kind of enjoying it.

On a ridiculously clear early December afternoon, Jasper Nitz showed up in my office. Sharon showed him in, sulking. His pale little face was even more pinched than usual.

"'S up, Nitz? Please don't tell me you have a question about the reading. I have nothing left to say about the language of madness—so much nothing, you can count it. One nothing. Two nothings. Ten nothings..."

"No, I."

"Oh. Okay, have a seat."

"Yeah, I."

"Let's engage in a little *educare*, huh? Yeah, I think a parable's in order here."

"But, I."

He shifted in the chair, shrugging, submitting himself.

"It goes a little something like this. You might've heard it. In fact, I know you heard it. It was a dark and stormy night. The skipper and I were on the bridge. The skipper says 'tell me a story,' and so I did. It was a dark and stormy night. The skipper and I were on the bridge. The skipper says, 'tell me story,' and so I did. It was a dark and stormy night. The skipper and I were on the bridge. The skipper says, 'tell me a story,' and so I did...'"

"I get it."

He looked daggers at me. Imploring daggers.

"Do you?"

"Not really. What am I supposed to do?"

"What are your options?"

"I don't have any."

"Ah-hah. You don't have any options, Plato, so?"

"So. So, I can't do anything?"

"Do you love her?"

"Of course."

"I mean, cherish her? You can't imagine your life without her?"

"Yes. I mean, no. I mean—"

"That a boy. You may as well face it, Jasper. You're fucked."

"I could—"

"Well, yeah. There is that. It even has a kind of romance. I mean, it's messy, degrading, illegal, and you still wouldn't be sharing the experience, to say nothing of the fact that sooner or later you'd find yourself hiding your stash from her. But I suppose even that is steeped in tradition."

My face flushed. This last was a detail from my parents' lives, probably not an absolute, and its appearance in my impromptu rant ought to have tipped me off that I was going overboard. But we're talking about my own best-trod nightmare terrain here. How should I have been? Rational?

Well, I wasn't. I stood over him, raving cruelly, gesturing wildly, until he batted my waving arm away like an angry little boy, which, after all, I guess he was.

"Listen, Nitz," I said. "I'm sorry. It really isn't any of my business. But since you're here in my office, I'll tell you this: I think you'd be better at it than she is."

The letter came that night. Evan hung around while I read it, making kiddie ghost-prints on the foggy windows, pogo-ing his heart out with Cump and two green ocelots, trying his dead-hardest to make things light, easier. I turned, with the two loose-leaf pages, to the wall. I wasn't in the mood.

Doll, we got a veritable Old West revival going on here. And for once, I mean that literally. Nary's grandson Ireneo it got into his head to re-stage the political riots of 1871. It's moronic. The fucking governor's paying for it. He's got all these school kids decked out as old territory Democrats rehearsing their number:

"se van, se van los Republicanos
para la Ascencion porque los
Democratas ganaron la eleccion."

And all to the tune of "Marching through Georgia." I swear these people don't have enough brains to unscrew a cap.

This fucking town is full of Danes. They're everywhere. They're in the plaza, jabbering away in Danish. They're in El Cabra, complaining about fish—or the lack thereof. The locals don't know what to make of it. But everybody likes the money.

Anyway, nix on sending me the trunk. I'll be in town next month. I've got a meet set up with Tom and Fee. Big plans for national Smiley distribution, but you don't want to know about that, I guess. What else? I gave Packy's Caddy to Denise. She tools around in it, happy as a clam. She's replaced the skulls and bimbos with unicorns and cherubs. But it's still a fuck of a big car. Sonia and Chris are getting hitched in June. I want to tell you now because I'll probably have to go back for that at least. You're invited and I figured we could go back together. The Totonacs are moving to Atlantic City next week. That'll last all of a month, I bet. I mean, can you picture Nary in New Jersey? Meanwhile, they let me have Arturo and I've been riding him all over the place like a regular asshole. I don't mind, though. He reminds me of you. I miss you terribly, Doll. I'll save out a button or two and maybe we can get down to a serious session of Evan-abatement when I hit town.

Looking forward,
Goliath

I put the letter down on the piano and the soon-to-be-abated Evan was right in my face.

"Think he'll come?"

I nodded.

"Think he'll stay?"

I shook my head, pushed past him, stared out the window. A garbage scow was stuck in the harbor. Kaspar wooed.

"Want him to?"

Watching the gray-capped river, I nodded again, slowly.

"Damn, Chica."

I turned and sank against the wall, leaning hard.

"Know what's funny about you, Molly?"

"What?"

Kaspar padded over to investigate.

"You lose people the way prize fighters lose teeth."

"You're right," I said, big dog in my lap. "That is funny."